Kaleidoscope

By the Author

Darryl Wimberley

KALEIDOSCOPE

The Toby Press

Kaleidoscope

First Edition 2008

The Toby Press LLC
POB 8531, New Milford, CT 06776-8531, USA
& POB 2455, London W1A 5WY, England
www.tobypress.com

ISBN 978 1 59264 244 1, *hardcover*

A CIP catalogue record for this title is
available from the British Library

Typeset by Koren Publishing Services

Printed and bound in the United States

Prologue

Athick fog clings like a dirty nightshirt to the flanks of the Alafia River. An Indian-summer scent rises from the water. Cottonmouths that would in cooler seasons eagerly feed on bream and bullfrogs fast in wait of deliverance from dog days gone too long even for reptiles to endure. To the west lies Tampa, swathed this summer of '29 in a gauze of mosquitoes and fruit flies, those plagues only somewhat abated among the palmetto and conifers bordering the banks of the Alafia.

An unlikely caravanserai convenes along the river's sluggish bend, a coven of vehicles clinging to a single, serpentine road, two ruts submerged beneath the fog in a pan of loam. Road wagons of all sorts drift in the miasma that attends—circus wagons, gypsy tugs, car homes, and trucks, their wooden beds sheltered by parasols of tarpaulin.

A handful of cottages and tents mingle with their mobile cousins on this boulevard of sand. Kerosene lamps are mostly wicked out for the night, though in one residence a signature illumination shimmers through needles of pine and shrouds of moss. It's a vast structure in comparison to the cramped quarters which are propped on wheels or stumps on all sides, a two-poled pavilion rising high above the neighboring canvas roofs. The bigtop tent glows like a Chinaman's lantern, illuminated from within by a necklace of white-hot globes. You could be drawn like a moth to that enticement. And if you were, you would see, cast onto the canopy's unsteady screen, an enormous silhouette.

An Amazon's shadow ripples with a sluggish breeze, perfectly proportioned, naked. She is bathing. A tub casts its own firmly delineated shadow with avatars of steam.

"It's all right," her voice coaxes from within. "You can come."

A pair of breasts lift huge and pendulous. The slap of flesh on water.

"Come on. Don't be afraid."

A runt-sized man hangs onto a tent pole inside the Amazon's palace. His larynx bobs with a swig of gin. His tie is loose and filthy and sopping sweat.

"You want me," she says. "It's natural. Can't be helped."

He shatters his hooch against the tent's pillar and an alarmed snort signals the presence of the tent's second, permanent resident; a chain shackles an enormous, African elephant to the big-top's second pole.

The beast snorts once again, tossing a pair of well-worn tusks.

"It's all right, Ambassador," she says.

The aging bull's ears flap like mammoth fans to cool the woman whom, until now, we've only imagined in shadow. She's not what we expect. She bathes, first of all, this Amazon, not in a tub but in the elephant's watering tank, an immense, iron-riveted cistern.

And her figure is not anticipated by the shadow cast onto the cloth of her tent, for this woman is huge. Six hundred and fifty pounds of wallowing flesh, her arms are the size of kegs. Her eyes recede like raisins pressed into a face as large as a pie. A mop of corn silk hair presses flat against a pail-sized skull. She sinks back into the steaming water and her breasts swell like buoys.

"Come on!" she urges her visitor. "Come on!"

He sheds his pants, first, as he clambers to the lip of the tank.

An erection preposterously out of proportion to his stunted frame stands like a flag.

"Oh," she purrs. "Hurry."

"Goddamn!" the runt exclaims and dives in.

He surfaces like a toy between her legs.

"Hurry!" she moans.

He plunges into her. Buries himself.

"Yes…" she hisses. "Yes, there you are! There!"

Ambassador jerks alarmed against his length of chain—

—and distorts the silhouette cast onto the canvas outside. A confused play of light and shadow casts the mismatched lovers onto a billowing screen. They sink into the outsized tub. Water thrashes furiously. A groan of effort or passion bursts from the tent's interior. And then the enraged trumpet of an elephant.

"AMBASSADOR!"

The canvas tent explodes outward with a wall of water. The Amazon gushes from her ruptured tank. Ambassador charges through a mangle of iron and, as the Fat Lady screams, stomps her toy-like lover into the sand outside.

Chapter one

"Play The Streets"—*To set up on
the street for an engagement.*

Jack Romaine tamped a sprinkle of Prince Albert along the length of a bummed paper as he scanned the *Enquirer* for the only news that mattered. There it was. *Reds Lose in Late Innings.*

"Damnation."

Another fiver wasted on the hometown team. A less compelling banner chronicled the latest effort to clean up City Hall—*George Remus Endorses End to Crony System in Cincinnati Government.*

Good old George. Was king of the bootleggers before he got busted. Before he killed his wife. Got away with that one, with the murder. And now here he was a Respected Citizen. A hotshot.

Some guys truly did have all the luck.

Jack struck a match to his cigarette and sucked hard. Fucking warm this morning. No breeze off the river. Thank God for the fountain. Jack frequently started his mornings here, on Fountain Square, with a smoke, a newspaper, and a hangover, idling beneath the fountain's bronze goddess, facing east over what was once the Fifth Street Market but had become a modern boulevard bustling with automobiles and people. A democratic mix. Stock brokers and pipefitters, bankers and hotdog vendors milling up and down the wide street.

But mostly it was the women kept his attention. Jack liked looking at the women on the street. Flappers with straight skirts and beads. Stockings pulled halfway down, some of 'em. Hair short as a boy's and capped with a cloche. You'd see 'em in the speakeasies buying drinks with their own cash, cigarettes prominent. Petting some sheik on the sly. It was smokin' in the boy's room, for sure. Some real lookers, too.

And looks were important to Jack. About the only thing he had, really, a movie star's face and physique. Marquee looks, the girls at Gilberts' said. A set of peepers the color of hazel set in a wide, square-jawed face which Jack took pains to keep unbroken, unspindled and without obvious mutilation. He had good skin. Smooth as a spanked baby's fanny, some Josephine once told him. And hair. A thick mane of hair parted straight down the middle and combed back slick and black with Brylcreem. Razor cut to taper at the nape.

As for threads, he did alright. Always second-hand, but that was peach, you never wanted too much of an air. You saw a lot of knicker and argyles, but Jack favored suits. He owned two. The rags he'd donned for the morning's business fit him best, a single-breasted sack coat in an Oxford summer wool over a double-breasted waistcoat. Shirt was a little long, a solid-white bosom starched stiff as a board, but he could bunch it up into the sleeves of his coat. No bowtie, he knotted a four-in-hand every morning to set off the wing collar. Trousers were corded and cuffed, though showing a little shine. Shoes were second-hand low-quarters always saddle-soaped and buffed. Of course, anybody with class needed some kind of lid and Jack had one, a black fedora he'd pinched right across the street at Gibson's.

Not much in the way of jewelry. A wedding band, which didn't signify much in these heady times. Not that Jack was obliged to wear a ring; his wife had died with the influenza nearly five years earlier. But it didn't feel right taking the thing off. Perhaps he needed to be reminded. Perhaps it was just the familiar weight.

Something.

Jack had a watch fobbed at a vest pocket, but it was just for show, the timepiece having been broken near the riverfront subsequent to some disagreement or another. Who needed watches, anyway? There was time enough for anything important. Always. Everything else could wait.

The only accoutrement of value besides his wedding ring was foreign, a kind of broach or pin acquired his last few weeks in the army. Jack kept that brass polished and fixed on his jacket's wide lapel. It wasn't like being a Mason or anything, nothing like that. In fact, Jack wasn't sure just *what* it was. Some herald embossed with a coat of arms, the inscription etched in a language with which Jack, apart from the empty rituals of Mass, was entirely unfamiliar. There was a story there if anybody wanted to hear it. Which nobody did.

Get back to normalcy, the president had urged after the war and people ever since were trying like mad to oblige. *Nooses give... Gas smells awful...You might as well live.*

Jack slipped his free hand into his pocket to finger a deck of cards. He tried to tell himself he wasn't worried about work. You could always get by with cards if you were good. If you were lucky.

Hey, it was good times all around, wasn't it? Roaring.

He wanted a drink. For a dime a streetcar would take you anywhere you wanted to go, but Jack was getting shy of dimes. He decided to hoof it. Anywhere along McMillan and Vine would do, but Jack decided on Wielert's Café. Wielert's was a dependable place. Boss Cox used to run the show from there, back when the Boss was still mayor. As he approached the café, Jack nodded to the familiar if nameless congregation loitering outside.

"'Lo, fellas," Romaine said, slipping through the knot of men to reach the not-well-disguised sally port that provided a boundary between the street and the goings-on inside.

"Minute, there."

A redhead rose slender as a reed from a cane-backed chair. A cane hat and knickers. Jack knew this one, at least.

"Murdock, what? You working doors, now?"

"Staponski says you don' come in."

"Hey. We're old friends."

"Staponski says you owe him."

Christian Nicholas Staponski. Nickname of Spuds. He ran the place.

"I owe the man, sure," Jack shrugged. "So's half the city."

"Yeah, well, your half ain't welcome."

"Look, I got a fiver. You chase me outta here, Spuds is not gonna like it."

"Give it to me. I'll give it to Spuds."

"I didn't fall off a turnip truck, Murdoch."

"The fuck you didn't," a voice rasped from behind.

Jack turned to find Nick Staponski filling the speakeasy's rude foyer.

"Well, you comin' in or what?"

Staponski turned back inside before Jack could reply, rolling on that bad hip. A narrow corridor opened onto the bar. Lots of foam-topped glasses along that polished run of hardwood. Smaller shots of moonshine or in some cases real whiskey scattered in between. A handful of stiffs killing time at the bar. Some sheik alongside a flapper trading shots and cigarettes like she was Diana Mayo.

"…'Tain' nobody's biiiiiizznesssssss…"

Spuds led Jack past a colored girl cooing beside a quintet of Negroes, to reach a peep-holed door. A single knock opened it. Jack passed into a low-ceilinged room cured with the odors of yeast and tobacco and sweat. Here's where you got the real action. Cards, numbers, horses. A Crosley radio buzzed on a long counter serving duty as the backroom bar, its vacuum tubes snatching a ballgame from the aether.

"…should remind you fans that the Reds are scheduled to play a regular season game with the National League champs in *October*—! Can you believe it? Next thing we're gonna be pitching strikes past Christmas trees. Incredible…"

"Who we playing today, the Pirates?" Jack asked almost on instinct.

"You don't care," Spuds growled, shoving Romaine against his rail-less bar. "Now where's my five?"

Jack's mouth dry as sandpaper.

"I got it for ya, Spuds."

"Not honestly, you didn't."

"I'm a working man, now. Got a job."

"Where?"

"Out in Norwood—'Playing Cards'. I'm a cutter."

"You're a cutter, all right."

"Got a pay check to prove it."

His first in months. And his last, too, Jack now fingering the deck of cards he lifted when he was fired.

"C'mon, Spuds. At least give me something to wet my whistle."

Staponski shrugged. "If you can pay."

"Gimme a beer," Jack replied and planted his last dollar on the bar.

Spuds nodded to his bartender. "Set him up."

Jack accepted his suds and turned his attention to the radio.

"…top of the eighth, it's a tied ball game, but there are no outs and the Reds have a man on second base."

"Who's at bat—? Dresser?" a fob-suited swell queried a couple of stools down. "If it's Dresser, forget it. Dresser can't hit the sack."

Fully a dozen men and a couple of women now gathered close to the radio. Money changing hands.

"Who the Pirates got on the mound?" Jack inquired mildly.

"Dawson," an emaciated elder coughed into his handkerchief. Jack spotted the red stain.

Jesus. A lunger.

Jack took a long draught of homebrew.

"Dawson's due," he announced. "Gonna get a hit, mark my words. Reds are gonna win."

Staponski hooted derision. "That's Romaine. Never saw a bet he didn't like."

Jack shrugged. "Put some money down."

"Not 'til I see my green first."

"C'mon, Spuds. Red's already got a guy on base. And no outs! Besides—you heard who the Pirates got pitching."

"Who cares?"

9

"A rookie. Joe Dawson. Guy's never won a game in late innings. Never."

Spuds maundered over that information, turned finally to his hired help. The bartender shrugged.

"It's better than his usual."

Staponski rested arms hairy as an ape on his bar.

"Okay, Romaine, I'll stake ya. Reds to win."

A chorus of voices chimed in, bets shouted out on either side. Jack penciling down wagers and odds on the margin of an *Enquirer*. Spuds leaning in close.

"It's my stake. Whatever you get comes to me, you understand, Jack?"

"Sure, sure," Jack took a buck from the lunger. "My plan all along."

But a newcomer's voice cut the action short.

"Don't count your money, pretty boy. The fat lady ain't sung yet."

Fist Carlton filled the bar's interior door, hands hanging white and scarred from the sleeves of a badly frayed overcoat. Everybody knew Fist Carlton. Everybody knew Fist's boss.

"You comin' quiet, Jack? Or I gotta work?"

Romaine knew, then, why he had been allowed with so little proof of currency into Staponski's back room.

Jack turned to his host.

"Didn't know you were running errands, Spuds."

"Big fish eat the little ones, Jack. You know that."

"Somebody better goddamn hold my bets, then," Jack protested. "I got a straight-up deal here, Spuds. You goddamn better not welch."

A massive, scarred fist snaked around Jack's neck like a noose.

"The fuck are you to complain?"

Chapter two

"White Money"—regular currency,
U.S. or Canadian.

Jack Romaine propped himself up stiffly beside Fist Carlton in a Duesenberg's vast interior, his intestines curdled in knots. There was no conversation, no explanation offered for Mr. Bladehorn's summons, which left Jack free to anticipate a wide variety of modes of hospitality. The steeple of Phillipus Church came into view, a golden hand and gilded finger extended toward the brooding belly of heaven. Jack judged that Fist was taking him somewhere toward Dayton Street, which he tried to tell himself was auspicious. They didn't kill you in places like Dayton Street, did they? For that sort of thing they drove you to the riverfront or out of town. And then when Fist stayed north on Vine, Jack was further relieved, calculating a destination somewhere in the Clifton heights of the city.

First bet he'd have won in a week if there had been any takers. Maple trees shaded one mansion after another on a gentle uphill drive. The river was far behind, now. When Jack turned he could just make out Mount Adams, far away to the east, overlooking the Ohio. Their climbing drive took Jack and his driver along an easy street of millionaires. Years ago men with money built up here to escape the heat, the fever. Some pretty fantastic digs, those guys put up. Two, three storey palaces on manicured grounds, fenced in and shaded with maples and elms. Long, gated drives. Pretty safe bet that behind one of those gates, in one of those palatial homes, was Fist Carlton's boss.

Word was that Oliver Bladehorn had run booze and broads in Chicago before relocating to Cincinnati. Jack had spent some time in Chicago. He had not profited from his sojourn in that city, but he had gained some wisdom. He learned, certainly, that it was much easier to deal off the bottom to any number of micks, wops, krauts, or niggers than it was to a single gangster. Jack had not turned a card with anybody moving whiskey since fleeing the windy city. And he was damn near certain that even in his blindest, drunkest excursions he had never gambled with Oliver Bladehorn.

Jack gathered enough confidence to run his ungloved hand over the smooth finish of the Duesenberg's mahogany dashboard.

"Is that a *radio*? In the *dash*?"

"Fuckin' hick," Fist growled.

"We could hear the game? We could listen right here in the car?"

"Not likely"

"Gimme a break, Fist!"

"Piss off Bladehorn, I'll be breaking your fucking legs."

Jack felt the knot that had partially relaxed retie in the pit of his stomach.

Oliver Bladehorn's mansion rose smooth and modern on the cusp of older properties and architecture. A wrought-iron gate fashioned in the shape of an eagles wing, or maybe a vulture's, was guarded. The Duesenberg passed through with barely a nod from a uniformed sentry to reach a private drive which glided toward a three-storey structure constructed in the art deco style that had become chic.

The place looked like it had been poured from a mold. A

bright white exterior. Couldn't tell if it was made of cement, or just whitewashed. Lots of glass. No hard angles, at least not on the outside. It seemed of a much lighter construction than older, crenelated homes that Jack had seen, but that may have been a deceit wrought by design.

They rumbled past a gaggle of women, forty or more, sipping tea on the broad lawn in their straight dresses and Mary Janes. Buttons'n bows. Resting from croquet, apparently. Mallets abandoned beside brightly striped balls.

"What's this? Your boss some kinda Free Thinker? Or does he just like petticoats?"

"You'll see what he likes," Fist said, and actually smiled.

They didn't stop out front. Fist wheeled the Doosey around to the backside of Bladehorn's modern residence and parked at the entrance to an enormous greenhouse.

"Go ahead."

Fist dipped the lid of his hat toward a well-screened door.

"He's waitin'."

Jack entered the hothouse just ahead of Fist Carlton. The morning's humidity was arid compared to the greenhouse's interior. A startling variety of completely unfamiliar plant life bloomed and tangled and spored from potting tables and peat. And hanging on every vine, limb, and blossom were veritable curtains of bright-colored wings. There were thousands, maybe tens of thousands of creatures pulsing gently on exotic orchids or thrashing on currents of saturated air, their hues electric against the greenhouse's transparent lens.

"Butterflies, Mr. Romaine."

Oliver Bladehorn sported a monocle and an apron over his pinstriped trousers.

"Surely even you can recognize a simple insect."

Jack resisted a reply. Butterflies were not, at that moment, the insect with which he was concerned.

Oliver Bladehorn was an odd combination of parts. A tonsure of hair was perfectly trimmed to laurel a well-waxed skull. He wore a suit and vest beneath his apron, even in this wet sauna, and yet Jack, who was already wet in his pits, could not detect a hint of perspiration on Mr. Bladehorn.

The gangster's face bulged from its bone-work like a rotting gourd. A drool of spittle seeped uncontrolled from a smile slit as though with a knife into that dying and desiccated countenance. Jack squirmed in spite of himself, wishing he could scratch under his arms, his balls. Bladehorn smiled wider.

"Danaus Plexippus," he had a refined voice.

"I beg your pardon?" Jack returned clumsily.

"And so you should, but I refer at present to the Monarch, Mr. Romaine. King of the butterflies. Danaus Plexippus. You see this one here?"

Bladehorn fielded a Monarch on the fly.

"The distinctive coloration? The russet wings set with these black veins? They are veins, you know. And then of course the black border, I especially like that, a black border with two rows of spots…" Bladehorn paused. "D'you know what they're for? The spots?"

"No, sir," Jack confessed. "I don't."

"Warns predators to expect an unsatisfactory encounter." Bladehorn freed his captive king. "The Monarch is unpleasant to the taste, you see. So even when you catch him—you pay a price."

A smile spreading through the seep of spit.

"I see," Jack pumped his head.

Where the hell was this heading?

Bladehorn regarded the man before him critically, thoughtfully.

"I have butterflies from all over the world, Mr. Romaine. The world—imagine. Men have died bringing me butterflies from Borneo and Madagascar. Died solely for my pleasure. At my…instruction. Beautiful creatures, the butterflies, I mean. They come from caterpillars, you know; contemplate if you can that transformation. Gives one hope that something beautiful, something worthwhile, can come from something mean and ugly. Perhaps even vile. You follow me, Mr. Romaine?"

"Don't believe I'm tracking quite yet, sir."

Bladehorn's laugh was abrupt and shrill.

"Why, I have high hopes for you, boy! I see in you the potential for royalty even though to all appearances I have before me only a worm."

Jack felt an added heat at his collar.

"Don't blush. It speaks to a lack of control."

"Go to hell," Jack blurted, and dropped to his knees as Fist drove a mitt deep into his gut.

Nothing quite like a punch below the sternum to get your attention. Your gut cramps, you want to shit and stars swim before your eyes in unfamiliar constellations.

Trying to breathe. Failing.

"He can break your neck, you know," Bladehorn resumed his lecture unperturbed. "I have seen Mr. Carlton break bones like twigs with those talented hands. Is that what you want, Mr. Romaine? Speak up, son."

"…Nnnn…no."

"Good." Bladehorn smiled. "Very good, in fact. Much better."

Jack pulled himself erect on a potting table. There was a trowel, there. A couple of pots. And a handgun. A revolver.

A firearm just sitting there in the open?! Was it loaded?

"Don't be a sucker, Mr. Romaine," Bladehorn swept the weapon into the table's molded drawer.

Jack's arms retreated in a clutch about his stomach.

"Whadda you…want with me? Mr. Bladehorn?"

"I have an opportunity for you, sir, a transformational opportunity, which is to say—a job. You have trouble remaining employed, don't you, Mr. Romaine? Staying on the payroll not one of your strengths, is it? And whatever pay you get, whatever your foreign mother-in-law can't extract from your gin-sodden pockets, whatever doesn't go to your whelp of a son, gets pissed away in booze or gambling.

"You are a welch, a drunk, and a cheater at cards, Mr. Romaine. Your debts chase you like the hounds of hell, as do the men you've cheated. Some of them very dangerous men."

Bladehorn padded drool from his lips.

"To a certain extent I can sympathize. Many a man turns to

drink after losing a loved one. And then with responsibilities, pressures, a man can make mistakes, can fold before a variety of temptations. I understand these things, I do. Makes life uncertain, at best, doesn't it?"

Jack was just beginning to be able to breathe.

"Mind getting to the point?"

Bladehorn frowned. "I was robbed. Property taken, family property. I want it returned."

"Why don't you ask Bone Breaker here to fetch it for you?"

"Cheek. Can be good. Even in an insect. Certainly, I could have Mr. Carlton, or any of my people, make the appropriate inquiries, but that would invite attention from authorities and competitors which at present I cannot afford. And then there is the question of privacy…

"This is a family matter, Mr. Romaine, a private affair which I would much prefer to keep private. I do not want people close to me knowing details of my family or finances. I certainly do not want my own people to know I've been robbed. Nor my other—associates. It could be misconstrued, you see. As a weakness."

Bladehorn paused as if waiting for a riposte.

Jack decided not to oblige.

"I need an outsider for this task, Mr. Romaine. With luck you'll be finished inside a day."

"You said something about pay."

"Naturally," Bladehorn tightened the knot on his apron. "I will advance you five hundred now against another five if you recover my property."

A thousand dollars? One *thousand*?! Jack tried to keep his poker face. He could do a lot with a thousand green.

"A grand, then. All right. For what?"

Bladehorn selected a trowel from the potting table. "A woman will be released from the workhouse—a Miss Sally Price. Fist will provide a photograph and particulars. Miss Price was the fiancée of a man who was once my chauffeur. Name of Jerry Driggers."

"I knew Driggers, what happened to that guy?"

"Shut yer trap and listen," Fist rumbled.

"I was married at the time," Bladehorn continued. "My wife died at sea, you might recall, with our son. Little over a year ago. Made all the papers."

"Didn't catch it."

"Ah. Well. My son was not destined for a long or healthy life and I married Claudia for her money. I was not aware until after my wife's death that she had hidden substantial sums of cash and negotiable securities in an apartment across town.

"I didn't know. Driggers did. Fifty thousand dollars and another quarter million in certificates for the Baltimore & Ohio Railroad stolen by my own driver from a safe beneath a bed which my wife while living never shared with me."

"Talk about cheek."

Bladehorn selected a pot of chrysanthemums. "Driggers planned to start his own bootleg operation. Before I could get to him, he was killed by some jackanapes on the river, some trivial dispute. Taking all knowledge of the cash and securities to a pauper's grave."

"But you figure Sally knows?" Jack supplied.

"About the theft, certainly. And probably how to locate the cash and stocks as well."

"What's she in for?"

"Skipping bail. Pity. If my people had gotten to her first, as we should have done…"

Fist shrank inside his overcoat.

"Say I find this Sally Price," Jack went on. "For the sake of shits and grins let's say that Sally actually does know where to find your property. That's true, she's got a fortune waiting. What makes you think she'll talk?"

Bladehorn smiled icily.

"Pick her up. Bring her to me. She'll talk."

Jack squirmed.

"Not the kinda job I usually do."

Bladehorn troweled damp soil into his pot of flowers.

"How much do you owe, Mr. Romaine?"

"Me? Owe?"

"You have markers out all over Cincinnati, of course," Bladehorn dropped his trowel. "But I believe more serious transgressions lie elsewhere. Chicago, perhaps? Where to my certain knowledge you owe a half-dozen businessmen upwards of a thousand dollars *each*.

"One of those gentlemen is an acquaintance of mine. Mr. Capone? Alphonso Capone? Notorious of late for his Valentine benedictions? Now, I realize that you are small fry, Mr. Romaine, and Mr. Capone has a large organization to run. Nevertheless. You owe. You're late. And I can tell you candidly that if you elect to refuse my offer someone will soon come to collect."

Jack tried a smile of his own. "A thousand bucks, or two thousand, won't pay off six large."

"It will get you out of town," Bladehorn returned blandly. "You can migrate, can't you, Jack? South for the winter. To Mexico, perhaps. Or one of the islands. Just like a butterfly."

Jack was looking at a short list of options.

"Awright," he gave it up. "I pick up the woman. Get her to you. That's it?"

"Entirely," Bladehorn reassured. "But in fairness I should warn that you may have some competition."

"'Scuse me?"

"Fellow used to work for me," Bladehorn replied offhandedly. "Arno Becker. Very unusual man. Very…disturbed."

"Uh huh. And this guy—he know about your property?"

"About the property, I am sure. Perhaps even about Miss Price. In fact, I wouldn't be surprised if he's there tomorrow."

"Tomorrow?" Jack's poker face crumbled to putty.

"At the workhouse, of course. Her prison. Didn't I mention? Miss Price's release is scheduled Tuesday at seven in the morning. Seven sharp. That information is supposed to be confidential, of course. But if I have it—"

"Gotcha." Jack felt as though he'd taken another punch in the stomach. "And what exactly do you mean by 'disturbed'?"

Water slid warm and bubbly down legs shaved smooth and hard as marble. Arno Becker was relaxing in a newly-drawn tub. He placed the razor on a wide windowsill and took in the view. It was a pleasant morning. The window looked down to an open market of the sort favored by residents of Over the Rhine. Their familiar accents wafted up to Becker along with the smell of beer and sauerkraut and freshly-baked bread. It seemed an irritant to interrupt his bath with its attendant pleasantries just to answer the door.

Arno Becker rose from the tub dripping water, the narcissistic product of blonde parents or their gods. The knock at the door sounded again and impatiently, but Arno remained unhurried in his naked perambulation across the hall, through a sitting room, past a coffee table, a drawer littered with forget-me-nots and a rocking chair seeped in blood.

A woman slumped in the rocker. An old woman, frail. Her wrists were bound with wire to the arms of the rocker. There were mutilations at regular intervals on her arms, her torso, her face. Her throat gaped open, blood soaking her cheap shift, and even in death her eyes held the terror of one who knows that her end will not come without ordeal.

She had just warmed the tub for a bath.

A fist pounded now on the door.

"EMMA!"

That Kraut accent. Low German. Jewish.

"Gott damn, frau! Kommen sie!"

"Ich komme, ich komme," Arno warbled a falsetto reply and opened the door.

An old man, bent and stunted with arthritis and ague panted in the hall outside his lofty rooms. A wrapper of sausage in one hand. A wedge of cheese in the door-banger.

"Mein Gott!"

Becker gathered the old man to himself like a fluttering bird, sweeping the fallen sausage and cheese inside the apartment with one well-turned foot.

"I have taken a liberty. As you see."

Directing the husband's attention to his butchered wife.

"I pay you!" the old geezer croaked. "God damn, I swear! I will!"

"Shhhh, I don't want another mess."
Arno clamped a pale hand over the fart's sour old mouth.
"I've just had a bath."

Chapter three

"Cut Up Jackpots"—*an exaggerated rendition of past events.*

A shroud of smoke hung nearly motionless in stale, late-afternoon air that had settled in the valley below the mansions high above the river. Not many suits or vests in this crowd. Most of the men in Jack's neighborhood worked on the docks or in factories or the slaughterhouse. They came home in catalog clothes, heavy overalls and trousers, Buster Browns and brogans and slouch caps, toting tin lunchboxes, wending their way through tribes of barefooted children playing stickball or chasing hoops beneath webs of electric wires and washlines that stretched between rows and rows of tenement housing.

Everywhere were posters and signs to entice the purchase of some good or service. Billboards beckoning from walls and rooftops to offer locals things they could not afford—refrigerators, electric razors—while reminding them of things they could not do without. Every home and sweatshop used Mr. Singer's sewing machine. Look in any kitchen and you'd find a cylinder of Old Dutch Cleanser; "Cleanliness Brings Good Cheer!" the copy promised. Of course, since The Dutch Lady herself was permanently hooded and facing the corner it was hard to test that proposition.

Jack's coldwater flat sweltered with thousands of others in this Appalachian enclave of the city. The Salvation Army had taken over a church across the street, reminding him daily that God did not give his children more trials than they could bear. With that great comfort and assurances of well-cleaned cheer, Jack skirted lackluster women crowding stoops littered with garbage to find the stairs leading to his flat.

In that one-room rental, an old woman bent over a steaming pot at a kerosene stove. With no separate kitchen in the flat, the stove and icebox looked out to a cot and pallet rolled up beside a broken couch. A sink doubled as tub for wash and bath. Aside from the bums lining up for a room across the street, the large pane window offered a view of the sun setting over the rooftops, that swollen fire filtered dark through coal-burned smoke. A skyline of tenements offered an uneven horizon.

"Mart'ahn—" the old woman addressed a dark-haired youngster at the window. Martin turned a page of his book, another one from *The Motor Boys* series, Mamere noticed. Any number of books and magazines were stacked along the wall beneath the window, Zane Grey westerns and *The Saturday Evening Post* taking their place with *The Motor Boys* and *The Radio Boys* and God only knew what other serial attractions.

"Mart'ahn, come to supper."

The nine-year old stifled a cough as he carried his adventure to the apartment's solitary table. Dark eyes to go with hair like his father's, raven-black and straight. A striking face, gaunt, prominent features. The cough came again—and again, this time not to be restrained. His grandmother took a square of cheesecloth off the top of the pitcher resting on their small table, poured water into a battered tin cup.

"Put that nonsense away."

"Yes, Mamere." He dropped his book to the floor.

Mama Erbet would have been at home in Napoleon's empire. A scarf covered the old woman's head, black skirt falling below her booted ankles. She wore a wool sweater, even in the heat, a woman gnawed to the rind. Bent. Desiccated.

There was electricity fed to the apartment, but except for a single plug-in dedicated to the radio that buzzed uncertainly beside the fire escape, the outlets were capped. The young boy took the chair nearest the radio.

"Supper first, Mart'ahn," the grandmother ladled the evening's meal into a modest bowl. It was a triumph, of sorts, the stew she served, a beignet improvised from the peelings of potatoes. The old woman ladled another portion. "You need to eat."

Martin Romaine spooned the gruel mechanically.

"Papa's 'sposed to be home by now."

"Your father is working."

"He said we'd play ball. He promised."

"He has to make a living," she offered without conviction.

The door opened at that moment, practically burst off its flimsy hinges, startling the boy and his grandmother to their feet.

"Papa!"

"Son."

"Can we play? You said—!"

"A minute, Martin, justa minute."

Jack Romaine tossing his hat to the table on a rush past his son to the radio.

"Papa?"

"Shhhh."

A squawk of static turning into discernible language: "…but it all ends when Joe Dawson—Dawson, can you believe it—? Comes up with a home run in the bottom of the eleventh inning…"

"That can't be!" Jack pounded the fragile table.

"…to win the game, Pirates 7, Reds 6 in extra innings!"

Jack sank into a chair, oblivious to his son and mother-in-law.

"Goddamn Dawson, I can't believe it."

The boy reached down and snatched the radio's cord from its socket.

"Martin! The hell, boy?"

"You said we'd play ball!"

"Mamere, tell him to plug that thing back in."

Mama Erbet rolled a frugal smoke from a tin of tobacco beside the sink.

"You said you'd be back!" Martin insisted. "You said you had a day off work and we'd play ball!"

"Oh, Christ, Sport, what can I tell ya? I was on my way. I got held up."

"You're lying."

"Don't call your father a liar," Mamere said by rote.

"You were drinking," the boy declared. "Or gambling—it was the game, wasn't it? You bet on the Reds!"

"Forget the Reds. I got work. A new job."

"But you promised—!"

"I KNOW WHAT I GODDAMN PROMISED! JESUS AREN'T YOU HEARING ME? I GOT WORK!"

The boy trembled suddenly, as if with a sudden chill.

And then came the coughs, wracking, persistent.

"Oh, jeez, Martin!" Jack reached clumsily for his son.

Mart'ahn darted past his father and into the water closet.

"Martin…"

"Leave him alone," the old woman ordered.

"Don't you start," Jack turned on his mother-in-law. "Don't you goddamn start!"

"You broke a promise." She held her cigarette from underneath, in the European fashion.

"Hey, I got collared by a gorilla, all right? I didn't have a lot of choice."

"And this is for your son to understand?"

"Gotta grow up sometime."

"Not with gorillas. My daughter would not want to see her son in the company of apes."

"Don't bring Gilette into this, awright? DON'T."

"She was your wife. The mother to your son, God rest her soul! She would want her son's father coming home when the sun is still up. Playing ball with his boy. Reading books! Not drunk and gambling and rubbing elbows with animals!"

"I'm getting a thousand smackers rubbing elbows. How would she like that?"

The crone sniffed.

"I believe it when I see it."

Jack reached into his second-hand trousers and threw a wad of cash onto the table.

"That's five hundred bucks. Minus a couple of beers. And that's just up front."

Her hand trembled at her throat.

"Mary and Joseph who will you kill?"

"...Nobody."

"These are not honest wages!" She backed away from the table. "This is not good money, you cannot tell me it is!"

"Buy a lot of baseballs, though, won't it? Or what about a glove? Martin's been wanting a new glove."

"What Martin wants is a father."

Jack clenched his fists. "You're busting my hump, you know that, old woman?"

"Who paid you this money?" she demanded.

"The hell does it matter?"

"Hah. A criminal."

Jack threw up his hands. "What am I supposed to do? Tell the man to take a hike? Kiss my ass?"

"Whatever is right," she replied. "That is what you must do."

"Bladehorn's not just some shill, Mamere. He's got me by the balls."

"Because you *gave* them to him! You and your drinking. Your cards!"

Jack reached for his fedora.

"I'm going out."

"Not with these!" She gathered the wad of bills off the table. "At least if we take blood money it will not go for gin!"

Jack displayed a twenty in his suit pocket.

"It's all right. I got change."

Twenty dollars will buy you a good time and by the time Jack Romaine made his way back to his uneasy roost it was well past midnight. He stumbled through the unlocked door, bottle in hand, to find his mother-in-law snoring on her pallet beside the window. Martin tossed fitfully nearby, laboring for an easy breath in his cot. That hair, so rich, so dark.

Jack saw the worn baseball glove that doubled for the boy's pillow. He placed his bottle carefully onto the floor, fumbled deep into a trouser pocket, and pulled something out.

It was a baseball.

"Won it on a bet, *mon petit*," Jack whispered to his son and slipped the ball beneath the boy's leather pillow. "Got it autographed, too. Joe Dawson."

Romaine weaved unsteady as he slipped his broken watch off its fob. He tapped the crystal impatiently.

"Papa's gotta sleep," he announced to the heedless room, and dropped like a loose suit onto the couch.

First light. A rising sun caught the ramparts on what anyone would be excused for believing to be a castle. Cincinnati's workhouse was an impressive stretch of architecture. Three tiers of cells housed inmates behind iron-barred windows that ran one-and-a-half football fields down the street. Corner towers rose to break up that long expanse, along with a mansarded center section. The walls were corbelled like ancient fortresses, and machicolations were cut at intervals as if hot tar or boiling water were to be poured down upon some unwitting invader.

Sally Price had not expected to leave the workhouse alive. She had spent a year-and-a-half looking over her shoulder, fearing a garrotte or knife. But the forbidding walls had proven safe, and now Sally was free, a woman of thirty, small, unattractive, with an adolescent's perennially blemished complexion, narrow eyes and poverty of hair.

A sour German matron behind a metal grille required Sally to sign for the same portmanteau she'd brought to prison; all her earthly possessions were lumped in that bag. Well, almost all. Sally had already changed out of the striped muslin which identified her as a thief. A plaid skirt and sweater had replaced her prison garb.

"Make sure it's all there," the clerk instructed.

A change of underwear. A pair of eyeglasses, broken. A woolen handbag that Sally did not open.

"That's everything."

A pair of guards lingered as Miss Price received her final dispensation through a porthole in the chickenwire grill. Three dollars and seventy cents. Earned during time served.

"Don't spend it all in one place," a screw mocked her.

"How 'bout my letter?"

The guard smirked. "Oh, Sally always gets her letter, don't she? Every month, hah, Sal? Like yer period."

Sally just waited. Silently.

The clerk scowled, "Awright," and shoved a manila envelope through the wire along with a pen and clipboard.

"Sign here. And again for your copy."

Sally signed the receipts slowly, elaborately.

"Gotta hand you one thing, Price. You keep it buttoned better than most."

Sally did not reply. It seemed, still, the safest thing to do.

The whitewashed wall opposite the Romaines' home beat back a rising sun. Mama Erbet stirred sleepily. Martin slumbered over the baseball he did not yet know nestled inside his glove. Jack woke up still dressed and holding his head. He looked at his son, his son's grandmother, and the cheaply framed photograph hanging on the wall above his sofa and bed.

It could have been a movie marquee. A striking young woman with raven hair and Hollywood eyelashes smiles buoyantly in the arms of a handsome American corpsman beneath the Arc de Triomphe.

Jack lingered over the photo a long moment. "Jill," he appealed through a mouth dry as clay. "Jack and Jill."

He left the sofa, wobbled over to the water pitcher handy on the sill and slurped water straight from its metal lip. Only then did Jack glance outside to notice—

The wall of the tenement on the other side of the street glowing pink with a well-risen sun.

"Shit!"

Sally Price emerged from prison to find an open street milling with people. What might at first have seemed to be a curb-side celebration was in fact a congress of citizens gathered to protest conditions inside the workhouse.

REHABILITATION, NOT INCARCERATION, a well-lettered banner fluttered damply. WORK WITH DIGNITY, urged a placard alongside.

Some of Cincinnati's wealthiest were turned out in a public display of progressive fervor to urge a change in the situation Sally had so recently endured. They seemed so earnest, these nouveau riche, so flushed with painless purpose, the women dressed in summer skirts and cloche hats, their necks draped in wreaths of beaded necklaces. The husbands congregating casually in Oxford baggies, or jodhpurs, their eyes shaded by derbies or motor caps.

Sally forged past the well-intended party, keeping her eyes on the ground just beyond her feet. It was hard after being imprisoned not to be distracted by so much activity. Ladies and gents were everywhere, tapping bunting onto booths erected in the landscaped park across the street, raising voices in warbled exhortation, or song, or prayer.

Adding to that congestion were leisure seekers and hangers-on. There were at least a dozen cyclists, real pests, showing off their ridiculous contraptions, drawing protests from trolleybus jockeys as they played chicken across the tracks. And vendors hawked their wares from all points of the compass, their wheeled stalls a barrier along the street.

Sally inhaled deeply. Food! The smells of sausage and chilli and cinnamon! But first the letter. Sally rummaged inside her fabric bag to find the manila envelope. She opened it carefully, almost reverently. And with the expected letter she found as well a handful of ten-dollar bills. Sally counted them quickly—

Fifty dollars!

It wasn't hard to find a private cranny behind a vendor's cart. Within moments she was gorging down the first real food of a year-and-a-half, the letter pressed smooth over her skirted knee as a Coney dog oozed chilli onto a napkin fashioned from the latest *Enquirer*.

> *Dear S,*
>
> *You're out! Sensational! I'll see you, but it won't be until sometime in the evening. Could be late. You'll have found the cash inside the envelope, so go enjoy yourself for the day and then check into the Hotel Milner. It's off Vine. There is a room reserved in your name. Check in some time around five o'clock, treat yourself to a good dinner and wait for me.*
>
> *Looking forward to seeing you,*
> *Alex Goodman*

Sally read the well-penned instructions once again. Then she returned the letter to its envelope, stuffing it along with the cash deep inside her blouse, pausing a moment, then, to consider—

It was a long time until five o'clock. How best to spend her first day of freedom?

Sally straightened suddenly. She walked with purpose to the front of the chilli dogcart. Waited for the vendor to acknowledge her presence.

"Yeah?"

"There a cross-town to Vine?"

"Trolley, yeah. Be by in a snap."

"And then can I take Vine to the zoo?"

"You want Number 78." He lipped a cigarette. "Straight up."

Jack Romaine did not find Sally Price as she negotiated a course through knots of gentlemen, ladies, and cyclists on her way to the trolley bus that arrived in a shower of sparks. Jack was pacing back and forth on the prison side of the street, a hound anxious to pick up a buried scent. Once again he checked the faded lithograph that Bladehorn had provided.

That was Sally. Bad skin, angular face, narrow eyes and mousy hair.

"Jesus," Jack had protested when Fist gave him the picture. "You expect me to know her from this?"

"She's the only one they're lettin' out," Fist returned. "Just be there."

But Jack was late, way late. It was nearly eight o'clock, the street already busy as a bee in a tar bucket, and he had no idea where to look for Sally Price.

A bell rang sharply. The trolley. Through a shifting crowd of cyclists and commuters Jack glimpsed a woman juggling a portmanteau and a Coney dog. Not too many women carrying suitcases, this morning. In fact—

"Gotcha."

Jack sprinted across the street just in time to take a bicycle's wheel square across his knee, rider and runner falling to the bricks together like a couple of footballers.

The rider cursing from a pretzel of broken spokes.

"Hell with you," Jack rose limping to plunge back through the cordon that lay between him and Sally Price.

Where was she?!

There! There she was, on the trolley!

She sat hindmost in a sandwich of commuters on the bottom level of a double-truck, a mousy woman almost smiling.

"All aboard."

Jack limped toward the two-decker streetcar. A pedestrian cut him off. Damn near knocked him down, in fact.

"HEY, BUDDY!" Jack challenged, but the guy just sailed past him, bounding like a goddamned deer from the sidewalk onto the streetcar.

He was tall, this late boarder, and blond. A boutonnière fixed gaily to his vest. A new derby hat and spats.

Their eyes met for a moment. Distant. Fleeting. But then wires sizzled overhead and Jack was still a stone's throw away as the car began its clatter up the gentle grade toward Vine Street.

"HOLD THE CAR!"

Jack now charging past the chilli-dog cart. The trolley was pulling away, gathering speed—!

"DRIVER! HOOOOOOLD UP!"

But the electric car clacked away noisily, accelerating uphill.

"JESUS, HOLD UP!"

Sally turned to see a man running up the tracks, his shouts muted by the racket of wheels and rails. He looked silly back there, like Charlie Chaplin. A handsome man holding his knee in a run for the trolley!

For a moment it seemed he might even make it. A final sprint drew Jack almost within reach of the car.

"SOMEBODY—GIVE ME—!" he gasped at a dead run.

But then he stumbled.

Sally laughed out loud when she saw Jack's comic spill, the hands splayed out to break that awkward fall onto the pavement, the Charlie Chaplin hat flying off that otherwise handsome head. Sally wasn't the only one amused by Romaine's painful spill. Passengers widely separated by class and income and prospects joined her hoots of derision in a shared moment of Schadenfreude. And why not? The man pulling himself off the asphalt had to be a klutz. A loser.

Prob'ly drunk, Sally was thinking. And anyway—

He had nothing to do with her.

Laughter trailed down the tracks, sharp and brittle. But there was one passenger who did not share the moment. The blonde man in spats did not laugh. It was not that he had missed the antics of the fellow running to catch the trolley. No, indeed. The tall, blond passenger with the boutonnière had noticed Jack as he leapt from the street to catch Number 78. He noticed Jack just as he noticed everything on the grounds outside the prison and on the street. But Romaine's predicament was not an object of humor for this gentleman, nor even of curiosity. Arno Becker's peculiar attentions were focused instead on the woman he had followed from prison. She had a strident laugh, he noted. Too much scalp showing for her years. And her mouth was smeared with chilli.

Jack Romaine raised himself on knees scraped raw, craning to spot Sally among the passengers in the trolley that *clack-clack-clacked* up the hill. His shouted curse died long before it reached the ears of anyone aboard. Already, passengers were returning to their newspapers and cinnamon buns, their interest in Jack's spill waning well ahead of his shouted profanity.

Sally's attention, certainly, was already shifted, leaning against her woolen bag to face the damp breeze drafted by the trolley's steady transport. She was savoring her new freedom at the car's uncanvassed window, eager to feel the river's air against her face. To smell its moldy aroma. Admiring the view of the Ohio, imagining herself installed on one of the shaded lawns banking that languid watercourse, or sipping tea in those well-made houses whose floors and toilets she used to scrub, those homes that, until recently, she could never hope to own.

The fifty bucks burning a hole in her rude purse? Was chump change compared to the reward to come; Alex had promised. A payoff for keeping her lips sealed.

So many things on Sally's mind, a maelstrom of competing emotions, expectations, and concerns. Arno Becker, on the other hand, was single-minded in his attention. His purpose.

Arno regarded Miss Price as he adjusted the carnation in his lapel. Should he approach her now? Or wait?

Perhaps wait, he decided.

Let her enjoy the ride. Relax. Lower her guard.

Meanwhile, Jack Romaine was hobbling back to the cart hawking chilli and dogs.

"What happened ta you?" the vendor challenged.

"When's the next trolley?" Jack grated.

"Half hour."

A half hour! Jack ran his hands through his hair. Well, that was it. He'd lost her. A deep, deep nausea stabbed him in the stomach. Bladehorn wasn't going to like this. Not at all.

Jack was about to limp away, but then the smell from the cart reminded him. The Coney dog. Chilli and cinnamon.

He turned back to the vendor.

"I was 'spose to meet my girl, see."

"Your girl."

"Yeah, plaid skirt and sweater? Flat-chested?"

The vendor's eyes narrowed.

Jack pulled out a crisp dollar bill along with the black and white photograph.

"Think of anything might help me out?"

He shrugged. "She might've asked about the trolley."

Jack peeled off another bill.

"Just tell me where."

The vendor gathered the bills in his cigarette hand.

"Try the zoo."

Sally paid her two bits and entered the Cincinnati Zoo. It was the city's pride, the zoo. Best in the country, people said. More animals than any zoo, animals you couldn't see anyplace else.

Sally adored those large mammals who spent their time in water, the hippopotami, the sea lions. The big cats were also a thrill, of course. And who could resist the chimps and bonobos? The one great ape? But it was the birds that always offered a particular fascination for Sally, especially the predators, the raptors. As a girl Sally had made her daddy stop so she could watch when the keepers fed live snakes to the secretary bird. She had relished that encounter, the crested relative of the falcon, earthbound, stamping its clawed feet onto the snake's neck, a sharp plunge of beak. Shaking the reptile to make certain of death. Then the feeding, the entrails bursting from their integument. Other children would hide their eyes, but not Sally.

But today she ignored the aviary, pausing instead to spend another nickel for food—a sausage in brown paper, a sweet roll, a root beer—before skirting the hippos' paddock and the albino rhinoceros to head directly for Swan Lake.

The city's zoo had been built on the acreage of a large dairy; Swan Lake dominated the interior, a body of water vast enough to accommodate sailboats and offering along its shoreline any number of retreats. On a weekend you'd expect to see hundreds of families milling about along the lake's well-tended shoreline. By midday there would be any number of boaters on the water. All forms of languid recreation.

But at half past eight on a working day, the shoreline was deserted. There weren't even any employees about, the staff still occupied with the tasks of feeding, grooming and medicating the largest gathering of exotic animals in the country. Sally, in fact, had not seen a single soul on her trek to the far side of Swan Lake. An ideal place for a woman seeking privacy. A retreat from prying eyes

She settled with her sausage and sweets on a bench tucked by an eddy of shallow water shaded by a grove of sycamore. No company but a gaggle of ducks that came for the crumbs that Sally threw into the water.

She retrieved the letter from her bag and spread it in her lap. Fifty dollars, and a hotel room waiting at five! Sally smiled. She counted her money again, chiding herself for profligate spending, separating the bills from the coins. Like Midas counting his hoard.

She finished the root beer, then returned to the letter, reading it once more before turning it over and smoothing the stationery on the bench's hardwood planks, careful not to soil the precious correspondence on the wrapper stained with the grease of her sausage.

Those small chores completed, Sally could for the first time in eighteen months simply relax.

No walls. No guards. So quiet. So still.

She closed her eyes and breathed. The air was clear, swept of haze or smoke by a mild breeze just hinting of autumn.

She must have fallen asleep because when next she opened her eyes there was a tall blond man standing near. Some swell in spats. Fiddling with a carnation.

"Gorgeous, isn't it?"

She jumped as if hit with a cattle prod.

"Didn't mean to startle," Arno Becker removed his derby.

"I didn't hear ya."

"I imagine not. I apologize."

Sally reached blindly for her letter, wadding it inside the butcher paper that wrapped her sausage.

"Not leaving on my account, I hope?" Arno remained amiable.

Sally dropped the letter and wrapper into the trash.

"Look, I ain't no whoor."

"Never imagined you were," he replied.

"We got no business," she gathered her soda bottle into her fist.

"Oh, but we do, Sally."

She froze at the unexpected familiarity.

"…I gotta go."

Arno reached out almost lazily to jerk the bottle from her hand.

She cried out sharply.

"Ever hear a panther, Sally? A panther in the wild screams exactly like a woman in agony. Monkeys, too. Monkeys can scream bloody murder. Not that anyone would hear a primate or a panther out here. We are so out of the way, aren't we? So…isolated."

"Whadda you want?" her pale face was grey.

"Why, the loot, Sal. The moolah. Your boyfriend's pickings, and don't tell me you don't know what I'm talking about."

"But I—AHH!"

She gasped, her wrist jacked up now between her shoulder blades.

"Fifty thousand dollars twists a lot of arms, Sally girl. Not to mention a quarter million in railroad stocks. So let's just forget the ifs, ands and buts, shall we? Now, where did Jerry Driggers hide the stash?"

"Makes you think he'd tell me?"

"Oh, you know something. Or maybe somebody," Arno found the knife inside his corded twill trousers. "I don't presume to know the details, but Jerry surely did and you were Jerry's gal, weren't you, Sally?"

"Jerry was just the driver; he wasn't the brains! He wasn't!"

"Who was, then?"

"Oh, God!"

"Come on."

"I can't!"

"They say you keep it shut pretty good, honey. Well. We'll see."

Jack Romaine scoured the zoo's grounds at a limping dogtrot, his tie pulled loose from a shirt soaked wet with sweat, his jacket slung over an arm.

Sally was here, somewhere, she had to be!

A trumpet blared to split his skull.

Well, she wasn't at the elephants' cage. Wasn't around the monkeys, either. Or at the arboretum—he'd checked all those exhibits. In fact, he'd checked everyplace. Unless she had doubled back—?

A fresh panic. Who was he kidding? She could have come and gone and he'd never know! What the hell were the odds, anyway, of finding anybody at a goddamned zoo?

What if he couldn't find her?

What would Bladehorn do?

Jack had a fleeting impulse to bolt. Five hundred bucks gave a man a good head start. He could take his son and mother in law, catch a train—To where?

You couldn't outrun bastards like Bladehorn. Jack had scrammed his ass out of Chicago and what had it gotten him?

Jack skidded to a halt and the thought occurred. More like a hope—

Maybe Sally wasn't here for the exhibits at all. Maybe she was just trying to lie low.

Jack wiped his forehead. Even assuming she was still on the grounds, how would he go about a search? There was a hell of lot of territory to cover. Acres!

Start with the lake, he decided. There was nobody on the water, yet. But the shoreline? Sure! A perfect place for somebody looking to stay out of the sun. Or out of sight. Out of the way.

So how many places could you find along the shore of Swan Lake? How long would it take to go all the way around?

Jack set off at a lope.

It was a half hour later and he almost missed her. Jack had finally reached the far-side shoreline, winded and drenched with sweat, when he saw a flock of pigeons vying with a pair of mallards over some sort of bread that lay scattered in crumbs before a park bench. A bag on the ground beside a trashcan. Or was that a purse?

It was the woolen handbag; Jack remembered. The one she was carrying when she got on the trolley.

"Get off, you," Jack swiped at the pigeons on the bench. Made sure no one was looking as he rifled Sally's purse.

Next to nothing inside. A pair of glasses, busted. Underwear. Some crumbs of bread. A waft of chilli and cinnamon. The scrawl of her signature on the prison receipt—Jesus, was that all? But at least he knew Sally was here. Or had been here.

Jack's heart hammered as though he were still in the infantry as he kneeled to inspect the ground around the park bench.

A carpet of elm and maple leaves were freshly turned to expose some injury to the soft earth beneath. You didn't have to be an Indian to see the gouges along the ground where something or somebody had been dragged away from the bench. Sally digging in her heels, maybe? And what was this? He wasn't a fucking Mohican, but wasn't that a boot print? Jack knelt to inspect an imprint too large for Sally or any woman he'd ever met. The heel's mold was stamped much more deeply into the sammy soil than the toe. Light on the toe, heavy on the heel. Like he was walking backward.

"Oh, shit."

Jack looked past the rim of the trashcan along the path of the troweled earth and boot prints to the lake beyond. It was shallow along the shoreline. You could see ducks breaking a smooth crease on water smooth as glass. And then he saw it.

"Mary and Joseph."

Jack shed his shoes and socks on the run as he plunged into

Swan Lake. What looked like a dozen strands of hair spread like a spill of oil on the water. Jack waded in knee deep to grab that meager purchase. He reached out. Gave a tug.

Sally Price's scalp popped free of a bloody skull.

Chapter four

*"Shill"—one who displays a
ticket to an attraction for the
purpose of enticing another.*

J ack heaved what little was left in his stomach into the trash can
beside the park bench.

"Oh, boy. Oh, boy."

Jack had seen bodies dismembered before, had seen limbs
blown off from artillery, had ministered to men with gangrene, men
hideously wounded in the trenches. But a body shattered by shell or
gunfire was impersonally violated. This corpse looked as though it
had come from an abattoir, flayed along the belly, deep cuts into the
tendons of her knees and hamstrings. That awful, naked skull.

Like a monkey skinned for meat.

Jack was pushing away from the bin when he noticed the half-
eaten chilli-dog inside, a wad of grease and beef wreathed in brown
paper and vomit. He glanced about the bench—no other trash obvious except a soda bottle still fizzing on the ground.

Some last meal, a chilli dog and a root beer. He turned his attention back to the trash.

"What's that?" Was that a scrap of stationery wadded inside the chilli-dog's wrapper?

Jack struggled to keep a fresh wave of nausea at bay as he retrieved the stained wrapper from the trashcan. You could see the watermark on the paper, *Eaton's Highland Linen*. Pretty fancy paper to waste on an ex-con, but then, you wouldn't want your friends talking behind your back. Jack returned to the bench, pinching his fingers to separate the stationery from its larded encasement. Moments later he had Sally's letter.

...Glad you're out...Money...See you...Hotel Milner...

"'*Alex Goodman*'?" Jack muttered aloud.

Who the hell was Alex Goodman?

Jack brushed off the letter as best he could before slipping it into the breast pocket of his suit. Arno would not have thrown this letter away, he was sure of that. If Becker had seen this letter, he'd have kept it. Sooooo...

Arno must have surprised Sally at the bench. She managed to toss the letter before the bastard got to work on her. Jack felt another wave of bile threatening. If he had been at the prison when he was supposed to be, Sally Price might have been spared her ordeal, at least at Becker's hand.

If he'd got up on time. If he hadn't pitched a drunk the night before, or played cards—!

But then Jack told himself that even if he had been parked on the prison steps, even if he had taken Sally by the arm, Becker would still have been there and would surely have tracked them both. Wouldn't he? And Arno certainly wouldn't let Jack get away with Sally without a fight; why, he would have killed Jack right along with Sally. Sure he would! And then there'd be two scalps soaking in the pond. So it didn't matter that Jack was hung over and late, did it? It hadn't made two cents' difference—that's what Jack told himself. That was the dodge he tried to sell.

But his gut wasn't buying it. And Oliver Bladehorn sure as hell wasn't going to buy it. Jack sank to the wooden bench. Sally was gone, nothing he could do about that, but what about this character Goodman? What was Alex Goodman's connection to this business? There was no doubt in Jack's mind that Becker got everything out of Sally Price that she had to give. Becker would be waiting for Alex Goodman at the Milner Hotel—unless, of course, he didn't need to. Unless Sally had sent him straight to the stolen cash and notes.

But had Sally ever known where to locate Bladehorn's property? It was apparent that Jerry Driggers had stashed the loot someplace, or with someone, but what made Oliver Bladehorn think that a thief sleeping with Bladehorn's wife would trust a cast-off girlfriend with that information?

The answer was that Bladehorn simply had no other lead to follow. But now there was a new name in the mix, a man who knew Sally, who obviously was taking great pains to remain out of sight as he squirreled Miss Price out of town. You didn't do things like that for shits and grins, so Jack was betting, hoping, really, that Alex Goodman was somehow involved with the theft of Bladehorn's cash and securities. Jack had to reach Goodman before Becker did, that much was clear. But how the hell do you get the drop on a killer you've never seen?

What did a butcher look like, anyhow?

Jack took a last look at Sally's corpse. He could not afford to stick around.

"Sorry, Sal."

He picked up his socks and shoes and limped along the shoreline back past the paddocks of the plant eaters and the cages of the big cats. The primate cage got his attention, chimps and orangutans fixing him with uncharacteristically silent stares.

Jack Romaine left the Cincinnati Zoo well before noon, hopping a single-truck streetcar heading south. He needed to put as much distance between himself and Swan Lake as he could. He was desperate for a drink. His hands were trembling in his lap and it wasn't even noon, but Jack could not chance an unwelcome encounter at any of his usual haunts.

There was a woman in the car with a baby carriage. One of those perambulators that were becoming popular. Big rubber tires, pneumatic. Big hooped canopy. An infant socked away inside, impervious to sun or rain, the mother letting the car's gentle sway prolong her baby's slumber. She placed something near its head, a teething ring, maybe? Jack tried to imagine his darkhaired son waking from a deep sleep to find his father's gift, the autographed ball waiting to be discovered beside Martin's pillowing glove. Might be the last token Martin ever got from his old man. Because if Becker didn't kill him, odds were Bladehorn would. After Fist broke his legs.

The joker in the deck was Alex Goodman. Fumbling a smoke from a damp pack, Jack tried to imagine how Goodman could plausibly be connected to the heist. Was he Jerry Drigger's bosom buddy, or Sally's brother-in-law, or third in a ménage à trois? Maybe he was humping Bladehorn's missus. Talk about an inside job. Or maybe he was a fucking priest, it didn't matter. All that mattered was that some time after five o'clock Alex Goodman would enter the Milner Hotel expecting to meet Sally Price and Arno Becker would be waiting.

Jack felt a coil of smoke and nicotine working down. He didn't know how he'd come out against a man who took scalps. It wasn't the killing itself that gave pause. Jack had killed before. The whistle blew and you were up and over and it was balls and bayonets and barbed wire. Machine guns and shrapnel. The screams of men and animals drowned inside the concussion of artillery and tanks and grenades.

But war was a corporate slaughter. You fought as a group; you died en masse. Jack had killed any number of faceless enemies by martial order, but never by himself. What would it be like to face Arno Becker on his own?

And even assuming he got past Becker, was there any guarantee he'd get the time of day from Alex Goodman? What would he do if Goodman simply refused to talk? Could Jack beat or torture a man for information to save himself, or Martin, or Mamere? Or would he simply turn Goodman over to Fist Carlton and wash his own hands clean? Jack wasn't kidding himself, these were sorry odds in a sorry hand, but he'd been called. He stubbed his smoke on the car's lacquered sill.

It was time to show or fold.

* * *

The Hotel Milner was on Seventh, just off Vine. What could he do to improve the odds between now and five o'clock? First thing, was to clean up. Jack's feet were still damp inside his socks, his woolen trousers clung to his calves, and his shirt was rank. He couldn't go to the Milner like this.

Jack thumbed through the bills in his jacket. He'd filched a hundred bucks from the advance money that Mamere stashed under her cot and so for the first time in a long time, was cash rich. He'd be able to get some nice duds. Maybe take a car to the Empress after and get something in his stomach. No point in meeting this date on an empty stomach.

Or empty hands, either. He'd need a knife, at minimum, and maybe a pair of knuckles. Could get those from Spuds. Might as well pay off his marker while he was at it, make the Polack happy.

Jack dropped stiffly from the streetcar at West Fifth, found a café not far from the Carew Building. Mostly tradesman and merchants downtown. Manufacturers and railroaders didn't get a lunch. Jack scanned the paper over eggs and hash browns and about a gallon of coffee. You couldn't look at a newspaper without smelling money. Story on the front page said by September the Carew Building would be a pile of scrap. A skyscraper in its place. Forty nine stories tall. Forty nine! What kind of gelt did it take to build a place like that?

He checked the sports and the horses and was lighting his third Chesterfield when a clock reminded him of the hour. He stubbed out his cigarette, downed his coffee to the grounds. He could not afford to be late.

It took a couple of hours for Jack to get himself clean, clothed and armed. He crossed Vine around four on his way to the Milner. It was a nice hotel. You entered the lobby on ankle-deep rugs spread across an oak floor buffed to a pleasant sheen. Paintings all over, large oils, mostly. Landscapes of the Ohio or Mississippi. The obligatory portrait of the governor and General Grant. All displayed beneath electric lighting that was incandescent and expensive and mostly unnecessary.

Fair number of folks milling in the lobby, which suited Jack's purpose. A banner over the entry to the bar greeted attendees to a convention of railroad executives. Pretty easy to spot that crowd, gents in their fifties and sixties with drinks and cigars and floozies flashing leg alongside. The usual complement of couples, married, courting or adulterating, drifting about.

Jack pulled a newly-bought Hamilton from his vest, checked it against a cabinet clock in the lobby. He returned the timepiece to his vest pocket, handling the fob like worry beads. Pausing to examine his reflection in one of the hotel's many gilded mirrors.

He told himself that he fit right in. The man staring back from the glass did not look like some jerk scrapping for cash or booze. It was a clean-shaven man in the mirror, a well-boned comer in a brand new single-breasted frock. A silk four-in-hand. Studs for the lightly-striped shirt and a new pair of Cole Haan shoes

He cinched the knot of his tie. Act like you owned the place, that was the thing. Like you belonged.

He crossed toward the desk inhaling a mixed atmosphere of French perfume and Cuban cigars and looking smart. Jack paused along his measured course to buy a paper from a selection near the concierge, leaving the girl a tip; sufficient but not ostentatious. Trying to remain unimpressed with the gents in tails and cummerbunds tapping ashes into potted ferns. The women flat as boys in the little black dresses that were all the rage. Their cigarettes coiling smoke from the tips of ivory holders. Boas and beads.

He'd give anything for a drink and there was a bar to oblige, flouting inspection just beyond the lobby. You couldn't buy booze, not even at the Milner, but you could bring your own. Jack would give much to join the murmur of conversation rising along that long brass rail, guys and gals consorting in mixed company. But he stopped himself, folding his paper as casually as he could manage before strolling past the bar to reconnoiter the front desk.

There were three clerks attending. Older man with the mien of a gatekeeper. Fella next to him looked fag. The third clerk keeping his eyes caged on the ledgers. No prospects there. Would have to be a bellhop, then. Jack took his time selecting the likeliest mark.

There he was, a kid kissing ass for tips. Chinstrap frayed at the edges. A tangle of unruly hair spilling below a cylinder of wool and tassel.

Jack strolled over.

"Sir?"

"Looking for a room."

"Check-in's at the desk, sir."

"Said I was looking," Jack displayed his wallet. "Didn't say anything about checking in."

The kid pushed Jack's wallet away.

"Not here."

"Where, then?"

"By the lift."

"After you."

The bellboy hefted a couple of bags on the way over.

"I don't have much time," the kid said.

"Room is already reserved," Jack pressed a buck into his hand. "Price is the name. Sally Price."

"You wanna number?"

"Yeah. And whether she's checked in."

"Wait in the lobby." The kid lifting the bags again in response to the elevator's descent. "Soon's I drop these off, I'll be back."

Jack found a chair in the lobby below a framed oil of a riverboat. Hiding behind his *Enquirer* and trying to ignore the sweat that threatened to stain his expensively starched collar. Didn't take more than a month for the bellboy to get back.

"Got something for me?"

"Gonna cost you another buck."

Jack was already slipping him the bill.

"There's a room, all right. Paid in advance. The lady ain't checked in yet, though."

"Anybody else checked in?"

"You, ah…you got a relationship with this lady, sir? This Miz Price?"

Jack produced a brand new five-dollar bill.

"Let's say I'm her husband."

The kid grinned.

"Husband? Really? Well, that's queer as turtles 'cause there's a gent already up there says he's her husband, too."

Upstart little fuck.

"Tell me something—his trousers. Were they nice and dry? Or did they look like they mighta been soaked?"

"Hard to say."

"Try." Jack keeping the fiver in his hand.

The bellhop glanced back to the desk, to the concierge.

"Gent looked spic and span to me. Not a suit, though, not like you. Just trousers and a linen jacket."

"But dry?"

"As a bone."

Of course, dry clothes didn't prove anything. Arno Becker could as easily have changed into dry duds as had Jack.

"What about the number?"

The bellboy scanned the lounge nervously.

"I dunno, mister, I don't want any trouble."

"Come on. We're almost there."

"…Room four-four-nine."

Jack took the lift to the fourth floor. He tipped the operator two bits and waited for the carriage to descend before turning down a hallway that still had fixtures for gas lighting. On the way to Room 449 an aging valet passed by, and a maid. Jack shoved his hands into his pockets on reaching the room, pausing at the door to make sure the hallway was empty. His left hand came out ringed in brass. A long, folding knife filled his right hand.

Seven inches of blade in the knife. He snapped it open, slipped it beneath the door's knocker and let the boar's head drop onto its brass plate.

No response.

Jack tried the knocker again.

"Who is it?" an androgynous falsetto queried from behind the door.

Was that Becker waiting inside? Or was it Alex Goodman? Jack had to throw the dice.

"Sally, it's me. Alex."

If Alex Goodman was waiting on the other side of the door Jack would have to break in. But if the fellow on the other side of the door was Arno Becker—

Jack waited.

Then it came, the snick of a deadbolt, hinges, the scrape of a bright chain. A sliver of light peeled from pillar to post and Jack kicked the door straight into Arno Becker's face.

"SUCKER!!" Jack slashed with his knife—

And got nothing but air.

Becker recovering from a somersault with a broken nose and a knife of his own. Left hand. A southpaw.

"Do come in."

He lunged and Jack took a piece of Becker's blade on his knuckles.

Arno smiled. "Pleased to make your acquaintance."

"Fuck you," Jack snarled, but he knew he had lost any benefit of surprise and already his heart was hammering anvils.

Pretty tight quarters for a knife fight. Footing was tricky, too, the floor polished and waxed slick as mercury, rugs loose on top. Arno circling like a shark.

Sizing him up.

"You're not Goodman," the blond butcher declared.

"The fuck would you know?"

"I saw you chasing a streetcar earlier today. Was grand entertainment."

"Get your jollies easy."

Becker snapped his knife from his left hand to the right and took a swipe—

But you couldn't survive the Great War and bayonets without learning something. Jack stepped inside the arc of Arno's blade and snapped a half-pound of brass solidly into the bone above the bastard's elbow.

Becker grunted in surprise, his knife spinning useless onto the polished floor. Jack waited for Becker to turn, the blond man scrambling to retrieve his weapon, and when he did Jack pounded two short, savage blows to the bastard's kidneys.

Arno cried out this time. Real pain. And then Jack measured a haymaker right to the gap between the blond-haired skull and the ox-sized neck.

Becker dropped like wet cowshit to the floor, knees bent, legs bicycling weakly. It had taken all of twenty seconds, but it felt to Jack like he'd been on the ass-end of a heavyweight fight.

He collapsed to the nearest chair and jerked his tie loose, heaving for air. When he was able to breathe, he rose on trembling legs to retrieve Arno's pigsticker from the floor.

That's when a steel-toed shoe caught him square on his shin.

It was Jack's turn to kiss the floor, rolling as Arno Becker smashed a chair to splinters only inches from his skull. But Jack had Becker's knife, added to his own. He scrambled to his feet with blades in both hands, backpedaling.

Arno croaked a kind of laugh.

"Now you have to kill me."

The second round raged even more furiously than the first. Becker ripped a club of oak from the leg of a Chippendale, chairs, lamps and vases shattering in the melee that followed. Jack would have traded both knives in his hands for a bayonet. Or an entrenching tool. More than one Kraut had lost his head on the edge of a doughboy's shovel.

But knives and knucks would have to do.

Arno wanted his frog sticker back, you could see it. You could see him timing Jack's lunge, just see the son of a bitch waiting for him to weary, for the snap to go out of that left jab so that he could smash Jack's wrist and take back his knife.

Jack obliged with a feint to Becker's left hand, always the left—the hand now holding Becker's club. Jab left, jab left. Little slower. Slower still—

Arno's hand snaked out faster than Jack could have imagined to trap his left hand. You could see the club following.

That's when Jack dropped to a knee and came from the floor with his knife in an uppercut to Becker's groin.

Becker's balls should have been sprouting from his trousers, but something hard and smooth deflected the thrust of Jack's blade like a stone skipped over water.

It was a cup. Goddammit, the bastard had armored his balls with a cup!

But Becker was still nicked, a seam bleeding bright and red above his navel.

"Not so deep as a well," Becker pressed a hand to his wound. "Nor so wide as a door, by any means."

But it was enough.

The butcher lurched back. A pair of French doors led to the balcony outside, a dead end apparently for Sally's killer. But Becker still had his improvised club. And Jack was spent. His arms heavy as lead. Stars swimming in and out of view before his eyes. Not to mention the knee and shin. One slip, Jack knew, and he could still wind up like Sally Price.

He couldn't take that chance.

He could wait. He had the bastard cornered and hurt, after all. Nowhere to go. But Becker was laughing! A mocking caw bubbling from a wide, sensual mouth, and it wasn't until then that Jack registered the fire escape.

The progressive city of Cincinnati had only recently required boarding homes and hotels to install those ingenious, cascading ladders of egress. Becker backed through the windowed doors and out onto the balcony.

"She begged at the end, you know."

Staunching his wound as he released a safety-latch.

"And you'll beg, too, whoever you are, before I'm through."

He rode the ladder down like a fireman's pole, a bright rasp of metal on metal to the alley below, and by the time Jack reached the balcony Becker was gone.

The bellboy regarded Jack Romaine. Suit and shirt ripped to shit. Face cut and bleeding.

"Sally must be hell on wheels."

"I'll pay for the damage," Jack pulled the kid inside.

"No skin off my nose."

"But I need to keep the room. I'm expecting another visitor."

"Another? Jesus, where's her husband? First husband, I mean?"

"He checked out."

"I dunno," the kid was having second thoughts.

Jack displayed a tenner.

"That's more than you make in a month."

"…What you want me to do?"

"Sometime right after five there's gonna be another gent asking for Sally Price. Make sure you're the boy brings him up."

You could see the one cog in the kid's brain turning over.

"There gonna be another brawl?"

"Don't expect so."

"Didn't expect this one, though, didja?"

"It's a different situation, all right? You ain't burnin' anybody."

The bellhop took the money. "But I was never here, got it? I never saw you. I never said a word about no room. Nothing."

"'Course not," Jack agreed amiably. "This is our transaction, shortstop. You and me."

The kid shoved a lock of hair back inside his hat.

"All right."

"That's the stuff," Jack approved cheerily. "Now, the name you want is Goodman. Alex Goodman. Or for that matter anybody asking after Sally Price."

"Goodman," the bellboy nodded sullenly. "Got it."

"You see 'im, you hear 'im, you just steer 'im in here to me."

"I want another Jackson when I bring him up."

"Done."

Jack watched the bellhop retreat down the hall. He hoped he'd bought the drip's loyalty, at least for the night. There was nothing else for it, really, nothing else to do. Jack closed the door.

Nothing but to watch and wait.

* * *

Couldn't have been fifteen minutes later Jack caught himself nodding off in the Chippendale lounger.

"Dammit."

He'd had trouble staying awake ever since the war. You never got enough sleep in the trenches, what with the misery, the disease, the enervating cold. More than once Jack had gone unconscious standing sentry, but that wasn't sleep.

The only thing kept him up was poker or whiskey and here he was in a fine hotel with no game, no booze, and the crushing urge to slumber. How long would he have to wait for Alex Goodman, anyway? Jack fished out his watch. Check in by five, the man's letter directed, but that didn't mean Goodman would arrive at five o'clock. He could be along later. Maybe a lot later.

Jack didn't need a mirror to know he was a mess. He was injured, exhausted. He had to get some rest. Just a nap, he told himself. If Goodman showed, the bellhop would wake him. Jack propped up the broken chair with a coffee table and then pulled up a generous ottoman. That would do. He shed his jacket, loosed his still-stiff collar and lay down.

He'd had worse beds, for sure; there were no sofas in the trenches. One of his worst fears as a corpsman had been to be buried alive in one of those filthy ditches, to be entombed in a barrage of artillery, sucking mud and muck into his lungs. A death by suffocation spurred with a single concussion of high explosive. Roused from sleep only to find death on a litter fashioned from a rag of blanket and ammunition cans.

Or to be flooded. Two days of thaw were enough to collapse any manner of tunnel or trench. Come spring, a single shower could trigger a flash flood and there you were, drowning like rats. Drowning, each man clawing over corpses to survive. Soldiers, comrades, scrambling over one another to get over the top. Clawing at the bones or putrefaction of corpses lodged alongside, an arm or leg now an improvised rung on a grisly ladder.

You were lucky enough to get out, there'd be snipers waiting. The machine guns.

Jack could see it now, a wall of water coursing down the trench.

And there's an arm, mummified, a hat rack reaching from the trench's unsteady wall. He leaps to grab that offered hand.

He reaches out. He grabs the arm.

And pulls Sally Price from the dissolving wall. She comes out naked and hairless. She's laughing, a pitiless laughter. A harpie's revenge and then—

A brass knocker jarred him awake.

"…Miz Price?"

Jack lurched up, disoriented.

"Sally Price?"

Jack scrambled from his makeshift bed, snatched the chain from its lock and yanked a bellman into the room.

A bellman in pillbox and stripes—but not the boy Jack expected. This was a guy old enough to be his grandfather.

"The hell are you?"

"Sir! Sir, please!"

The old fart raising a hand as if to ward off an angry fist.

Jack didn't blame him. God knows he must look like somebody just got finished fighting a dog.

"It's all right," Romaine tried to calm the geezer. "Take it easy. I was just expecting somebody else is all."

"Sure, mister."

Scanning the room, now. Taking in the shattered furniture. Blood on the floor, on the couch.

"Look, you wanna be a problem?" Jack let him see his brass knucks.

"NO! No, sir."

"Then just forget about this mess. Forget it."

He peeled off the ten-spot slated for the kid and pressed it into the old-timer's trembling fist.

"Relax. You don't know nuthin'. You came up here asking for Sally Price and her husband meets you at the door. That's me. I'm the husband. You didn't even go inside, see? Now whatever you got, pass it on."

"Just this."

The bellhop stretched like a first baseman to drop a sealed envelope into Jack's hand.

"And where'd you get it?"

"Some character. Didn't give a name."

"Gotta do better than that, pops."

"He was just some guy, I don't know! Had this loud jacket and baggy slacks an' one of them straw hats like you see with a flower big as yer fist stuck in the band. He caught me on the street."

"The street? OUTSIDE?"

Jack burst from a gaggle of coats and tails milling on the street outside the Milner Hotel. It was already dark, gas lamps mixing with electrics along the street. The sidewalk swelling with ladies and gents, streetcars and automobiles. Jack scanned the avenue up and down. Not a loud shirt or baggy slacks anywhere.

Not a straw hat in sight.

Jack sagged against a lamp pole, pulled the envelope from the torn pocket of his suit jacket and tore it open with his teeth.

"Hello."

A train ticket was neatly folded over a crisp set of bills and a handwritten letter. Jack counted the cash first. One hundred... *Two* hundred and fifty bucks! Romaine folded the cash away as he scanned the ticket. Looked like Mr. Goodman wanted Sally to head south. Tampa.

Then he read the letter. It was penned in the same precise hand as the correspondence he'd fished from the garbage bin at the zoo. Jack raised the script to catch the streetlamp's limn.

> *Hi, Sally Babe, I had to nix my plans to meet you in C. I hate to disappoint, but there you are. It's just a delay. Looking forward to seeing you at the Kaleidoscope. But for tonight, enjoy the Milner— eat all you want, it's on the tab! Tomorrow you'll be coming to me. Get up early. You have reservations for a sleeper on the Louisville & Nashville. Travel light, it's a long ride. I'll have a man waiting to pick you up.*

And don't worry about a thing. It's all over, Sally, girl. All taken care of. Thanks, kiddo. For everything!

Alex Goodman

Jack double-checked the ticket. Tampa.

"I guess that's south enough."

But where the hell and what was The Kaleidoscope?

He stuffed ticket and letter back into the envelope and for a good long moment considered running south with Martin and Mamere. Just take what was left of the money Bladehorn had given him and blow town.

But that hadn't worked in Chicago, had it? Wouldn't work in Cincinnati, either, or Tampa, not even with a five hundred dollar head start. Guys like Bladehorn didn't let the small fish go; they couldn't afford to, not with all the big fish watching for any sign of weakness.

Jack was going to have to face the music; he had fucked up with Sally, no way around that one. But if he didn't want his legs broken he had to convince Bladehorn that the trail to his property led to Tampa and Alex Goodman.

All said and done, Jack had done his job, hadn't he? He'd gotten the goods from Sally, even if second hand. He'd faced Arno Becker in a knife-fight, for Chrissake. Cut that competitor out of the chase. Surely, Bladehorn could manage the rest on his own. He could send Fist to Tampa, couldn't he? Why not?

Bastard could use a good sweat.

Jack limped into Spuds' place early the next morning. Now that he was paid up he was welcome to use the phone. He rang straight through to Bladehorn's residence. No party lines on The Hill. Fist Carlton took the call.

"I got some news for Mr. Bladehorn."

"Where you at?"

Took an hour for Fist to pull up outside Spuds' place, those massive hands spanning the Duesenberg's steering wheel like a player on a piano.

It was a long and silent drive to Bladehorn's mansion. No one on the grounds this morning. No croquet. No accoutrements of polite society. Fist kept his hands in his pockets as he escorted Jack to the hothouse out back.

Bladehorn was busy pinning insects onto a board. A jar of butterflies took their place on a raised table littered with piles of peat and moss. A brilliantly veined Monarch was being crucified on a cross of cork mounted above the potting table. Bladehorn was oblivious to the creature's last flutters. He listened to Jack's stammered excuses absently as he studied the train ticket, the letters. Leafing through the bills with gloved hands as Jack amplified his encounter with Arno Becker.

"I give you a simple job and I read about it in the papers. Though I grant that not many men have survived an encounter with Arno Becker," the gangster allowed, dabbing a kerchief to the spittle gathering at his mouth. And then, "Too bad you couldn't kill him."

Fist Carlton seemed disappointed at his boss's measured response. Probably because he had looked forward to beating Jack to death himself.

"Now tell me everything again. From the beginning."

So Jack ran it once more, a nearly accurate account of the previous day's events, concluding—

"That's about it. Last time I saw Arno he was riding a fire escape. But he doesn't know about this Kaleidoscope place, or Tampa, Mr. Bladehorn, you can bet on that."

"You are the gambler, Mr. Romaine, not I."

"Look at it this way, Mr. Bladehorn; if Sally knew where to find the money, Becker's already got it. If you saw what he did to her, well—you'd know."

"Mmmm. So what did Arno get from the poor woman?"

"He got a name, Alex Goodman," Jack answered. "And before Becker was done he knew Goodman was 'sposed to meet Sally at the Milner. That's why Arno went to the hotel, to wait for the sap. Lucky I got there ahead of him or we'd have Goodman's scalp to go with Sally's."

"Even so, you should have been at the prison when Miss Price was released."

"If I *had*, Becker'd have killed us both."

"Perhaps. Probably, even." Bladehorn selected an orchid from a tray heavy with mist. "Nevertheless, you were tardy."

"The thing is—Sally's not your horse, Mr. Bladehorn. Never was. You want your property you need to find Alex Goodman."

"So you say."

"Look how he strung Sally along: First, he tells her he'll meet her at the hotel, but he doesn't show. Instead, he sends in a letter off the street with a wad of cash and a ticket to Florida."

"To what purpose?" Bladehorn kneading a trowel's worth of peat into a pot. "If Sally did not know where to find my property, as you surmise, then why would Mr. Goodman involve himself with her at all?

"Maybe to kill her," Jack shrugged. "Or maybe to split the pie; for all we know Sally and Driggers were partnered with Goodman from the beginning. But the point is, Sally's only link to your cash and certificates is through Alex Goodman and Goodman's going out of his way to stay out of sight. Read the note; he's not even going to show his face at the Tampa station. Tells Sally there'll be 'a man' to meet her. What man? Who? I'm tellin' ya, this is a guy wants to stay out of sight. Got to be a reason."

Bladehorn transferred the orchid to the pot and laid his trowel aside and Jack decided to press his case.

"Another thing, Mr. Bladehorn, about the letters. You look, you'll see there's no return address on any of 'em. No address inside to write back, no phone number. And then the very last letter Sally gets travel money and a train ticket, so you know what I'm thinking?

"I'm thinking this guy Goodman has got your property, all right, and he's on the lam. He's hiding in some swamp near Tampa. Someplace out of the way. But it won't be long before he cashes in those railroad certificates, you can bet on that, and when he does you can kiss off ever seeing a dime of what your wife took from you. A man can't run far on five hundred dollars, but a quarter of a million—? Son of a bitch will be out of the country."

Bladehorn regarded his jar of specimens. Wings black and gold and tapping, tapping against their transparent prison.

"An interesting theory, Mr. Romaine."

"It's your best shot, anyway," Jack tried to disguise a sigh of relief. "Now, sir, I've been jake by you, haven't I? But now that we're square I'm thinking I should leave the city. Start over."

"Very sensible," Bladehorn agreed. "But first you'll need this."

Holding back the cash as he handed Jack the train ticket intended for Sally Price.

"What are you tellin' me, Mr. Bladehorn?"

"That you will be traveling to Tampa, of course."

"Really? 'Cause, I was thinking more like the west coast. San Francisco, maybe? Or Los Angeles, somebody said something about the movies."

Bladehorn shed his gloves to open the lid on his jar of captured monarchs.

"You're going to Tampa on my behalf, Mr. Romaine. You will go, you will find Alex Goodman, whoever he is, and you will bring back my stocks and cash, or what's left of it."

"That...wasn't our deal," Jack edged back.

"Do I need to remind you of your considerable debts, young man?"

"I owe Mr. Capone. Not you."

"Not so."

Bladehorn collected a butterfly deftly and when he resealed the jar took care to display the telegram beneath.

"All your notes," Bladehorn invited Jack's confirmation. "Over six thousand dollars of debts paid. By me."

Jack snatched the telegram and the gangster smiled as the weight of his unexpected largesse sank in.

"You no longer owe Mr. Capone a dime, Mr. Romaine. You now owe...me." Bladehorn's smile was malignant. "You will recover what my unfaithful wife tried to conceal from me, my boy, and I shall forgive your debts plus pay the balance of the thousand originally bargained. Now, I would say that's a handsome proposition, wouldn't you? Eminently."

"What if I can't find anything?" Jack could feel Fist at this back.

"Then I shall find something of yours, won't I? Some*one* of yours, I should say. And balance the ledger on those terms."

Jack lunged. Fist Carlton jerked him back like a dog on a leash.

"Touch my son I'll kill you, you sick fuck! By God I will!"

"An impotent threat."

Bladehorn rummaged a pin off his table of flowers as Fist dragged Jack toward the flimsy door.

"Goodbye, Mr. Romaine."

The gangster raised his captive butterfly to the board.

"Good hunting."

Chapter five

Moolah—*cash or loot, usually stolen.*

How long will you be gone?" Mamere was looking especially severe this morning in her perennially funereal attire.

"Couple weeks. Month at the outside."

Jack hesitated before reaching over his duffel bag to take a photograph off the apartment's wide windowsill. His son Martin, framed in tones of sepia. The dark hair, like his mother's. Handsome kid. Like a movie star.

Mamere lit a cigarette off the stove's sputtering burner.

Jack returned the photo carefully to the sill.

"You've got four hundred in the kitty," he nodded to the tobacco tin that she imagined secured their assets as securely as a vault. "I took the rest."

"Will you have enough?" she exhaled.

"I got the ticket, plus some of the cash I held back."

"You mean that you stole."

"Stealing from a thief ain't stealing. 'Specially from a bastard like Bladehorn."

"Stealing is stealing."

Jack finished his inventory without retort. Three suits, the last of which, having gone through a fight, was patched worse than the other two. Shirts and skivvies. Toiletries. Rummaging through the bag he spotted the knuckles, bright and heavy. The knife he verified by feel, the gnarling of its scales long familiar.

"I want you and Martin out of the city. Just 'till I get back."

"Why?" she stiffened further. "Why should I do such a thing?"

Jack reverted to vulgar French. "(So that no one may harm him.)"

She replied in kind. "(So. You have put your own son in harm's way?")

"*Oui, Mamere.*"

The use of the familiar lowered her guard a fraction.

"(Are *you* in danger?)"

"Just take care of Martin," he replied in English.

She considered the matter a moment.

"Francois's family," she said finally. "In Cleveland. You remember the place? His address?"

"Yes."

Francois was his wife's elder brother. He had not spoken to his brother-in-law for years.

Mamere exhaled a cloud of cheap tobacco. "They are family."

A sudden constriction in his throat. Jack swallowed.

"I'll wire if I have any news. Don't try to reach me. Don't write anything down."

Jack shifted his duffel onto his shoulder. Established his fedora on his head.

"When Martin gets back from school tell him…tell him…"

"I tell him," the old woman said, and turned away.

Chapter six

Rube—*a mark, a chump, a loser.*

Seventy-three dollars got you a sleeper from Cincinnati to Tampa. A first-class ride. Jack boarded the seven o'clock *L&N* which gave him more time than he wanted on the haul to Atlanta. Too much to think about. Too much time on hands used to handling cards or whiskey. Jack tried to keep awake, tried to keep that photograph before him, of Martin, of Gilette.

The terrain rolling by outside his Pullman coach became more and more unfamiliar. He felt himself drifting on iron wheels further and further from steady bearings, the gentle vistas above the Ohio River giving way to blue mountains which had by sunset transformed into a flat and ochre pan of clay.

There was no discernible industry on the approach to the city of Atlanta. The urban landscape of the Midwest had long given way to wheat fields, small towns, and, now, to pockets of agriculture hemmed in at intervals with small, dirty towns peopled at their fringes with Negroes. Negroes everywhere. At the stations. By water-filled ditches. Jack's odyssey south seemed to him lined with colored men and cane poles, their catches of fish got with a snatch of line and a can of worms.

He had thought no region could be more humid than Cincinnati, but the further he locomoted into the Deep South, the wetter and warmer it got. The laced curtains in his compartment hung like rags on a clothesline. Moss sagged on the live oaks outside like the beard of a drowned man.

Jack took off his collar. He wanted a drink. He wanted to gamble. He began to wish for any variety of companionship, some intercourse with his fellow-travelers, some conversation to pass the time. But those imperatives warred with a sterner dictum, which was to remain sober, alert, and inconspicuous, which compelled a distance from his fellow passengers.

There was plenty of temptation. Someone had brought a gramophone into the dining car. It didn't work well, a worn spinner of "Bye, Bye, Blackbird" jumping grooves with the train over iron tracks. But a swell of young people kept on without regard, the women shedding their Berlutis and stockings to dance the Charleston and sipping from their sheiks' silver-tipped walking sticks. Ignoring entirely the admonitions of stone-faced conductors. Those determined to revel ignored the porters and searched for more recruits to their own inebriated cause.

"Come on, fella," a redhead with an Eaton crop plopped into his lap. "Don't be a flat tire."

Parties didn't stop, after all, just because you were in sweaty transit. The lost generation were determined to have a good time, even if they made themselves miserable doing it. But Jack declined their invitation. He could not afford the seduction of some flapper out for a good time. The last thing in the world he could afford was to cross some jealous boyfriend or husband. Harder to ignore were the card games played as casually as checkers all over the car. That, and the booze. An atmosphere of temptation, cigar smoke redolent in the heavy air, the seductive movement of makeshift chips among snifters of brandy or collins of bourbon.

There was another reason to say alert, of course, and his name was Becker. Jack found himself looking over his shoulder for Sally's killer. He would not have been surprised waking in his sleeper to find that blond, evil face sharing his pillow. The man was preternatural, immune to normal attacks.

Death's happy whore.

Every blond-haired passenger gave Jack the sheebies, which he kept telling himself was not rational. How, after all, could Becker know Jack was on this train? And even if Becker had tracked Jack onto the Pullman, surely by now Jack would have spotted the bastard. Wouldn't he?

Why, then, did Jack keep looking over his shoulder?

The cars switched locomotives at Atlanta, continuing on the Central of Georgia to arrive after midnight at Albany where the Atlantic Coastline Railroad took over, it's '467 engine pulling Jack deep into the Sunshine State at seventy or sometimes eighty miles an hour past small towns with place names completely unfamiliar: Monticello and Perry. Live Oak and Hampton and Ocala. Wildwood and Coleman. Jack opened his wallet. There were two photographs lodged inside. One of his son Martin. And then Gilette. She posed stiffly with a pair of other nurses in their whites and hats. He had other photographs but this was the first and his favorite.

Sitting there in the diner, looking over his shoulder, Jack wondered how things might have been if his wife had not been taken from him so soon. Would he have remained a family man? Would he have stayed in New York working a foundry or on the docks or perhaps a shoe salesman downtown?

The photograph had been taken in France, in Tannerie, at a field hospital. Jack had mustered from Camp Upton in New York with forty thousand other patriots or draftees or those wanting to prove something to themselves. The 77th Division deployed from ships and rail-lines and even horseback to fill the trenches criss-crossing countryside once travelled by Napoleon. The division had engaged heavily fortified Boche for nearly a month in the Oise-Aisne region. Tens of thousands of men were shredded in that encounter. Gilette had been assigned to a French first-aid post behind the lines in Tannerie. A church had been converted for the purpose. The walls were peppered with German artillery, part of the roof was blown away, but the Virgin inside, serene in marble tranquility, was untouched. You heard stories like that all over France, that the statues of saints and virgins were impervious to German guns. It had been beneath Mary's open hands that Jack entered the infirmary.

You smelled the wounded long before you saw them. The ripe stench of pus mingling with the astringency of alcohol. Woefully few doctors in attendance, fluttering by intermittently in their long white coats. It was the nurses who were ubiquitous, working virtually as surgeons themselves in the daily, sometimes hourly, dressing of wounds. Nurses, mostly women, prying shards of metal or bullet from suppurating injuries. Nurses treating tetanus and gangrene and peritonitis. Everything from cracked kneecaps to trepanned skulls. Jack was not himself wounded. He had been commandeered with a half-dozen other men to secure a truck of supplies being sent to the hospital. The trucks were always clearly marked with the universal cross but supplies were short on both sides of the line and were subject to ambush, even by French civilians.

The efficiency of trench warfare could be measured in the tons of material needed to treat casualties. Gauze was delivered over sea and land in lots of a thousand yards, along with cuvettes and gloves and platinum needles. And morphine, of course. Lots of morphine. Enough alcohol to float a city of gangsters. Supply lines were subject to any number of ruptures, however; even hospital ships were subject to attack and so Jack found the nurses at Tannerie attempting to sterilize bandages corrupt with pus or excrement in vats of boiling water. Constant streams of wounded were unloaded as so many cords of wood from trucks and cots, doctors making instant judgments as to the likelihood of survival—this man too far along to help, this man rushed for immediate amputation. The rest waiting in pain, sometimes agony, comforted only by memory or religion or most reliably the human contact of the mostly-female and mostly French nurses who lived on soup and bread and sixteen hour shifts.

Rows and rows of American and French and sometimes even German soldiers languished in cots littered row upon row beneath a cathedral ceiling festooned with the limp standards of the Allies. The place was eerily quiet. No complaints from those martial beds. The muffled coughs of those able to clear their throats and chests, the sputum of those sequestered with tuberculosis. Murmurs in varying tongues of men dictating letters, or dying. Those soon to be discharged reading letters or playing cards. Sometimes you'd see a man sipping a malted milk or peeling a rare orange. Mulling over a copy of some hoarded magazine or newspaper or, of course, letters from home.

"Over here."

Jack actually heard his wife-to-be before he saw her. She was petite, even for a French woman. Built like a pear. Hair tangled as a ball of yarn trapped beneath the peaked, starched hat. But the eyes were the thing. Green, like the kind of green reflected in a still stream banked by some brilliant forest. An emerald green.

Her patient was muttering some gibberish in a language Jack could not identify. He was a soldier, that was clear enough, shrouded in sheets and bandages with tubes like tapeworms draining a lung. A leg had been amputated and was seeping. He clutched a medal like a rosary. A scrap of ribbon embossed with a star over a scrap of brass.

"You can help me." She spoke to Jack in passable English. It was not a request.

"Is he a prisoner?" Jack had asked.

"No. Arab. They left him here to die, but I've brought him back I think."

She made Jack wash his hands. "Hand me the instruments when I tell you," and before you knew it she was in the guy's guts, pulling out scraps of cloth and integument.

"Jesus Christ," Jack tried to hold his gorge.

"It was worse before. Wasn't it, my Muslim friend?"

The man growled something.

"Cheerful, isn't he?"

"He wouldn't speak to me at all in the beginning," she replied. "They don't trust the French."

"And yet they fight for them?"

"They fight for any reason at all."

"You need anything else before I go?"

"We need everything. All the time."

The Arab died not long after that first encounter. Gilette was not sure what to do with his things. Usually there was a forwarding address, some next of kin. But for the Arab, nothing but a box in a hole in the ground.

"He was awfully attached to that decoration," Jack remarked. "Maybe you should bury the medal with him."

"No," she shook her head sadly. "He thought it would keep him alive. Toward the end, when he knew better, he made me take it."

"What's it for?"

"Men who are wounded, they get one."

He saw Gilette perhaps half a dozen times in her hospital ward, always with supplies. She was a native of the area, turned out. Lived only a bicycle's ride from the hospital. "'Who would you choose for a husband'," he read the question from a worn edition of *The Spiker*, "'a Frenchman or an American?'"

"A Frenchman," she replied without hesitation. "He eats less."

Just before the 77th moved on he managed one last trip to the hospital for the allowed excuse of visiting a wounded buddy. He brought chocolate instead of linens or morphine. Then he made Gilette promise that he might see her when, as he put it, the job was done. She seemed surprised, even a little amused, when a month after Versailles he arrived at her shepherd home. A cottage of wood and shingle. A small vineyard. Goats and sheep. She was much changed in her new setting, reduced from a position of competence and command to a peasant. He offered her New York and after only a moment's hesitation she said he should speak to her parents.

They married in the same sanctuary where she had labored during the war and honeymooned on the boat to America. They were pregnant less than a year later and then had come the terrible epidemic. Gilette directing her own care until the very end.

"You are a terrible nurse, *mon cher.*"

"And why is that?"

"You care too much."

She reached over to a bed stand and produced the Arab's ribboned medal.

"The '*Insigne du Blesse Militaire*'," she pressed it into his hand. "To remind us of our wounds."

The photograph slipped from his fingers to the dining car's hardwood table. Jack's hand wandered to the brass pinned, still, on his lapel. He glanced about. Car was nearly empty; Jesus, was it that late? Jack checked his watch before he slipped Gilette's photo beneath his son's. Then he dropped a buck from his wallet for the steward and left the diner.

Jack Romaine collapsed fully clothed into his sleeper's narrow berth. The gay voices of floozies and their gents smothered in the deep rumble of iron wheels on iron rails. The sway of the car. Rock along, rock along. All he needed was a little rest, he told himself. Just a little…

An emerald green outfield frames an immaculately groomed baseball diamond. Jack sees his son heft a bat over homeplate. A boy of summer in a uniform trimmed in scarlet. Soft hair spills from beneath a woolen cap; Martin waves to his dad. Jack smiles back proudly. The catcher dons his mask; Jack cannot see the barred face. But he recognizes the hands that give the pitcher his signal. They are huge hands. Misshapen. And as Jack stands paralyzed in the stands at left field he sees the pitcher begin his windup. An athlete, for sure. Big man. Hair and skin pale as bleached bone.

Arno Becker hurls a fastball straight at the batter's head.

"Martin! MARTIN!"

Jack tries to warn his son. But there is no sound, no rush of air, nothing to strum his vocal cords to life as the ball sails in slow motion toward the unblemished boy at home plate—

"TAMPA in one hour. Passengers for TAMPA."

A porter rousting travelers from their dreams.

Jack stumbled from his rack, splashed water on his face from the valet's basin. A change of shirt and then he was back to the dining car. The windows set at intervals along the car's length divided the passing scenery into separate frames like splices from an ongoing film, a series of pictures flashing inside motionless panes depending entirely on the train's six driving wheels to impute activity and life. In the course of Jack's restless slumber oak trees and Spanish moss had been replaced by palmetto and pine. A land still owned by Seminoles flashed by now—

Clack-clack, clack-clack, clack-clack.

He reached for a cigarette then decided against it. He already felt like he was breathing syrup. The heat was stifling inside the car. He wanted to get *out*. To climb atop his Pullman, rip open his coat and collar and bring a gale of stream-driven air bursting into his lungs. To see something beyond a virid blur of vegetation.

They had to be near the coast, but it was impossible to tell. A wasteland sentineled with conifers crowded right up to the railbed leaving only a ribbon of sky turning amethystine overhead. Not a living thing moved, not even a buzzard, the climate torrid under plum-colored ribs of cloud.

Every window in the car was wide open and every female present had a fan in her hand. Jack abjured coffee entirely, giving in to the foreign taste of iced tea sweetened with molasses and served by a Negro steward who, to Jack's irritation, never seemed to break a sweat. A *Tampa Tribune* offered some diversion. Two columns in that rag were spent extolling the marvels of the Southern Star, the nation's largest airliner. A marvelous flying machine, the paper declared. Could carry twenty passengers in comfort from Tampa to Chile.

Jack shook his head. Who in their right mind would trust his life to an aeroplane over water?

Other stories related to local concerns. The effects of the Mediterranean fruit fly continued to merit attention and comment. Thousands of acres of orchards destroyed, Jack read. Fortunes lost overnight. But of course the rich always imagined themselves to be immune; two full columns were devoted to slavish praise of Tampa's Mirasol Hotel. "A revival of Mediterranean and Moorish architecture," the piece declared with authority, "with Venetian Gothic influence." A big draw for royalty and rich people, apparently, but the rest of Tampa's real estate was feeling the effects of speculation.

And it wasn't just real estate that had investors nervous in the sunny city. According to the paper, the city was reeling, financially.

The Citizens Bank & Trust had closed its doors the previous July; depositors were clogging the courts to regain their life's savings. Jack snorted derision. Everyplace else in the country was rich. What was wrong with *these* clowns?

But in other respects Tampa looked a lot like cities anywhere. The Volstead Act was no better enforced in the southland than in the Midwest. The same busts, the same bosses. Gambling was big, which was interesting. *'Bolita'*, a game unknown to Jack, apparently paid big odds. One of the kings of the little ball, Charlie Wall, was set free after a jury could not find evidence or stomach to convict him for the wholesale dealing of narcotics.

Booze, gambling, drugs. Same as anyplace.

There were the usual gossip columns keeping their readers abreast of the sportsmen and celebrities vacationing or occasionally working in the city. But not all visitors were equally welcome. There had been an uproar over a screening of *Uncle Tom's Cabin*, local members of the United Daughters of the Confederacy objecting to that depiction of the Ku Klux Klan. D.W. Griffith's *Birth of a Nation* was accordingly substituted as a more palatable alternative.

So much for local news.

Jack arrived at Tampa's Union Station just in time to experience a cloudburst. Jack had never seen a sky so gravid with precipitation. The train had to be backed into the Tampa station, creating a delay which grated on already frayed nerves. A geyser of steam sent a brakeman cursing as the engineer cleared the train's valves of mud. Beyond the brakeman's retreat Jack could see a long concourse scrolling into view, a weaving line of passengers and hangers-on and, unexpected, cordons of men in uniform. Campaign boots and khakis. Springfield rifles sprouting bayonets.

"Nash'nul God," the porter answered his question.

And what did they need the Guard for?

"De fruit fly."

"Be one hell of a fly."

A magnificent ironwork of sliding gates came into view. The train hissed and hooted and slowed to a stop in a thunderstorm. The porter swung off easily. Jack followed behind the cover of tourists and bankers scrambling uselessly to avoid the driving rain, a tie draped around his neck like a hangman's noose. Something like a warm, wet blanket settled beneath the brim of his fedora only to be stirred by a sudden gust of unseasonably frigid air. Lightning *craaaaacked* and thunder boomed and Jack jumped with other travelers for the cover of the concourse.

He scanned the dock. A virtual sea of expectant eyes straining to find friends and family among the debarking passengers. A confusion of greetings, whistles and shouts of recognition adding to the confusion of wind and rain and thunder. Somewhere among these milling folks was somebody sent to meet Sally Price. Be too rich to spot some lackey hefting a jerry-rigged salutation—*For Miss Price.* Jack never had that kind of luck. He was beginning to feel a rise of panic. The crowd was thinning, family, friends and business associates pairing off and dispersing. Jack looked in vain for a craning neck, any sign of some hanger-on who might be the man sent to pick up Sally Price. Some expression of anxiety or disappointment other than his own, when Goodman's proxy realized that the woman he was sent to meet had not arrived.

But the only face still turned to the train was Jack's own. And with the storm driving everyone else for cover he was beginning to look awfully conspicuous, a newcomer soaked and solitary amidst a residue of baggage boys and porters.

"Hep you with sumpin', suh?"

The Negro again. The porter.

"No, thanks, Uncle," Jack replied and tipped the man two bits.

Whoever was sent to meet Sally was gone by now, but Goodman had assured Sally he'd see her at 'The Kaleidoscope'. There couldn't be that many joints by that name. Maybe the porter could steer him. Jack was about to re-engage the Negro when an upbeat voice called out—

"Help with the bag, bright boy?"

Jack glanced about. Not a soul in sight.

"Hey, pinhead," the voice chirped, practically from his pocket, "You wanta hand with yer satch or what?"

The smallest man Jack had ever seen spit the biggest plug of tobacco he'd ever seen into a spittoon ten feet distant. Pealed that brass like a gong.

"What about it?" the spitter pulled his sleeve across the stain at his mouth. "Two bits, I'll tote yer bag."

"For two bits you can live in it," Jack replied.

"Oh, that's rich," the dwarf did not smile. "I never heard that one before."

He was not a smidgeon over three feet tall. Bright red hair, a real carrot top. Overalls made him look even shorter than he was and his shoes must have been made for a child. He was oddly constructed, thick-framed, but with limbs stiffly bent, like the trolls of fairy tales. Jack noted the wrists. Swollen. Truncated.

"What's your name, little man?"

"Tom Thumb, why should you care?"

"I make it a habit never to piss off anybody half my size."

The little man grabbed his crotch.

"And how would *you* know?"

That got a chuckle, even from a traveler bone-tired and anxious.

"Tell you what, I got the grip, but I could use a ride."

"Where to?"

"…The Kaleidoscope."

The troll rolled his shoulders slowly. "Kaleidoscope, uh huh. And what brings ya?"

Jack shrugged.

"Friend said I should come down."

"Say, you're not in the pictures, are ya?"

"Hell, no. You?"

"Sure, spent the night humping Mary Pickford. That's why I'm hustlin' bags at a train station."

"You got a name?"

"Call me Tommy. Tommy Speck."

"Jack Romaine."

A bolt of lightning broke over the tracks like a rifle shot.

"The hell?" Jack ducked.

"Keep yer britches." The dwarf jerked a thumb over a knot of shoulder. "I got a truck."

The second the little shit got his two bits he lost interest in conversation. Jack was following Speck down the tracks in silence when he saw a freight car getting more than the expected attention. A squad of hefty men in souwesters converged on the dock, hustling to rig what looked like a heavily timbered drawbridge from the dock to the door of a just-opened freight car. A solitary woman directed that bustling gang. A tall woman, very tall. She wore no headgear. In fact, she wore nothing in deference to the downpour. A cotton shift was soaked with rain, the fabric clinging like a second skin to her flesh. A long, firm frame. Her hair could have belonged to an Indian, raven and straight and down past her waist.

"The hell is that?" Jack blinked water from his eyes.

"Are you comin'?"

"Just a sec."

Jack formed a visor against the rain with the brim of his hat. A bolt of lightning briefly spotlighted the long-haired attendant. She was waving to someone inside the railroad car. A greeting? A command? Lightning cracked again, and thunder, and then a four-wheeled wagon creaked out of the car and onto the drawbridge. Bales of hay piled above the wagon's sideboards to stack along something inside—some*one* inside, Jack corrected himself—some human figure propped on hay bales as though they were pillows.

"Holy Mack."

She filled the wagon, an enormous, folded aggregate of flesh. The rain plastered dishwater blond curls to a forehead as broad as the belly of a tub. You could put a row of silver dollars in the creases of her arms, her neck. She turned imperiously in the downpour to gaze down the tracks. It seemed, distant as she was, that she looked straight into Jack's eyes.

"Princess Peewee," Tommy anticipated his question.

"'Princess Peewee'? 'Tommy Speck'? Christ, does anybody have a real name down here?"

Speck snorted disdain for that convention.

Seven men with ropes strained to retard the wagon's descent

down its rain-slick incline. Once that oversized cart was safely onto the loading dock, a heavy truck pulled up, its sideboards clapping inside their vertical restraints. A giant stepped out of the passenger side of the Ford, a no-shit Negro giant. Jack could not guess his size except to realize that the giant's head and shoulders towered over the far side of the truck's battered cab.

The giant strolled to the rear of the truck's bed, a massive length of chain draped over his shoulder. In a matter of seconds the links were secured from the wagon's yoke to an anchor jerry-rigged in the Ford's bed. Then the giant spread a tarpaulin as gently as a blanket over the reclining royal. A tender, almost reverent ministration.

Jack spilled water in a silver spout from the lid of his hat.

"You know these people?"

"That's a question either dumb or dangerous."

Dangerous?

And then the lady-in-waiting leapt light as a doe from the dock into the truck bed. She leaned over the reclining Princess, restraining a fall of long, raven hair to leave a kiss on that wide forehead.

"She a switch hitter? The looker?"

"None of my business."

"She got a handle?" Jack tried another tack.

"Luna. Luna Chevreaux."

"*Mon chere la lune.*"

"She'll be your boss," Speck said.

"Boss? How you know I'm looking for work?"

"Everybody comes to Kaleidoscope works, Jack. Or whatever *your* name is. And we all work for Luna. If you ain't willing to do that—train pulls out in six minutes."

Jack scanned the track. Except for these freaks the concourse was deserted.

"Fine, then," Romaine spilled water from his hat. "But I'm driving."

Tommy's Model-T was rigged with a hand-operated clutch and brake whose function the dwarf left Jack to divine on his own. They drove due east from Tampa before turning south. The lightning and thunder had abated, but not the downpour, water falling in buckets to inundate two wide lanes of a modern asphalt highway.

"Just finished last year," Tommy was once more chatting away as if he'd known Jack all his life. "Before the highway—? Rain like this—? You'd be up to your axles."

The car swayed on narrow tires in a brutal crosswind. Jack struggling to keep the vehicle centered on what looked to be the silver belly of a snake.

"Goes all the way to Miami," Tommy informed him. "That's why they call it the Tammy Ammy. Tampa-Miami. Get it?"

"Got it," Jack replied shortly and the dwarf howled laughter as if some hugely ingenious joke had just been passed between them.

"How long are we gonna be on this thing?" Jack asked when his passenger settled down.

"All the way," Speck replied brightly. "I coulda taken a shortcut over McKay Bay, but with this rain—"

"Gotcha," Jack replied. "And 'bout how far's the Kaleidoscope?"

Tommy regarded him with some humor.

"You don't know nuthin', do ya?"

"Just took a gamble," Jack replied coolly.

"Well, we've only got ten, maybe twelve miles to go." Tommy propped a child-sized shoe on the dashboard.

"And exactly who are 'we'?"

"Oh, that's sharp," Tommy chortled evilly, and something about his thwarted torso sent a crawl up the back of Jack's neck. "Very sharp."

Twenty minutes later Tommy directed Jack off the hard pavement to a series of ruts gleaming silver with water. A river coursed along one side.

"The Alafia," Tommy informed him. "The Little Alafia, actually."

"Where's the Big Alafia?"

"Other side of the Little Alafia. Dumbass."

A soft sand road carried them through a sprawl of trailers

and trucks occupying spits of sand that spidered at random on lots spiked with pine trees and puddles of rain. Every manner of portable transportation littered those small squares of loam: trucks, caravans, wagons.

The hell was this place? A camp for gypsies?

"Turn here."

Jack turned onto a sandy boulevard leading to more permanent structures. A few cottages on one side of the flooded ruts, shacks actually. And then Jack saw a tin roof rising beyond. And then he saw something else.

"God Almighty."

A tiger pacing a cage not ten feet off the road. Jack jerked the wheel on instinct. Tommy grabbed his arm. A surprising grip. Like a goddamn vice.

"'S'matter, Jack?" the little man regarded him coolly. "Ain't you been around animals?"

Speck released his arm and Jack geared down, centering the truck on its sandy boulevard. There were more animals to be seen on either side of the loam. Horses and llamas corralled behind a fence. A cage of monkeys, their simian stares impenetrable. A flamboyance of flamingoes. A single lion, indifferent to his captured kingdom, the rain, or anything else.

Jack heard an elephant, he was sure of it!

That jungle trumpet.

And then a bolt of lightning flashed like the bulb of an overgrown camera to klieg another structure down the road, rising above a screen of pine trees, separate from the other structures.

"That a tent?"

"Yep," Tommy offered no further explanation and then, "Okay. Pull up here. No, dummy, *my* side."

Through his window Jack could make out a broad veranda. Then a steep shell of tin sheltering two stories of clapboard, some kind of flag on top. The truck's window fogged with his breath; Jack wiped it off. There was another structure tacked onto the back of the building across the street, more of an afterthought than an improvement.

The entire exterior looked to be papered in garishly rendered advertisement posters splashed on randomly, fantastic scenes of burlesque or *faux* exotica. A row of bulbs sputtered above the entering door.

Jack could see a sign:

*** THE KALEIDOSCOPE COOKHOUSE & CAFE ***

—and then in smaller case beneath.

RUBES NEED NOT APPLY

"Go on in," his diminutive guide piled out of the truck. "You're lucky Half Track'll still have some hash on the burner."

Jack turned up the collar of his coat, his city shoes plunging in mud to the ankles as he dropped from the truck's cab. By the time he had slogged across the flooded street, Tommy Speck's Model-T was already clattering away to some unremarked destination. Jack jogged up the pine-planked steps that rose to the Kaleidoscope's verandah. He had barely gotten beneath the bib of that porch when the front door banged open.

"What the—?!" Jack began but the challenge he intended died in his throat.

A bald, black man about seven and one half feet tall filled the door like a silo.

It was the giant. The giant from the train station.

"'Scuse me," Jack found himself backing away. This was the same Goliath he'd seen tending the fat lady's wagon, he was sure of it. But how in hell had he beat Jack to the café?

Did the son of a bitch fly?

The Giant brushed past with barely a glance.

Jack shook himself like a terrier, took a deep breath, and managed a single step inside the diner. And froze.

He could not move. It was as if roots had grown from the soles of his feet into the yellow heart pine beneath. His first impulse was to vomit, to purge himself. But Jack fought that sudden nausea, that sure betrayal.

This was not what he expected.

This was not what he expected at all.

It wasn't the place itself that stopped Jack in his tracks. The interior was in most respects no different than an ordinary café—a horseshoe counter, tables and booths, hotplates and coffee pots. There were the usual photos you'd see in any eatery hung all over the walls, a mix of boxers and baseball players, and movie stars, of course, those silent sirens. In those respects the place was ordinary.

But the people inside were not.

If you could call them people. The first thing Jack saw on entering the café was what he took to be a great shaggy dog, an Airedale at first glance, until he realized that this was a man, a human whose face was reduced to a snout shoved from a shaggy mat of hair. And the Dog Man wasn't alone. In fact, there wasn't a human being in the place who wasn't twisted or distorted or malformed or diseased in some unsettling fashion.

Every table served a freak of nature, every countertop, chair and stool. A limbless man stretched like a python in a faux leather booth near the Dog Man. Chatting with The Serpent was a more fortunate albeit armless creature who, as Jack stared, brought a cup of coffee to her lips with her toes. Boothed opposite The Serpent and Twinkle Toes, a human bulletin board lounged, a shirtless being of uncertain gender whose skin was raised as if in Braille to convey a variety of curses, admonitions and advertisements; 'TRAILER FOR SALE—SEE CHARLEY BLADE', Jack could read that message across the hermaphrodite's chest from thirty feet away. And another, 'HE LIVES! JOHN 3:16'.

In contrast, a woman alongside the Human Slate seemed to have been flayed alive, her skin oozing lesions and injury. Siamese twins cooperated over a bowl of some kind of goulash, two grown women joined quite literally at the hip. In a variant of that anomaly, a shirtless man sat at a table with a stillborn sibling sprouted like some monstrous tumor from his chest.

Jack stifled his rising bile.

"You don't like the company, go someplace else."

The challenge came practically at his shoulder. Jack turned to find a good looking blonde fondling a snake the size of a ladder—and three tits. Which in the latter case confirmed for Jack that it really was possible to have an embarrassment of riches.

"So what is it, Slick?"

The boa sliding over her bare shoulders.

"You goin'? Or stayin'?"

"I'm here to work," he swallowed.

"Work with me," she lifted her breasts for inspection. "So round, so firm, so fully packed."

One of the midgets sighed.

"Swear to God, I had a million dollars I'd buy six acres of them tits and walk around barefoot."

"In your dreams, Sleepy," she snapped and returned smiling to Jack Romaine.

"But you, sailor—"

She lunged her mouth to his and held him like a leech. He tried to tear away, but something pulled him to her. Closer…closer! It was a cool noose, and smooth. And it moved.

"JESUS!"

The snake hissed in his ear and the freaks roared laughter.

"Kiss me like you like it and I'll take him off," she offered.

"Take him off, bitch, or you can kiss my ass."

"Oooooo," she cooed. "I like this bad boy."

"Let him go, Cassandra."

The order came with bored authority from a woman with no legs who rolled from behind the counter, lipping a cigarette atop a platter rigged with roller skates.

Cassandra hissed along with her snake.

"You want your pet? 'Cause I was just looking for somethin' to put in my stew."

"Mystery meat!" somebody chortled and the others joined in.

"Mystery meat, mystery meat…!"

"Shut up or you'll be shittin' beans and grits," the truncated woman warned and the house settled down.

"Come on, Merlin," Cassandra pouting as she uncoiled her constrictor from about Jack's neck. "Looks like this Johnny's lost his pencil."

"Don't mind Cassandra," the woman shoved herself back toward the counter. "She doesn't get laid enough."

And then, glancing back to Jack.

"Comes to that, I don't either."

Clearly there were rules here that Jack was expected to learn.

He trailed his savior to a stool at the counter.

"You must be Half Track."

"Bright boy."

"Jack Romaine," he leaned over to offer his hand.

She snorted. "Okay. Well, 'Jack', meet your neighbor; that'd be 'Penguin'."

A female on the stool beside him extended a hand with fingers completely webbed in flesh.

"Charlene Amethyst Bouchet. 'The Penguin Lady', I'm sure you've heard of me? I was in Jersey last week, but we got shut down, so I'm bedding early."

"Tough break," Jack guessed a reply.

She shrugged. "Somebody's palm didn't get greased."

"Always a possibility," the Dog Man sympathized with a heavy accent. "Unless, of course, you're with Barnum or one of the larger shows."

"Yeah, yeah, yer famous, Jo Jo," the web-handed performer turned to Jack. "These circus riffraff. Always putting on airs. Not I. I've worked the Big Tent; I admit it. But I'm carney to the webs of my feet."

"Hey, Cracker Jack, you gonna jaw all night?" Half Track interrupted. "Or are ya gonna eat?"

"I could use some chow," Jack was glad to change the subject. "What you got?"

"Frog legs are always good," Penguin suggested brightly.

"I'm sure they are."

"What? You never had frog legs?"

"Can't say as I have."

"Should try 'em."

Penguin reached behind the counter to fetch a jar filled with frogs.

"See?" she used her hands like flippers to capture a green-skinned entree.

"You cook him or what?'

"No. I take him with water," she gathered a glass.

"Water?" Jack kept a poker face.

"Well, beer's better but, what the hey," she said and popped the frog into her mouth. A swig of water, then, and the amphibian was down the hatch.

Jack's gills went green as the cookhouse roared laughter.

"Nice trick," he managed, finally.

And then came a squeaky voice apparently from somewhere inside The Penguin Lady's bulging throat.

"'Let me out! Let me out!'"

She heaved once and the frog spilled from her mouth alive and well and hopping for freedom off the counter.

The freaks cheered. Jack felt suddenly dizzy. Disoriented.

"Here," Half Track shoved a steaming bowl beneath his face. "This'll put some hair on your feet."

"Maybe I'll just go with some coffee."

"'S'matter, Jack?" a new voice challenged. "Something kill your appetite?"

Luna Chevreaux had shed her rain-soaked shift for a dry change of cotton. She strolled across the café, bare-shouldered and tall. Jack could not miss the high mound of breasts, the curve of belly beneath. Raven hair falling straight as a Seminole's down that long, long back.

But there was something about Luna which Jack had been unable to see when he first saw her at the train station, a detail that in the mix of elements and distance was camouflaged. It was her skin.

Luna's skin was not tanned as might be expected from years in the sun. But she was not white, either. And she was not black.

Her skin was blue.

Not the blue of bannered flags nor of robin's eggs or summer skies. Something like a muddled bruise stained the lady's skin from the tips of her sandaled feet to the roots of her jet-black hair.

"What? Got a rip in your knickers?"

"No," his mouth was dry. "It's nothing."

"Liar," she said and a hiss rising from one counter spread like steam around the knotted interior.

Even leaning on the counter Luna looked down on Romaine.

"You don't really think anybody buys your little come-along, do you, Jack?"

"Come along?"

"You're no carney."

Hisssss.... Jack measured the distance to the door.

"Why'd you come here?" she pulled a stool over.

"I'm...s...tarting over."

Her smile was brittle. "Everyone here starts over."

"Then I'm no different than anyone else."

Luna shook her head.

"Where you're wrong, mister. See, in this place *we* are the normal people. We live here. We eat and drink and shit and screw along this little stretch of water and sand and nobody, *nobody* looks at us like we're odd or retarded or cursed.

"*We* are the everyday folk at Kaleidoscope and you, Jack, or whatever your name is, are the freak."

Jack met her agate eyes.

"Fine. I'm the freak. Now, what about a job?"

She reached out to examine the wartime souvenir pinned to the lapel of his suit.

"Where'd you get this?"

"I stole it," he answered shortly, and she almost smiled.

"Half Track—"

"Yes, boss?"

"Have Tommy get him a room. But no credit."

Her moon-blue hand journeyed from his lapel to linger over the knot of his tie.

"This one pays cash."

Chapter seven

First-of-Mayer—*a newcomer on the show.*

Jack emerged from the café to distant thunder, like a bowling ball striking faraway pins. No lightning remained to strobe the sandy street, but large, solitary drops of rain slid in silver balls off tin roofs or needles of pine. The single road that connected the various vehicles, wagons and shacks of the settlement was by now a muddy quagmire. If this was the place that had been Alex Goodman's hideout, Jack was not impressed. Anybody slick enough to steal a quarter million in bonds shoulda been able to find a better stash than this motleyed hole.

He dodged puddles crossing the sandy rut separating the café from a shack across the street. "The Sugar Shack" Half Track had sent him to, not much more than a lean-to propped as first among equals to a handful of other shelters of rough timber and tin. A screen door wobbled on flimsy hinges to let him enter what passed for an office. An abbreviated counter and cigar box fronted a pegboard draped with a dozen brightly tagged keys.

Tommy Speck climbed off an orange crate to give a key to an odd couple waiting at the counter.

"I never know what to do with these guys," Tommy declared cheerfully as Jack scraped the mud off his cityslickers.

Two heads turreted to acknowledge Romaine's arrival. Two identical faces. But only one body.

Jack found himself once again staring.

"Jacques and Marcel DuBois," the dominant male introduced his genial twin.

They looked to be joined side by side about the chest, some Frog version of Chang and Cheng. Not youngsters, these two, Jack would guess somewhere into their forties, though it was impossible to say for sure.

They were dressed ludicrously for the climate, twin collars stiff above some bastardized version of a black wool suit. Twin cravats winked diamonds Jack was sure were paste. It was easy to see that they shared a single pair of arms and legs.

Jack wondered what else they shared.

He nodded politely. "Jack Romaine."

Two heads bowed in unison.

"Some pair, ain't they?" Tommy grinned from his crate. "Musicians, too, both of 'em. Violin. They take turns with the bow, 'The Siamese Svengalis'. Class act. Thing is—I never know when they come in here. Do I charge 'em for a single? Or a double?"

The midget burst into a cackle of laughter, slapping his bowed leg. Hooting at the top of his toy-sized lungs.

"Glad you're so pleased with yourself, Speck."

But the little man was unfazed. "'Single or double'! That's pretty good. Gotta work that inta my gig."

Tommy shuffled over to the cigar box that functioned, apparently, as a cash register.

"Two bits," Speck informed them.

Marcel turned his head nervously to his twin.

"(But we cannot pay!?)" That lament murmured *en Francais.* "(We have no money?!)"

"(You are ill, brother. We need a room.)"

84

"(Still. What can we tell him?)"

"You two can moonshine later," Speck growled. "Right now I need two bits for the night."

Which got no response from the twins.

"Fifty cents?" Tommy tried again. "Half-a-Washington? Can't you guys parley voo English?"

"I'll cover it," Jack spoke up. "Go ahead and make it for two nights. For them and me."

Jacques and Marcel looked up startled.

"Parlez vous francais, monsieur?"

"(My wife was French. She taught me a little. And I have a mother-in-law from Normandy—)"

"(Poor man!)"

"(—she taught me a lot.)"

The twins' laughter was light as a pair of starlings.

Tommy scowled. "You bastards yakking it over me?"

"(There is…nothing at your expense, monsieur.)"

Tommy turned to Jack.

"The joke's not on you, little man."

"Better goddamn well not be," Speck took Jack's money. "And the next time you call me little, yer gonna be sleeping in the shitter."

Jacques and Marcel received their key graciously. "We heard performers could find respite here," Jacques bowed to Jack.

"Really? Where'd you hear that?"

"Monsieur is too modest," Marcel blushed.

It was odd to see one face blushing while on the same set of shoulders the other face remained composed.

"We heard a benefactor inhabited this place," Jacques took up his brother's thread. "But we did not expect such generosity so soon. *Merci. Merci beaucoup.*"

"My pleasure."

Jack stood aside as the twins took a bag each to crab out of Tommy Speck's miniature office. Looked like a pair of Chaplins, the twins did, waddling out into the rain.

Jack tapped a cigarette from a pack of Chesterfields.

"What was all that about a benefactor?"

"No idea," Speck got busy at his board of pegs.

"Seemed pretty sure they'd find somebody willing to help."

"Work the midway long enough, you're bound to find a sucker someplace. Here—"

Speck tossed Jack a towel.

"One per room. You don't like the sheets, laundry 'em yourself. There's a pot under the bed if you need it. Outhouse out back."

"Anyplace I can wash up?"

"Fuckin' rainin', ain't it? Or you can use the stock tank."

Romaine spent the rest of the night in his shorts on a litter that might have been rescued from the trenches. An east-facing window and a blistering sun the next morning were not enough to rouse him from that rude cot. He had dumped his wallet and watch beside an alarm clock on the orange crate that served as a nightstand, stripped to his shorts and collapsed on sheets that needed to be boiled in lye.

The room was not much more than a closet, a perfect square roughed in. Already the shack was heating up, the tin walls and roof an oven in the sun. One large, unscreened window faced east onto the boulevard outside. A curtain rigged from a flour sack bent the slender dowel nailed into that pine frame. Jack stirred damply in his skivvies, deep in some lunar dream.

But then something like the trumpet of Gabriel blasted the tin walls.

"Jesus!"

He tumbled or was spilled from bed.

Another blast shook the timbers.

"Fucking Christ!!"

He staggered to the window to see an enormous bull elephant on the street outside. An African behemoth. The beast raised its trunk for another trumpet and Jack could swear his hair blew back.

"Up and at 'em, bright boy!"

There was Tommy Speck, about the size of a bucket, leading a beast the size of a small house down the street.

"The hell—?" Jack groped for his watch.

"You got thirty minutes if ya want breakfast, Buster Brown," Tommy informed him loudly. "After that it ain't nuthin' but the sweat off yer balls."

Jack slipped on his travel slacks and a clean undershirt and hustled across to the Kaleidoscope. He steeled himself against any fresh surprise he might encounter on entering the carney's café. No matter what he saw, Jack told himself, he would not react. He needed information from these people and he wasn't going to get it if he acted like a chump.

Jack entered the cookhouse and immediately spotted Half Track negotiating one of the several ramps that allowed her to tend the counter and grille. The sight of an ordinary-looking man nursing a smoke and coffee at a neighboring booth was reassuring, though the purpose of the wheelbarrow next to him was not immediately obvious. And then Jack saw a snout centered in a mane of shaggy hair rising from behind the counter.

"Morning, Jo Jo."

A low growl answered, the head dipped from sight and it took the scratch-scratch-scratch of paws on a pine floor before Jack realized his mistake.

"Easy, fella!" he backed away from around a hundred pounds of half-bred mutt.

"Off, Boomer," Half Track commanded and the dog plopped like a rug to the floor.

"Sorry," Jack offered as he found his stool.

"Fucking rube," she shook her head.

Jack decided he might as well take this one head-on.

"Got a thing against rubes, Half Track?"

Half Track pushed him a cup of coffee.

"A rube is a mark, lot lice, whale shit. He's anyone who's not a carney. He's a tag, a meal, a cheap trick. He sure as hell ain't one of us."

"Long as we're clear," Jack raised the scalding caffeine to his mouth. "So what's for breakfast?"

"Cash only."

"I've got cash."

"In advance, no circus terms for you."

Jack forked over two bits.

"Everything comes with grits." She hauled herself up to a griddle big enough for Paul Bunyan. "So don't bitch."

Turning then to her other customer.

"Freddie? Coffee?"

"Nah, I'm 'bout jazzed out."

The man took a last sip of java, stubbed out his cig. Jack offered his best marquee smile.

"So. You off work for the season, too?"

The man regarded him coolly. "First off, I ain't a working man. As any carney would know. Second, if I want conversation, I'll ask for it."

With that the fella dragged himself out from behind his table and revealed the purpose of the wheelbarrow.

"You lookin' at, dickhead?" Freddie grunted as he squatted to heft his load.

What Freddie loaded into the wheelbarrow was his own scrotum. Jack could not help watching as the slender man lugged a set of balls the size of a bale of hay into the barrow's shallow bowl. Jack had heard of elephantiasis, and who hadn't slipped into a sideshow to see the usual distensions of arms or fingers or clits or dicks, most of which he had assumed were faked. But there was nothing phony here. With his own eyes Jack was watching Freddie load fifty pounds of his own testicles into a wheelbarrow.

"See ya, Half Track," the freak offered over his shoulder and followed his gonads out the door.

"Now there," Half Track paused in admiration, "is a real performer."

She slid a platter piled with eggs and grits and bacon and pancakes down the counter.

"Five cents," she said before Jack could touch his coffee.

"For what?"

"For refills."

"I haven't had a refill."

"Not yet, but you will. That's what 'advance' means, ain't it?"

"Any other rules I should know?"

"I imagine, yes." The answer came from the front door. Jack swiveled his stool to see Luna Chevreaux strolling over.

She was dressed like a dyke. Trousers and brogans. Khaki shirt cinched in on that insect waist.

"Any coffee left, Half Track?"

"On the way."

Luna slipped a folding knife from her trousers.

"We were speaking of rules."

"I was, at least," Jack nodded.

She stretched over the counter, speared an orange from a bowl.

"Well, there are rules in any society, aren't there? For instance, you might have figured out that in Kaleidoscope you're either a working man or a performer. If you last, which I doubt, you'll be a working man. Important not to forget your place."

"Okay," Jack nodded.

"Another rule. Do not for any reason bullshit me. I don't care if you robbed a bank, fucked somebody's wife or killed a copper, but do not piss on my leg and tell me it's fucking dewdrops."

One long peel unwinding the whole time from the peeling orange. Jack swallowed his coffee. "Fair enough."

"Now. What do you have to offer us, Mr. Romaine?"

"Hard to say. I've never worked at a beddy before."

"You bed down when you aren't working'," Luna corrected him. "Winters the shows close up, people have to go someplace. Circus tramps, they usually winter over in Sarasota. That's fine if you work the wire or throw a knife but nobody wants freaks around. Most natives see you outside a tent they shit themselves. Half of them think we're cursed or subhuman or spawned from the devil. Hypocrites, all of 'em. It's jake getting your jollies watching Jo Jo's mug or Frankie's balls, but, hey! don't bed down in my neighborhood!

"Till this place we had no place. I first came down here it was no more than a fishing camp. Back then we just had tents. Giant was the first one to put down a shack. Then Tommy and his wife.

First thing you know freaks from all over the country started bedding down here.

"Won't be long before Kaleidoscope is an honest-to-God town. Maybe one day even have a mayor and cops! A fire department. And nothing but carneys running the joint."

"'Kaleidoscope Fire Department'? Too much."

"What—you think this is a joke?"

"I didn't say that.

"Hell, you didn't," Half Track sniffed.

"Every seen a kaleidoscope, Jack?" Luna dropped the perfect peel of her orange onto the counter. "Every looked through a kaleidoscope?"

"When I was a kid, maybe."

"All those shapes and colors look mismatched, at first, don't they? Out of place. But then you put 'em in a barrel and turn 'em and you get something beautiful. That's what we are. That's what we want Kaleidoscope to be."

She pulled her stool close to him. He could smell the nectar of orange in her gypsy hair.

"So how'd you find us, Jack? Who told you about Kaleidoscope?"

Jack stirred his sunnyside into the grits. "Ran into a guy at a speakeasy said he used to travel with the circus. Went on and on about this place near Tampa. Place to beddy when work dried up."

"You could have picked up that much anyplace."

"Tellin' ya, I got it from this guy."

"This Doe have a name?"

"Well, like I said I only met him the one time and we were both hitting it pretty hard," Jack squinted as if trying to recall some distant memory. "But seems like he told me his name was 'Alec'. Or maybe it was Alex. Yeah, that was it, Alex. Alex Goodman."

Jack was sure he saw something ripple across that blue skin.

"And how well did you know this Alex?" Luna's voice was casual.

"I just ran into him, that's all. I don't even know if he's a carney."

"What he is, is dead," Luna declared.

"…Run that by again?"

"Alex Goodman is dead."

A cold fist reached into Jack's entrails and twisted them.

"You sure?" he asked like an idiot.

"Oh, yeah," Half Track affirmed. "Ambassador killed 'im just this Monday past."

Jack didn't need a calendar to realize that if Goodman bit the dog Monday he wasn't in Cincinnati on Tuesday.

But somebody had been.

"Who's this Ambassador?" he stalled for time.

"Our elephant," Luna answered, watching him closely. "Big bull, you've seen him?"

"Heard him, anyway," Jack replied but his mind was racing on different tracks.

He only had Luna's word that Goodman was dead. On the other hand he knew that *someone* claiming that identity had sure as hell been in Ohio at the Hotel Milner late Tuesday. If it wasn't Goodman, it had to be somebody standing in for him.

Maybe the same Johnny who was supposed to meet Sally at the station?

"How'd it happen? With the elephant?" he tried to buy time.

Luna shrugged. "Alex must have spooked him."

Half Track cackled. "Time he was through there wasn't enough left of that drunk's bony ass to bait a mouse trap."

Jack felt the color draining from his face.

"Concerned, Mr. Romaine?" Luna was close to him now. That bruised skin. Uncomfortably close.

"Just shook is all," Jack wished he had a drink.

"Odd reaction, don't you think, Half Track? From a man says he barely knew Alex."

"It's the way he got it, that's all," Jack tried to cover himself. "Stomped to death by an elephant? I wouldn't wish that on anybody. Not on my worst enemy."

Luna folder her knife into her pocket. "Toss me a mug, would you, Track?"

Half Track tossed her boss a chipped coffee cup. Luna caught it and reached past Jack for a fill. Leaning all the way across. Her breasts hanging in his face. Her hair. That hyacinth smell.

But that skin. Thick as mustard.

She poured her coffee leisurely, withdrew. Then she placed her cup next to Jack's. Pulled her stool even closer.

"Accidents happen, Jack. All the time. Could happen to any-body. Could happen to you. Hard work, Jack. You'll be sucking hind tit. Swinging mallets and shoveling shit from dawn 'til dark. You still wanta stay?"

Jack lifted his own mug. Nothing but dregs left.

"…I got no choice," he said, finally.

Luna leaned away.

"I think that may be the only truthful thing you've said since you got here."

She slid from her stool.

"We're starting a one-nighter, Saturdays only. Nothing fancy, just once a week. Under the stars. You'll need some work clothes. And brogans, you ain't gonna last a day in those shoes."

"When do I start?"

"Tomorrow. Five sharp. That's in the morning, Jack. I'll know by noon if you can brodie a freak show."

It was barely light the next morning when Jack dragged himself to the cookhouse for grits and coffee. It was already hot. Not a breath to stir the flag mounted on the café's roof.

Tommy Speck was talking a mile a minute. Cleary taking great pleasure in having Jack on his leash.

"So I'm a, what—a brodie?"

"Close enough. A gopher, a working man. Bottom of the heap. The lingo's meant for the road. Like this ain't really a cookhouse—a real cookhouse'd be in a tent or maybe a wagon. But what the hey. We're carnies, even when we're bedding."

"Bed sounds pretty good, about now."

"Forget it, pretty boy. You got to earn your keep."

"So are we like a circus?"

The word 'circus' got the attention of a pinhead nearby.

Tommy leaned forward. "Not the circus, awright? We ain't the fucking circus."

"Sorry."

"This thing we're doin' is strictly midway. No Big Tent. No Liberty Ride. Nothing fleabag, but not no Sunday school, neither. What we are is hully-gully and hootchy-kootch. Freaks and performers and candy butchers."

"So I'll be working a carnival?"

"You'll be building the carnival. Lot's already laid out. Got most of the sawdust down. Once the stalls are up and everybody's got his act up, we'll be ready to go."

"Expecting a crowd?"

Speck shrugged. "Who knows? But if we fold we don't have to hit the road. No tear down, no gas or traincars or wagons. 'Course by spring we'll have itchy feet, but till then—it's step up and smile, gents. And keep yer hands in yer pockets!"

It was not yet six in the morning as Jack lugged a sledge hammer and a coil of rope through the midst of a midway in the making. He spotted a familiar figure just ahead, lumbering behind a wheelbarrow.

"Hey, Freddie," Jack spoke up as he pulled alongside and was snubbed without comment.

"What's Freddie's beef?" Jack asked when he caught up with Tommy Speck.

"Freddie? You mean Friederich?"

"I mean the carney hauling his balls in a wheelbarrow."

Tommy glanced back. "You don't chitchat with Friederich," Tommy informed him coldly. "You don't gab with anybody's a performer. You ain't earned that right."

Jack blanched, "I was just being polite."

"Not your place," Tommy snapped. "Especially when he's on his way to his pit, right over there."

Jack followed Tommy's finger to a life-sized linotype stretched over a newly-built stage. It was a shocking photograph; if Jack hadn't seen the man with his own two eyes he'd swear the lino was faked. A man perched naked on a pair of cajones larger than an ottoman! A banner above making the unnecessarily exaggerated claim:

—SEE FRIEDERICH THE UNPARALLELED—
THE MAN WITH SIXTY POUND TESTICLES

"Goddamn class act," Tommy declared. "The real thing, front-row. Brings in the marks like tits and beer."

It was not a big carnival, not much more than a forty-miler, as Tommy described it, which made no sense at all to Jack as the grounds were definitely not forty miles across. Barely forty goddamn yards across. Not that size made all that much difference, at least not for a brodie. Carnivals were all laid out in similar fashion, Jack learned, a wide, straight artery interrupted along the sides at intervals with pits or stalls or tents offering cheap temptations.

It all began with staking out the lot. Tommy Speck was Luna's designated pro which meant among other things that it was Tommy's prerogative to assign and measure out the positions of the various games, shows and concessions along the midway's front and back end.

"The 'Front End' starts right inside the gate," Tommy instructed his brodie on the run. "Front end's for family, hotdogs, cotton candy. The talkers hit 'em once they get their goodies, work 'em to the stalls or shows. But this morning I got you brodying the Back End."

The back end was reserved for more exotic entertainment, the strippers, torture shows and such. Most prominent among the back-enders were the geeks, glommers and freaks who were the stars of Kaleidoscope. There were stalls going up all over the place. Brightly painted banners stretched between poles hung with kerosene lanterns. Bunting and banners erotically illustrated with promises of forbidden fruit.

"Hi, Jack."

The Penguin Lady in a costume of seagreen and sequins smiling behind a barricade of oilcloth and timber.

"'Lo, Pencil Dick."

This from Cassandra. A banner overhead gave hints of her blarney: "SEE CASSANDRA, THREE-BREASTED PRIESTESS OF THE DELPHIC ISLES."

The back end, clearly, was a place to lose innocence, or find it. A place where rubes found themselves both attracted and repulsed by aberrations of flesh which they had not thought possible. There were no gimmicks here, Tommy insisted. No flimflam. It was here that a giddy young girl might write her beau a valentine on The Human Slate's permeable chest. It was here that crowds shrieked as Pinhead drove nails up his nose. Here was where you'd find The Snake Lady and The Wild Men of Borneo, Circassian Princesses and Cannibals.

Here was where, once a week, Half Track The Severed Torso and The Penguin Lady resurrected their roadshow acts. And it was here, too, in canvas tents, that young men crowded to experience their first hootchy-kootchy. Jack saw the enticing banner: LUNA THE MOON MAIDEN.

"One thin diiiiime," Tommy barked. "One tenth of a dol-laaaah…. 'S'matter, Jack?"

"Nothing," Jack dragged his attention away. He should be thinking about Sally Price and Alex Goodman and Oliver Bladehorn.

And Martin and Mamere.

"Grab a bucket of nails," Tommy directed him. "And a shovel, too. Looks like we need to spread some more sawdust."

Every performer was jealous of his position on the midway, everybody cursing or cajoling to put his pit in the choicest location. On the road those negotiations could get nasty, but here, in this beddy, the performers seemed content with, or resigned to, Tommy Speck's high-pitched verdicts.

Jack began his apprenticeship as a brodie shoveling sawdust in the blistering sun. By noon he was hammering nails and stretching canvas for the pits and booths designed to part marks from their money. A whistle from a calliope brought sandwiches and ice water for a twenty minute reprieve. Then it was back to work, this time nearer the front end and in the construction of what was euphemistically described as "GAMES OF SKILL!!"

"Oh, there's skill, all right," Speck chuckled going on to

demonstrate how easy it was to dull a dart so that it would not lodge on its target board. Other games of skill were rigged from the get-go. Take the old bottle-throw, for instance. What could be simpler than knocking a milk bottle off a crate with a baseball?

"Can I try?" Jack asked.

"Sure," Tommy smiled and let him waste a dozen pitches and a half-dozen strikes before he told Jack that the bottles were weighted at their bases with lead or cement.

Assembling the barrel toss gave Jack a chance to see a variation on the pitch-and-toss. All the rube had to do was throw a baseball into a barrel and get a prize. How hard could that be? But the barrel was rigged with a false bottom as resilient as a trampoline so that a ball thrown from the specified distance invariably bounced out.

Not everything was a flattie. "This here 'Fish the Bottle' is hanky-pank," Tommy noted, which in the carney's twisted lingo meant it was honest. "Gotta let the schmucks win something."

"Looks like you'd lose money."

Tommy shook his head. "Way you come out on a hanky-pank is you only give away brummagem for prizes. But there's more money stackin' the deck. Like I say, Luna ain't got us runnin' no Sunday School."

She sure as hell wasn't. Jack saw more varieties of cheating along that fifty yards of sawdust than he'd seen in a lifetime of poker. Foot-pedals stopped the Wheel of Fortune anywhere the carney wanted. The skilos' arrow never stopped on a winning color. The rifles at the shooting gallery shot blanks. You could swing the mallet as hard as you wanted on the High Striker, but its iron weight wouldn't travel two feet skyward to gong the bell, win you a Teddy and get you laid by the gal who always thought you were something special unless Half Track released the tension on the knob that adjusted the friction along the traveling wire.

The carney who worked the gaff on one flattie would play the stick on the one next door, winning some rigged game of skill or chance as a come-on to rubes eager to part with their money. Even brodies were allowed to look down on rubes, a breed of person universally courted and yet held in contempt.

There were other things to learn, besides, expectations of behavior related to propriety and decorum that had the force of law. Some of these *obiter dicta* Jack had already learned. The rest Tommy Speck supplied rapid-fire.

Rule Number One: A brodie never, for any reason, talks to a mark.

If a yokel got riled it was generally Luna's job to patch him, though of course The Giant was always available if muscle was required. But most rubes were easy to smooth. Amazing what a free ticket to the torture pit did to mollify some outraged cowboy or what a teddy bear could do to squawk the occasionally mortified Sunday schooler.

Rule Number Two was easy: Never forget Rule Number One.

There was a pecking order in this world that was ignored only at one's peril. Top dog was the owner and operator. That was Luna Chevreaux. Jack learned that Luna didn't actually own a thing on the property, but every concession, sideshow, game and ride on the midway paid her fifty percent of its profit.

In return for that consideration Luna bankrolled most of the acts. She handled the books, the drunks, and the local John Q. Luna was operator, lot man, patch and ride superintendent rolled into one. She did everything from inspect the Tilt-A-Wheel to bribe the Hillsborough sheriff not to bother looking for liquor in the hootchy-kootchies that offered strippers to single men driving all the way from Tampa for a walk on the wild side. Everything was a fix, Jack learned. A con. A scam.

Except for the geeks.

The lepers of polite society were the aristocrats in Kaleidoscope and there were no fakes. Pinhead actually did hammer real nails up his nose. Penguin's limbs were webbed from birth and Half Track had no fake bottom within which to hide a healthy pair of legs. The Half Woman and The Dog Man and The Svengali Siamese Violinists and The Alligator Man and Freddie Bronkowski with his wheelbarrowed balls—these along with giants, midgets, and other misfits were the royalty of Kaleidoscope. And first among these peers was the carney's most enduring and profitable attraction, the Matron of the Midway, the Colossus of Sex…The Amazing—! The Inimitable——!

Princess Peewee.

More widely known as, simply, The Fat Lady.

Her banner advertised a weight of six hundred and forty-seven pounds

"Jesus Christ, is that possible?"

"That ain't even the heaviest," Tommy confirmed. "But Peewee's special. She's got class."

The word "class" did not come to mind when Jack recalled the wallowing mound of flesh that he had seen wagoned off a freight car, but even a rookie knew there were times you kept your trap shut.

Romaine finished his first day as a brodie with a sunburn, blistered hands and an overarching preoccupation—in the course of that long day he had gleaned not a smidgeon of information regarding Alex Goodman, much less any surrogate. Jack dreaded his first report back to Cincinnati; Oliver Bladehorn would not be happy to learn that a pachyderm had stomped his only solid lead to pulp.

The only encouraging news—somebody down here was clearly hiding something. Who was the rumored benefactor bailing geeks out of hard times? The Fiddle Twins assumed Jack was the moneybag, but who was it really? If Alex Goodman hadn't been in Cincinnati to meet Sally Price, then who had? It didn't take a Pinkerton to figure that Luna had hired Jack largely to make sure he didn't get answers to those questions. She had Jack by the balls and he had to play along. He wasn't going to find any leads to Bladehorn's stash from the outside of this closed-in camp, after all. If there was something down here that belonged to Bladehorn, somebody inside this tight knit of misfits had the beans and Jack had to make them spill.

He fell into bed exhausted, but could not sleep. Tommy roused the new brodie the second day at five sharp to work another day just like the first. By the third day Jack was close to folding.

What if he'd simply hit a dead end? What if there was nothing to be found in this fucking place but snakes and mosquitoes and freaks who never rubbed two honest dimes together in their lives?

Problem was, there was no other place to look. You couldn't

stash fifteen large and a quarter million in bonds on your lonesome. Somebody in this con-wise camp had to know something.

But what are the odds, Jack, that they'll talk to you?

By the fourth day, Jack decided it didn't matter what the odds were. Sometimes you got a bad hand you couldn't fold; you just had to keep on playing hoping to draw that ace or else slip it up your sleeve. Jack decided he'd work on Tommy Speck. Four days of constant labor had diminished the distance between the two men. Tommy liked to talk. He liked to drink, too, and to gamble. Those were diversions which might be worked to advantage.

The G-tent provided his opportunity. On the road, a G-tent was a kind of social hall for carneys, a place to trade the virtually constant gossip that characterized the freaks' conversation, and a place to gamble, which was their continual recreation. Brodies were generally discouraged from socializing with performers. The card table, however, proved a major exception to that rule.

The tent was raised on the backside of the midway, just behind the menagerie and the mechanical rides. The canvas was glowing like a jack o' lantern from kerosene lamps as Jack stepped inside. Tommy was already in high form over a stein of homebrew, descanting to everyone in earshot on the differences between carney life and circus life right down to the knots used to secure the stakes anchoring their always-separate tents ("...Ya never see a carney usin' that extra hitch!"), swapping stories with The Giant and Jo Jo and Frankie about the great carnivals and their owners, names completely unfamiliar to Jack—Mr. Jones, Mr. Ferari, and the feisty Hody Hurd.

"Fuck with that lady, you'd be redlighted overnight," Tommy promised. "You'd be nursing a hangover in the stockcar, just sleepin' it off at sixty miles an hour, next thing you know the sidedoor's open and your ass is wrapped around a telegraph pole!"

"Lady knew how to take care of business!" Cassandra chortled, those three breasts rising and falling in perfect, firmly packed unison.

"Got sawdust in her veins," Tommy echoed the sentiment. You might miss the small, plump woman smiling quietly at his side. In all their conversation, Tommy had not once referred to his wife.

Eileen was her name, Jack learned that much from Penguin. Had been married to Tommy for years but was only just now *embarasso* with their first child.

She was a small woman, barely four feet tall, which still made her a head taller than her husband, but Penguin told Jack that Eileen was not a dwarf.

"Not all little people are dwarfs," Charlotte informed him. "You can tell by looking at her joints, the way she walks—she's not like Tommy. She's a midget."

"Will their child be a dwarf?"

"Won't know 'til the pickle pops."

Jack was tempted to sample the carney's homebrew but settled instead for a firkin of tea sugared like molasses and poured over ice. He found a crate near Speck and his wife and settled in, feigning interest as the little man recalled his days with Guy Dodson and May Cody Fleming. Jack laughed along with the other carneys as Tommy aped or skewered the various managers whose railroad cars took shows all over the country. Speck knew them all. He knew the corporate side of the midway, as well, tracing the Byzantine ownership of the Royal American or the Amusement Corporation of America with the same rigor that a biographer would bring to bear on Carnegie or Mellon.

The more the dwarf drank, the less precision was involved, naturally, Tommy turning from fact to fiction, spinning yarns that always tied to girls and cards and booze and claiming a ringside seat at every significant event in history.

"I was *in* Buffalo in 1901 when they shot President McKinley."

"Ought-One," Half Track repeated and pressed the date onto The Slate's palimpsest skin with a spoon.

One outrageous lie after another. Or perhaps they really were outrageous truths—no one seemed to care.

Every freak, knife-thrower and sword-swallower present had stories to tell, weaving incidents with histories and genealogies completely foreign to any outsider. There was a pair of faces though, new arrivals, who seemed very familiar to Jack.

They were twins, good looking brunettes, bright, happy faces. Kind of sexy.

He nudged Half Track.

"Know those two?"

"What two?"

"By Jo Jo. Sitting back to back."

She followed his finger and snorted, "They ain't sittin' back to back, moron. They're *joined* back to back."

Even Jack had heard of the famous Hilton Sisters, and now he recalled where he'd seen them. It had been a vaudeville in Chicago. The twins headlined the show, two sweetly harmonized voices forever linked. He'd even bought a photograph afterward, that photo along with the attached promotional material intended to show how perfectly "adjusted" and "normal" the sisters really, truly were. Jack recalled the picture clearly now. Two young ladies dancing back to back with a pair of smiling, well-dressed beaus.

And here they were, another pair of Siamese freaks, sitting not ten feet from Jacques and Marcel. But unlike the Svengali Violinists, the Hilton Sisters were famous.

Were they rich as well?

Jack edged over to Tommy Speck's wife.

"Somebody said those are the Hiltons, over there," he pointed.

She smiled affirmation.

"They're pretty big, aren't they?"

She smiled again. "Tommy said you weren't too sharp."

There you go. Another dead end. But Jack had to keep playing.

"Jack Romaine. Don't believe we've met."

"Eileen. Pleased to meetcha."

"Is it true the sisters are gonna be in the pictures? I heard something about a talkie."

"They're real troupers," she nodded.

"Not a bad life," Jack offered.

"Depends," she shrugged and something in her tone changed.

Jack leaned over. "They got problems?"

Gossip. That was all it took for Eileen to open up.

"Word is they're damn near hostage to their managers," she

said, and her little nostrils flared. "They never see a dime of their take. They're put up in this mansion in San Antonio but it might as well be a prison. Poor kids never see a fella unless it's for some promotional. Never get loose from the show unless the Meyers orchestrate it.

"Took a month to give those pricks the slip. The girls—? The Meyers think they're in Saratoga. Luna brought 'em up to see an attorney in Tampa. See if she can cut 'em loose from Meyer and Edith. Those two! They ain't even the girls' real parents, for God's sake!"

Lots to glean, there. Such as, for instance, how Luna Chevreaux had come to know any attorney prominent enough to represent the Hilton Sisters. But before Jack could even go about finding a way to frame that question, Eileen was back to her husband and another run of carney lore.

People and places. Name after name. Bill Lynch and the Lee brothers. Carl Sedlmayr. Nat Worman ("…you need somethin' fixed, get it to Nat…")

Jack learned the histories of Tom Thumb and Little Egypt sitting in that side-open tent. The freaks talked and talked, and as the lanterns wicked low and shadows pushed from the corners of the canvas their voices began almost imperceptibly to override the sight of their extra or missing limbs, their lesions, their anatomic anomalies or folds of skin. These were the voices of a genuine family, Jack began dimly to realize, an extended family flung on railroad cars and gas wagons all over the country, a soiree of misfits returning with the frost each year for renewal in a familiar, if not familial reunion.

There were celebrities on the billboard, but not on the backside. The Hilton Sisters who were worth hundreds of thousands of dollars fetched their own drinks right along with Half Track and Penguin. They got ribbed and kidded just like every other performer. And there were other named stars present as well, performers with royal status in this offbeat world, who were met with equal equanimity.

Jack Earl himself dipped into the pavilion just before midnight, higher by a foot than The Giant, looking taller still with a ten-gallon hat perched on his lantern-jawed head.

"Just in the neighborhood," Earl replied to a casual question.

"Thought I'd play me a hand or two of some cards. Get some of my money back from Tommy Speck."

"How long ya got, Earl?" Tommy was already clearing a crate for a table.

"Not long enough."

It was odd to see a man eight and a half feet tall pull up a fifty gallon barrel for an ottoman.

The world's tallest man tipped back his ten-gallon to feature a weary face.

"Got to hitch up with Barnum's in Sarasota."

"Tell that shithead he can wait," Cassandra challenged, as Tommy pulled out a deck of Players.

"Tell P.T. I'm takin' you fishing."

"Been fishin' with you b'fore, Cassandra," Earl winked. "An' it damn near killed me."

The whole tent roared laughter. A slow smile eased The Giant's craggy face. The deeply set eyes roamed the tent briefly before they settled at last on the only unmarked face under the tent.

Without warning, Jack Earl reached over and took Jack Romaine's dealing hand.

"Don't remember seein' you anyplace," Earl turned Jack's hand palm-up without waiting for a reply.

"I'm just a working man." Jack resisted the urge to jerk his hand away. The tent was suddenly still as a house of stiffs. "Just started, really. Tommy's showing me the ropes."

Earl shrugged as he shuffled the cards.

"Ever'body's got to start somewhere," he said. "Word of advice, though. If yer willing."

"Sure."

"Get yerself an act. Walk nails, shit turds out yer mouth, somethin'. You don' wanta be a brodie forever."

The pronouncement seemed to be received as a kind of benediction. A buzz of life and laughter resumed as if wound up from a gramophone's seashell speaker and within seconds the tent was as raucous as ever.

"Deal the man in, Tommy," Earl said, and Jack took a familiar seat.

They played a few hands. Small talk. Then Jack Earl turned to address Tommy Speck's wife.

"Ran into yer brother the other day. In Saratoga. Said he was pitchin' for the Reds."

Jack kept a poker face.

"He's just tryin' out," Eileen blushed pleasure. "But Aaron's good."

"Got himself a hell of an arm," Tommy agreed.

"They could use one," Earl rejoined and Eileen laughed with everyone else.

Jack let a couple of cards slide before he risked an aside to Mrs. Speck.

"You from Cincinnati, Eileen?"

"My family lives there," she nodded brightly, and Tommy broke in smoothly.

"Cain't exactly call it home, though, can we, babe? Bein' on the road alla time."

Jack passed it off with a friendly nod. He waited long enough to finish a few more hands before he folded.

"I gotta hit the hay, gentlemen," he announced, and with that excuse left the Specks and the other carnies to themselves.

Skirting the pines back to his shack, Jack mulled over the information he had gleaned from the evening's society. There were a couple of things, he decided. First off it was apparent that Tommy did not want Jack to know his wife hailed from Cincinnati. Why? Could be a simple matter of coincidence that Eileen Speck was a citizen of the Queen City. And what about Eileen's brother? A traveling man, apparently, playing games from Ohio to Florida. Could *he* be Alex Goodman's go-between? Had Goodman been using Eileen's brother or someone in her family to shepherd Sally Price?

Then there was that business with the Hilton sisters. Why had the twins come to Kaleidoscope in the first place? What made them think that Luna Chevreaux had the resources to end their indenturement?

Something stirred in the shadows beyond the needles of pine. Moving between the moon and the trees. Jack pivoted carefully. Luna regarded him from a distance, nearly invisible in the late night's lunar shadow.

How long had she been watching?

"Better get some rest, Jack." The arc of a cigarette hissed to the sand. "Brodies start early."

Chapter seven

Gimmick—the control on a crooked game of chance.

The next morning put Jack behind a shovel and mallet trying to keep up with Tommy Speck as the little man pushed to complete preparations for the Saturday show. It was nearly noon when trucks came rolling down the sandy lane and Jack left his hammer and shovel to unload hay and oats and staples for the cookhouse.

"For a beddy, this place takes a lot of work," Jack observed.

Speck grinned. "Kaleidoscope's more than a beddy between seasons. It's supply and credit, billboard and employment. It's a listening post and a way station for people who don't fit anyplace else. And it ain't just geeks comin' down. Take a look over there—"

Jack followed Speck's direction to see a young athletic man pulling swords from a tarp-covered truck.

Jack nodded. "He's no geek."

"He's a performer. Circus ain't got no monopoly on talent,

have they? We got plenty to see. Take a look at Charlie, you wanna see somethin'."

The young man had tossed off his shirt and was carefully inspecting a sword that looked as long as a yardstick.

"Oh, shit," Jack said and as if on cue the youngster leaned far back, opened his mouth and with perfect aplomb slid the blade down his throat to the hilt.

"Real comer," Tommy grunted approval. "Kid got four swords down this summer. *Four.* Plus a dagger. That's real talent."

"But it's a gimmick, right?" Jack protested. "I mean, the blade slides up in the handle or something, is that it?"

Tommy snorted. "Not a carney. I knew this swallower once, been at it for years. He gets up one morning, lines up his tools. Little June bug lights on one of his blades. Little bitty, no more than a pin. It's showtime; Larry opens his gullet and down goes the sword—with the bug."

"What'd he do?"

"Same as you. Or me. He coughed.

Jack winced.

"Yep. Gutted himself on the spot. Rubes got their money's worth that day, I can tell ya."

"Hey, Tommy!"

The bare-chested performer was replacing his sword with its fellows.

"Tommy, you got a minute?"

"Minute, maybe," the dwarf seemed suddenly cool.

The man grabbed his shirt as he jogged over.

"Charlie Blade," he extended a hand graciously to Jack.

"Jack Romaine. Pretty impressive act you got."

Tommy spit a wad into the sand. "Charlie, whatchu want?"

"Need you da see Luna for me," Blade clasped his hands like he was at prayer. "I juss needsum snatch. Little bread. Justa tide me over."

"You were here just last month, Blade. Month early, why weren't you workin' a show?"

"Luna knows."

"Yeah, well, yer wearin' out yer welcome."

"Jussum green till the moon turns. I gan worka show Saturday. You gan hav' all my take."

Jack recognized the slurred speech. The dilated pupils.

"You want somethin' from the Boss, yer gonna have to ask 'er yerself." Tommy rendered his verdict coldly.

"Thags, Tommy, thassa good idea. I juss see Luna, then. Ask her myself."

But Tommy was already walking away. Jack had to hustle to catch him.

"What was that about?"

"Money," Tommy dismissed it too quickly. "Charlie's always short."

Something else going on? Tommy might need a drink to let something slip, but Jack already had Charlie Blade's number.

The next stop on the runway introduced Jack to another newly arrived performer. "The Great Flambé" was a ravaged old-timer with a lion's mane of silver hair, hurling fire from his mouth like a dragon onto a miniature castle fashioned of papier-mâché.

WHOOOOOSH! and the citadel burst into flame.

"What you think, Master Speck?" Flambé's address was formal, a European accent. He barely acknowledged Jack, stepping back instead to admire the effect of his work.

"Tits," Tommy approved. "And maybe you could put a little moat around it, too? Let the rubes throw in a dime every time you torch 'er."

"An excellent suggestion!" Flambé beamed. "You are genius, Master Speck!"

Only then deigning to acknowledge the working man alongside.

"And who is this choice specimen in your thrall?"

"New man."

"Name's Romaine," Jack spoke up but did not extend a hand. "Jack Romaine."

"How all-American," the older man's smile displayed perfect teeth. "My familiar to my friends is *Flambé*. Be delighted to become familiar. My trailer is just past the lion's cage. You will recognize the artwork."

"Uh. Thanks."

Jack hung on Tommy's shoulder as they walked away.

"'Become familiar'......that mean what I *think* it means?"

"What, you ain't had yer huckle berried?" Tommy chuckled. "Just grab your hammer, Pretty Boy. Time you finish this next job, Flambé's not gonna want you anyplace close."

The job waiting led Jack beyond the bounds of the nearly-finished carnival to a barricade of yellow heart pines pierced by a narrow gauge of railroad track.

"Where's this go?"

"Follow 'em and see," was Speck's reply and a minute later Jack spotted a pennant wafting from the twin-poled tent he had first seen on his rainy arrival at Kaleidoscope.

He glanced over to Tommy. "Got some more acts in the big-top?"

"No, this is a private residence."

"A residence? You're kidding."

"No, Peewee lives here. And Ambassador, too."

"The elephant?"

"Yeah, he stays with the Princess. Kind of like her companion."

"Pretty weird, don't you think?" Jack risked a provocation, "A woman living with an elephant?"

If Tommy saw the bait he didn't take it.

"I dunno," the dwarf's shrug was noncommittal. "Peewee and Ambassador—they get along real well. She's got her bed right where she can talk to him. She needs something, anything—change of clothes, pitcher of water—he brings it over gentle as a lamb. She wants a bath, he puts her in the tank. Takes her out, too, good damn thing. Take a crane and a crew of men, otherwise."

A wagon of hay waited outside The Fat Lady's residence. A ring of barrels surrounded a corral of packed earth. Clearly, the place was used to train an act; there were oversized balls stowed to the side, what looked like riding crops the length of fishing poles stowed on the perimeter. There was also a plow and harrow that looked oddly out of place.

The tent was larger than Jack had imagined, must have been a hundred, hundred and twenty feet wide. Two lines of quarter poles supported the canvas between the side and center poles. No water bags. The tarp pulled tight on guys strung like piano wire all around.

"Tight as Dick's hatband," Tommy checked the sun's height. "Shouldn't be this tight this late in the day. Speakin' of late in the day, must be near noon. Take a gander."

There was someone ahead of them on the narrow rail. It was The Giant, pushing what looked like a luggage cart along the iron track. Getting closer, Jack saw a feast of food steaming from that hand-pushed truck, whole chickens on a platter beside bowls of carrots and mashed potatoes. A separate roast. A string of sausages.

Jack shifted his mallet.

"He feeding an army?"

"Nope," Tommy smiled proudly. "It's all for Peewee."

"For the week?"

"For a meal. One meal." Tommy beamed. "Magnificent, ain't it?"

"Can't wait to see."

"Grab the flap for Giant."

Jack jogged ahead of the cart. Two sheets of tarp sang on metal rings allowing entrance into the rude palace. The Giant pushed his moveable feast into the gloomy interior without a word of thanks or acknowledgement. It was darker inside than Jack expected. Tommy nudged him in the direction of what looked to be a stack of ordinary iron bars.

"Grab some of them tie-downs."

The bars turned out to be thick as Jack's arm and six feet long. Jack noted the eyelets welded on top.

"Luna wants us to put in some extra security for Ambassador." Tommy went on to give detailed instruction for a perimeter of stakes designed to prevent another rampage by the aging elephant.

"But all you got to do is hammer in the iron. Spots are already marked. Then we'll thread lines through the eyebolts to tie the old boy off."

"I never tied off an elephant."

"And you ain't gonna start with this one; that's the trainer's job."

By the time Jack managed to heft a single iron stake onto his shoulder, The Giant was leaving. The black man nodded almost imperceptibly to Tommy, but for Jack—nothing. The brodie might as well have been invisible.

"Not much of a talker, is he? The nigger."

"Call him nigger to his face and you'll see.

Another reminder to Jack that he was an outsider in this strange community. A series of sheets appeared ahead, ghostly demarcations strung on what might have been clotheslines set up near the center of the tent. Tommy pulled up short and Jack almost stumbled into him.

"Watch yer step."

"Sorry."

"Now, yer about to meet the Princess, awright? Our biggest draw. Our most respected performer."

"Fine, sure."

"It ain't fine and it ain't ever sure," Speck contradicted him coldly. "Peewee can be tricky. She's feeling sociable, you'll be all right. But if yer smart you'll just shut up, do yer job, and get the hell out. And do not gawk. She's on her own time, now, and in her own house. Show some goddamn respect."

Tommy left him there, halfway between the inner sanctum and the canvas skin behind. The only light coming into the tent shut off, suddenly, when Speck closed the flap on his way outside. Nothing left to guide Jack then but the ghostly pale of the wall ahead.

He was already sweating like a French whore in church. The interior, though dark, was sweltering. There was no sound, either. No trumpet of jungle beast. Not a sound from The Princess. Jack found the narrow strip of track with his city-slicker shoe and followed that iron ribbon to the sheeted boudoir waiting ahead.

A flickering glow from inside, a lantern.

"Well, ya comin' in or what?"

He slid the sheet aside and saw her, Princess Peewee grazing like some pampered bovine off a cart chocked on its rails directly beside a bed reinforced with enough timber to build a barn.

A Raggedy Anne doll propped ludicrously on a pillow that was a napkin next to Peewee's tub-sized head. Another surprise—there were books all over the bed, books half-opened on the bed itself, books stacked from the sawdust floor, more books in the shelves of her headboard. A couple of the authors were familiar; some man's wife had given Jack a copy of *The Great Gatsby* after a furtive encounter, an absolute must, she had told him, the defining book of our generation, but he hadn't got around to it. Peewee, on the other hand, was clearly committed to the hardback propped open on top of her breasts.

Jack turned his attention to the water tank. The tank was situated at the foot of the bed, a Brobdingnagian cistern at least thirty feet in circumference. Deep as a man was tall. You could see where the iron cylinder had ruptured, new rivets bright as silver dollars up and down to repair the broken seam. The welds did not look professional. Jack wondered if it would hold.

Peewee's jaw was working like a heifer's. A breast of chicken competing with the book in her free hand.

"Well, now, Ambassador, this one's new."

It wasn't until Peewee's remark that Jack actually saw the beast. Talk about missing the elephant in the fucking room! But in fairness it was a big room, and dark, and until he moved the water tank had concealed Ambassador from easy view.

The earth trembled as the bull ambled, that's how you'd have to describe it, to the head of Peewee's bed. At least twelve feet high, the creature would have to weigh, what—four thousand? Five thousand pounds? Jack could only guess. The tusks alone would have made some bushman a fortune, great prongs of ivory anchored on either side of the massive proboscis.

Peewee sat up and Jack saw the title of her book, *The Age of Innocence.*

"Edith Wharton," Peewee supplied the author and Jack wondered if he was being encouraged to communicate.

"Wharton, you know her?"

"Ah, no. No, Princess, who is she?"

"Writer. Free thinker. Henry James calls her his angel of destruction which makes me think he needs her a hell of a lot more than she needs him."

Peewee broke off a drumstick.

"Well, you gonna gawk or you gonna work?"

"Don't mind me," Jack apologized, and hurried over to the stack of eye-bolted stakes that were to become the puny restraint for Peewee's guardian.

He stripped to the waist and got to it. There were a dozen bars which had to be pounded into place with their dozen or more tethers. Tommy had arranged the stakes to allow Ambassador a range through his normal circuit. Beyond her initial remarks, The Fat Lady appeared to ignore him entirely, returning to her competing appetites with a relish that was audible from yards away.

Within minutes he was pouring sweat, but Jack was determined not to beg for either water or rest. He tapped a spike gently to stand, then swung the sledge back and rode it down. The impact of steel on steel was lost in the vast interior, a mere *tink*, like a distant hammer on a ten-penny nail.

Over and over he drove the heavy sledge, one iron stake after another coaxed inches at a time into the yielding earth. Then to thread a chain heavy enough to hold a barge through those waiting eyes. Rounding the circuit until after some interminable interval he was returned again to the side of The Fat Lady's bed.

Jack grabbed his back as he straightened from his labor and found Peewee regarding him in unabashed inspection. Two small, bright eyes pressed like berries into that pie face.

"Should keep the big fella on campus," Jack gestured awkwardly in the general direction of the elephant. "If he's rigged right."

"That's what they said last time." Peewee closed her book.

"I'm not the man actually tying the tether."

"Never imagined you were. AMBASSADOR—"

The beast turned to her voice. You could feel a sudden stir of air with the movement of the animal's enormous ears.

"Time to train, baby."

She raised a hand, extended it straight from her shoulder.

"OUTSIDE."

The elephant snorted once, the explosion from that long trunk scattering peanut shells and sawdust. The impact of padded hooves, then, and Jack found himself backing away as the bull ambled past to find the iron track that would lead him out of the tent.

"Impressive," Jack reached down to collect his shirt.

"Leave it off."

"'Scuse me?"

"Your shirt. Leave it off."

Jack dropped his uppers to the floor.

"Turn around," she said. "Well, go on, face me."

He hesitated a fraction before he complied.

"That's enough. Now stand a minute."

He stood with sweat pouring down his face and torso, pooling in crevices along his collarbone and belly. For a long time she didn't say anything. Just lay there Roman fashion, examining him as though he were a piece of meat. Occasionally Jack imagined that he heard a grunt of satisfaction. Or a sigh of indifference.

It didn't stop her meal. She finished off a prime rib as though it was an appetizer. Those jaws working like a cow chewing its cud, the grease crushed from the fat coursing down her face.

Jack thought she had to be the most repulsive thing he had ever seen. And yet something was stirring that he could not stop.

To hell with this. His job was done, it was stifling hot (how did she stand it in here, anyhow?) and he was getting the fuck out.

But then she spoke and he knew he could not go.

"You're not the rube knew my Alex, are ya?" she inquired through a mash of potatoes.

Jack froze.

"Cat got your tongue, Pretty Boy?"

He flushed. "Never claimed to know the man. Just ran into him, is all. Had a couple of beers, got talking, he said I might could get work down here. Why? He mention me?"

Her smile was lascivious and Jack felt something crawling at the nape of his neck. But there was an erection, too. A hard bone growing in his trousers. He shifted to conceal that embarrassment.

Her eyes twinkled.

"We were real pals, y'know. Alex and me. Intimate, ya might say."

A man? With this pile of flesh? Jack didn't want to think about it. But his dick seemed to have a mind of its own.

"Don't be embarrassed, sailor. Happens all the time."

"What do you care what Alex said?" Jack tried to steer her attention away from his crotch.

She shrugged. "Only natural to ask. When you have a lover you wonder what he says to his friends, his buddies."

"We weren't friends."

"I bet you weren't," she replied, and the menace was unmistakable.

She shoved the cart aside as easily as a tray.

"You feel sooooo dirty, don'tcha? And sooooo superior. Five'll get you ten you'll wash yer horn first time you get the chance. And then you'll laugh behind my back."

"Nobody's laughing," Jack retorted.

"Bullshit, all rubes laugh."

"I'm a brodie."

"You're a rube."

"Makes you think so?"

"I can read your mind."

"I thought that was Cassandra's gig," Jack retorted.

She smiled. "Why don't we see for ourselves, then?"

Peewee used her sheet to wipe the grease from her hands. Then she hauled herself erect, the timbers beneath her bed complaining from that effort. Breasts falling like sacks of meal into her lap. Then she closed her eyes. Pressed dimpled fingers to her temples and then, *sotto voce*—

"'How could anybody want to fuck *her?*'"

Opening her eyes. That menacing smile.

"Is that about right, 'Jack'? That pretty much what's in your head? 'Course, I notice your dick's saying something different."

She lowered her massive arms.

"You come here swinging a sledge like you never used one before, doing everything you can to keep your eyes off me. 'That bitch,' you're thinking, 'Eating like a hog. How could Alex want HER? Was he drunk?'"

"Was he?" Jack snatched his shirt off the ground.

"Not too drunk to get a stiff on."

"Man had passion."

"He had passion for *me*, you prick, and that's the part makes you itch, doesn't it? That's what's got the sweat rolling off your balls."

"You're painting me in a corner here, Princess."

"Oh, so I'm supposed to just bare my soul, tell you about my kinky sex life, my diet and my lovers and you can sit there with a straight face and a hard on and lie your ass off, and I'm not supposed to care?! Let me tell you something—"

She lurched forward and Jack jerked on instinct to retreat.

"Alex was good to me! He gave me what I wanted and I gave him what he wanted and anything else, *anything*, is nobody's business."

"So you get to keep your secrets, is that it? But I don't?"

The smile on her painted lips spread like a gash across her face.

"You're in Kaleidoscope, Mr. Jack Romaine. Nobody keeps secrets from me. Not in the end."

Jack emerged from Peewee's tent shaken and unsure and wary of encountering her unsupervised elephant. But, as Peewee had indicated, Ambassador was being trained. Jack was surprised to see that the same queer who swallowed fire was also a mahout. The silver-haired fire-swallower was standing before the bull elephant beneath the stand of pines which separated Peewee's palace from the carnival proper. The same barrels Jack saw on approaching the tent were apparently on tap for Ambassador's routine.

"Flambé."

"*Si, senor.* I would invite you once again to enjoy my hospitality, but as you can see I am occupied. And to be honest you should take the opportunity for a bath."

Flambé tapped the enormous animal gently on the trunk—"Salute, Ambassador."

—and a padded hoof raised to extend as gracefully as any ballerina's.

"So you are a trainer, too?"

Flambé tapped the trunk again and Ambassador went back to all-fours.

"I started with elephants. I am not the best, but this one is easy. Well trained.

"AMBASSADOR. LIFT."

The bull offered his trunk. Flambé stepped aboard like the damn thing was an elevator and within seconds was high above the earth.

"Man of many talents, isn't he?"

Jack turned to the unfamiliar voice and found a new face at his shoulder. A new and unremarkable face smiling pleasantly from beneath a felt derby. Jack looked for missing or extra body parts and found none. So. An abnormally normal man. In his thirties, probably. Jack's age. His hair was shaggy about his ears. He was a couple of inches shorter than Jack, very slender. Dressed for the heat in khaki tans. He carried a leather satchel.

"Talents?" Jack tried to remain aloof.

"Flambé, I mean," the newcomer had a smile that pulled crows' feet from his eyes. "The man swallows fire, tames elephants. Fashions castles from newsprint and flour."

Jack nodded. "He's an article, all right. A fool, too, in my opinion. I can't believe anybody'd trust that elephant."

"You mean Ambassador? Oh, he's gentle enough."

"Gentle enough to stomp a fella to death."

"That was an extreme circumstance."

"Glad to hear it," Jack replied laconically.

The bull lowering his silver-haired trainer gently to earth.

"You're new to the beddy?"

"If you don't know that, you're the only one around here doesn't."

The man laughed easily. "Unfortunately, I am normally the last to hear anything."

He took off his hat to offer his hand.

"Doctor Bernard Snyder. Please call me Doc."

"Doc it'll be, then. I'm Jack Romaine."

The doctor took Jack's offered hand—

"What's this? A brodie with blisters?"

"I'm new to the carney, actually. Kind of starting over."

"Same for me," Snyder examined the hand with the appearance of serious concern. "Left my first practice in Louisiana to start another here. You need to clean these. Infection down here can get ugly."

Jack took back his hand. "I was a corpsman."

"Ah. Military."

"The war, right. One nobody talks about. Are you the only medic here?"

"Pretty much," Snyder replaced his derby.

"See some interesting stuff, I 'magine."

The physician stiffened a fraction. "I wouldn't know what you mean by 'interesting'. These people are my friends. Family, even. I don't view them as artifacts."

Of course not, Jack thought. You're the one regular around here they have to talk to. The guy they have to trust.

"I didn't mean the performers," he lied. "I just meant that the carney's interesting. And dangerous, too. Must be a million ways a man can get crushed or burned or cut. That's all. Really."

Doc Snyder's smile spelled relief at that qualification.

"I got you, sure. And you're right; I see more than the usual trauma. Have to be at a lumber camp to compare, I think."

Jack smiled encouragement. "Take that guy got killed by the elephant—"

"Alex Goodman," Snyder nodded gravely. "Sad case."

"You know him?"

"Not well," the doc shook his head.

"You see him? I mean, after he was killed?"

"Certainly. I'm the coroner for the county as well as the resident physician."

"Jesus," Jack turned his attention pointedly to the elephant before them. "Is there anyway to know what set the damn thing off? Was Goodman cruel to him? Provoke him, somehow?"

Doc shrugged, "Only one near enough to see anything was Peewee. She was pretty traumatized, as you can imagine."

"Seems like she's pretty tight with the elephant, though."

"Unfortunately a bull can turn, even on a longtime trainer. It's tragic, but the animals do go rogue, especially the older ones. When they do they can become very dangerous."

"Kneel." Flambé's command floated through the pines and Ambassador sank gently to his forelegs, his silver-haired trainer offering a snack to the beast's exquisitely discerning trunk.

"If he's a rogue, shouldn't he be put down?" Jack wondered aloud.

"Beg your pardon?" Doc turned around.

Jack jerked a finger toward Ambassador. "Well, once an elephant goes rogue, he *stays* rogue, right? He becomes unpredictable. Happy as a clam one minute. Spooked the next."

"I suppose that's one way to characterize it."

"Then why hasn't Luna destroyed the thing? Why would she risk having a rogue bull kill somebody else?"

Doctor Snyder did not reply.

Jack slipped on his shirt. "'Course, what do I know?" He presented a movie star's smile. "I'm just a working man."

Chapter eight

The Doniker—*a toilet.*

Saturday brought the rubes from Tampa and surrounding burgs to the exotic pleasures rumored to be available in the freak town of Kaleidoscope. The Hillsborough County Sheriff hovered over the midway as though it were a whorehouse that he had half a mind to shut down, but apparently Luna had the fix in. The local John Q kept their distance and the show opened without incident and 'under the stars', the midway raucous with grinders and pitchmen luring natives to part with their cash in return for thrills, chills, or cotton candy.

The talkers were in their pits, pitching varied come-ons for the alibi games, sideshows and of course the carney's *piece de resistance*, the ten-in-one where Peewee took her place of honor with the other geeks on display.

"Romaine. Get the lead out."

Tommy Speck was harder to shed than a flea, but Jack had managed to break free of his diminutive chaperone long enough to send Bladehorn a telegram. There was actually one telephone in

Kaleidoscope, in the cookhouse, but Jack did not want to risk using that contraption, not only because he knew the carneys would be listening, but also because he wanted to avoid any kind of conversation with Oliver Bladehorn. His plan, after all, was to stall for time, and it was a hell of a lot easier to lie by wire than over a telephone.

Western Union kept an office just across the sandy street from the apartment propped on top of Luna's café. The agent who now tapped out Morse code in the Union office used to be a circus performer before a night on the high-wire put him in a wheelchair. Jack didn't trust HighWire entirely; no matter what animus existed between carneys and sawdust-eaters, Jack was pretty sure that High-Wire would not cross Luna for his sake. But Jack didn't have much choice in the matter. A letter would be too slow and too easy to intercept, so Jack settled on HighWire and Western Union as his best means to communicate with Mr. Bladehorn.

Trying his best to be discreet, Jack almost ran into Luna Chevreaux on his way to the telegraph office. He spotted Luna's long blue figure huddled with Doc Snyder, the two of them just emerging from the cash wagon which of course was not a wagon at all, but an earthbound office of tin and timber that housed the steel vault that secured every nickel and dime earned by the carnival.

They were deep in conversation, Luna and Doc. Probably about money, Jack reasoned. Most of the big acts and their performers wouldn't be coming to Kaleidoscope until some time in November, and many of those would not interrupt their bed to work at all. Luna's once-a-week stand was more a hedge against expenses than a bid for serious income. Nobody was going to get rich at a beddy, that much was clear. Not from the carnival, anyway.

Jack ducked from sight as Luna escorted Doc Snyder across the street to the big truck, the Ford that Jack had first observed trailering Peewee in from the Tampa railroad station. Jack had no idea who owned the truck, or even if it *was* actually owned. It was used to haul in staples from the Tampa market and for the transport of much heavier materials related to construction or plumbing essential for the beddy's maintenance.

Could be any number of reasons for Doc to need a ride to

Tampa, Jack mused, but somehow he doubted that a run for lumber was among them.

Was Doc taking the community's cash for deposit? Was there a bank somewhere in Tampa connected to an account in Luna's name? Or, perhaps, in Alex Goodman's name?

Luna was still engaged with Doc as Jack slipped unobserved into the telegraph office. Cost four bits to send his carefully calibrated message to Oliver Bladehorn:

HAVE REACHED TOWN OF KALEIDOSCOPE STOP SOUTH
OF TAMPA STOP OUR MAN HAS BEEN SPOTTED HERE STOP
NO WORD OF PROPERTY STOP WILL WIRE WHEN I FIND
MORE STOP

It wasn't going to make Bladehorn happy; Jack knew that. But it would buy some time.

Jack made sure his circuit back to the midway was inconspicuous. He was passing the young and talented sword swallower when The Great Flambé waved him over.

"Greetings, Mr. Romaine."

The older man was stripped to the waist. Not in bad shape, Jack had to admit.

"Have a proposition for you."

He chuckled at Jack's reaction.

"Nothing like that. It's about your career."

"I got no career," Jack said flatly.

"Precisely. Do you recall Mr. Earl's admonition? If you intend to fit in this society, you are going to need to perform."

"I can't even juggle," Jack replied.

"Ah, but you have a natural presence," Flambé assured him. "I can see it. You may not be in the movies, Jack, but you are on-camera, I can see that. You are performing all the time. Quite the actor, actually."

Was the old homo offering a compliment? Or a threat?

"What'd you have in mind?" Jack glanced up and down the row of festive tents and stalls.

"I think you should swallow fire," Flambé replied, and pulled a pair of iron rods from a basin of water.

"Not interested," Jack replied.

"Then get interested."

Was a woman giving that command; Luna Chevreaux appeared as if by magic at his shoulder.

"We already got too many mouths to feed, Jack. If you wanna stay, you're gonna have to pay your way and that means you got to get an act."

"Didn't say anything about that when you hired me," Jack objected.

"Didn't invite you down, either, did I? Did anybody?"

How much did she know? How much did she suspect? It didn't matter; he had to find a way to stay near the beddy.

But eating *fire*?!

"You know Flambé's been handling Ambassador," Luna went on. "He's the only trainer we got left, which means somebody's got to pick up his act."

"It's mostly spectacle," Flambé assured him. "Not like swallowing swords, not at all. There is a certain technique, of course. And be foolish to say there aren't risks."

Jack took a gander at the rods. They were slender, some sort of light metal. A doweled handle at one end led to a not-quite-closed loop at the other extremity, a kind of hook. Flambé wadded a strip of cloth into that clutch.

"Your torch", he demonstrated.

Then the veteran performer slipped the lid off a covered can and soaked the cloth with a clear fluid.

"Your fuel," Flambé declared and Jack could smell the gasoline.

"I don't think this is my act," he demurred.

Flambé smiled as if he'd heard not a wisp of reservation.

"The essential thing with swallowing flame is to keep the fumes out of your lungs," he instructed. "Get any vapor at all inside your lungs, the fire follows down and you get an ignition like in the cylinder of an automobile. Only your lungs aren't made of steel."

"Not the way I wanna travel," Jack tried to back away but Luna blocked his retreat.

"You wanna stay, Jack? Then *try* it. Try it or leave."

"I've seen what gas can do to a set of lungs," Jack grated. "I've seen plenty."

"Said you wanted to start over."

"Just have some minor concern about burning out the inside of my lungs is all."

"I've seen men survive." All of a sudden Flambé was all business. "Not saying the odds are good, naturally."

"I know the odds."

"Well, then, if you want to improve your chances the trick is to keep up a gentle exhalation. Some performers hyperventilate in preparation, though I suggest against it. Just fill your handsome chest with air. Like this—"

The old trouper's diaphragm rose visibly.

"—Come on, Jack. Let's see those marvelous pectorals."

Jack could feel Luna at his back. He ran a dry tongue over dry lips.

"I'll try," he said. "Just once."

"Fill up," Flambé encouraged evilly.

Jack pumped air into his lungs until it hurt.

"There, there, don't overdo. Once you've got a constant pressure of exhalation your only worry is to avoid the burns that can come when the fire exits your mouth."

Jack's chest collapsed like a balloon.

"That's *all* I got to worry?"

"Your chest, Jack. You've let it collapse. So once again—Inhale! That's right, overdo. Now, all you need to do is make sure your mouth and lips are wet."

The silver-haired devil was silver-tongued, too. About a foot of tongue, which he rolled salaciously about his lips; Jack fought a tide of crimson that was rising in his face. His own mouth felt dry as toast.

"Take the torch."

Flambé wrapped Jack's already blistered hand around the instrument. That weight. Heavier than he expected.

"Now for the match. Luna, would you assist?"

A match scratched to life and Jack jumped as if stung.

"Easy, Jack," his tutor cautioned sharply. "It'll be all right. Just listen to me. I am lighting your torch."

Jack could feel the heat. It felt like a blowtorch.

"Now you must insert the torch at just the right angle into your mouth."

Flambé illustrated with an unlit rod, tilting his own head back to illustrate.

"Just that slant, you see? Neophytes generally use their free hand to guide it. Like a blind man lighting a cigarette. Don't want to miss, do we?"

"No," Jack croaked.

"Don't speak," Flambé commanded. "You begin a gentle exhalation even before entry, very light. Constant pressure. We there? Good. Head back. Back, Jack. Hold. Gentle exhale. Now when the fire comes push it out. Here it comes…"

Flambé trapped Jack's hands in his own to guide the torch in. Air seemed to torrent from Jack's lungs like a fire hose and a yard of flame leaped from his mouth.

Jack jerked the torch free.

"Bravo!" Flambé applauded. "Now once more. For confidence."

He could see Luna watching him. Was this her way to run him off? Wasn't going to work. He had a family at stake, Martin and Mamere. Not to mention his own hide. Jack thought of Gilette. He thought of a church full of men coughing up their lungs.

No way he was going to let this muddy bitch bust his hump.

"Head back," Flambé commanded.

"Give me the torch," Jack replied.

It was a true solo, this time. But going in Jack nicked a tooth with the iron torch, his head dipping on instinct—

"LOOK UP, JACK."

He could feel the fumes in his throat—

"BLOW IT OUT."

Jack blew air from every orifice in his body, his mouth, his nose, his ears. His ass, if he could.

WHOOOOOSH!!!

The gas vaporized on contact with the atmosphere to throw a spear of flame from his badly singed mouth.

Then it was done. It was over. He was alive.

Jack swayed dizzily.

"I gan thmell 'air," he wheezed.

"God's little way of getting your attention," Flambé's comfort seemed deliberately ambiguous.

Jack worked his mouth.

"Blithtahs, doo. I god blithtas."

"A journeyman's scars," Flambé assured him. "This was an excellent start, believe me. An outstanding premiere."

Jack felt weak in his legs and was surprised to find Luna's hand steady on his back.

"Well, Jack. Now you know the life."

Jack doused his own torch in the basin and walked away under his own steam. He wasn't twenty yards down the midway when Tommy Speck came bustling out of The Snake Lady's pit.

"Jack?! Goddammit, where you been? Grab a shovel, for chrissake. Move it!"

Evening fell with the ever-entwined aromas of hotdogs and cotton candy. Every pit, tent and concession was draped in primary colors, splashed in bright paint and lit with white-hot lamps. The rap of talkers warred with the jangle of the rides and the shrieks of rubes throwing away their money. The Tilt-A-Wheel turned slowly before a harvest moon, the midway's Milky Way. Jack was back to his role as a working man, again following Tommy Speck from one menial task to another. He had just repaired one stall when Tommy rushed him to the heart and soul of the midway. A gaudy banner offered its oil-painted advertisement in lurid detail:

THE CONGRESS OF HUMAN CURIOSITIES

The men and women familiar to Jack from the cookhouse

counter, those sturdy folk who threw horseshoes outside their trucks and trailers, or gossiped in the G-tent, were transformed now under the influence of paint and oilcloth and costumes into creatures of a disturbing and alien world. Half Track looked positively foreign from the waist up, as 'Princess Monica, The Half Woman of Saint Albans'.

A talker unfamiliar to Jack lured natives to the stage where Marcel & Jacques shared hands and heads over a cello.

"BROUGHT to you by SPECIAL engagement from the Louvre, the Somme and the streets of PAREEEEEE! The most amaaaaaaazing Spec-Ta-Cal! Siamese Twins JOINED at the breast since birth and BLESSED with the gift of music these ENTIRELY original creatures PERFORM AS CAN NO OTHER MUSICIAN IN THAAAAAA WOOOOORLD!!"

Beethoven's *Ode To Joy* rising sweet and clear as a child's tears above the raucous clamor of barkers and rubes and the distant hoot of a calliope.

"C'mon," Tommy snapped. "Ain't you ever heard a fiddle?"

A few steps away from the Svengali Twins came a display with a different appeal:

SEE THE INCUBI! LIFE IN STASIS!

A score of fetuses floating like fairies in jars of formaldehyde.

"Pickled punks, we call 'em," Tommy barely spared a glance.

Jack's stomach rebelled.

"Need a douche?"

"You're an asshole, Tommy."

The little man just laughed.

Performers worked the right-hand tickets, geeks worked the left. Jack saw Blade at work, swallowing a sword that looked long as a fishing pole. Jack had to reflect that his own, recent introduction to the arts made him more appreciative of the younger man's skill and aplomb.

On the other side of the sawdust a hootchy-kootchy offered the always-popular strippers. "Luna'll perform sometimes," Tommy mentioned offhandedly.

But not this evening, Jack noticed. Tonight the natives would see Cassandra at work.

Tommy was keen to see Flambé's act.

"He's been workin' on somethin' special."

And indeed he had. The Great Flambé's act combined his twin capacities to tame elephants and fire. Jack watched with Tommy as the veteran rode Ambassador's tusks to take a tin of gasoline off a bunted barrel.

"Ahhhhhhhh!" the crowd cooed in anticipation.

The torches came next. Twin pillars.

"UP," Flambé commanded, and rode the bull's tusks a dozen feet into the air.

Jack watched Flambé balance on his ivory pedestal, fill his mouth with gasoline and without a moment's hesitation swallow a flaming torch. Fire spewing from his elevated perch to incinerate a papier-mâché castle set twenty feet away.

The crowd roared its astonished approval and Jack with them. The son of a bitch was a pleaser, no doubt about it.

The Penguin Lady did her shtick in a sideshow down from Flambé's act. Jack had never seen Charlotte in other than modest and ordinary attire, but here she was, hair down and stretched nearly naked on an oil-painted iceberg, dry ice wafting over the set to provide the illusion of chill in the tropics.

A wooden puppet boot-blacked to resemble a penguin cuddled between Charlotte's webbed extremities. As the marks milled outside her pit, The Penguin Lady drew her scenario with Delphic indifference.

"…What kind of creatures are these, little ones?" The Penguin Lady regarding the natives as though they were the creatures on display. "Who are these myrmidons who stare at us as we seek to take our bed?"

The puppet answering in Charlotte's thrown voice.

"These are the most wonderful and terrible of beings, my lady. They are called…people."

Some nervous jitters, then, from an audience suddenly quiet.

"Tell them to be careful," The Penguin Lady stretched lasciviously. "What they seek may not be what they neeeeeed...."

Down from The Penguin Lady, a headless woman rose from her chair to the amazement of all. Her barker really had the rubes going—

"...HEADLESS at birth HEADLESS FAYE is kept alive ONLY by a LIQUID NOURISHMENT developed by Doctor Anaximander Albatross Ethelreld, Ph.D., M.D., L.L.D. and communicator with the SPIRITS BEYOND!!!"

A coil of hoses gurgled fluids into the severed neck.

Jack leaned close to Tommy's ear.

"Is that real?"

Tommy chortled. "The fuck, Jack! You *are* a rube!"

So it went. A troupe billed as the "Original Wild Men of Borneo" threw bananas at the crowd. Turned out there were at least a dozen troupes of Negroes claiming to be the last and cannibalistic inhabitants from that ill-defined location. On the other hand, he also saw legitimate performers like Pinhead drive nails up his nose. The Armless Man he'd first seen at Luna's café had the rubes going when he pulled somebody from the audience and with nothing but the toes of his feet proceeded to untie the mark's shoes and re-tie them! Then he slipped off the rube's tie and re-knotted it!

A pair of dwarfs, friends of Tommy's, weighed in for an incredulous circle of admirers at a *combined* weight of—

"One hundred forty-nine and a half pounds!"

And at the other extreme was Princess Peewee.

Tommy stopped Jack short at Peewee's elevated stall. The Fat Lady sat spraddle-legged above the crowd with no pretense at royalty. A loose shift left all the folds and creases corpulent and plain to see. She wore no underthings, Jack noticed, and noticed, too, that she didn't seem to care.

655 POUNDS—a pair of scales were rigged to exaggerate, but only slightly. Jack could see that The Princess was the largest draw of any sideshow; must have been a hundred natives jostling to get a gander. And she definitely knew how to cater to their several inter-

ests, rocking those huge breasts to and fro as she fanned herself with a faux feather of ostrich.

"Say, Peewee!" some yokel yelled from the crowd. "Will ya MARRY me?"

"Depends if yer BIG enough," Peewee shot back, and the rubes roared laughter.

Dollar bills fluttered like pollen into a tub placed below Peewee's rude throne. Coins were tossed onstage.

"Look at these people," Tommy said proudly. "They eat her up."

Not a hint more of acknowledgement from The Princess to her admirers, however. Not so much as a nod to the men and boys who filled her tub with bills and silver. She lapsed to a feigned indifference, now that she had them on her leash. Those golden curls plastered close to her skull. Royal and aloof. Quite literally above the fray.

Jack nodded to the half-filled tub.

"Want me to sack the money?"

"Not tonight. Tonight you're the bruno."

"Okay, I give up, what's a bruno?"

"From the mines, dickhead. Coal mines? The fella that shovels coal into the cart."

"Don't see any coal mines here."

"Well, you ain't workin' for a mine, are ya?"

"So what am I shoveling?"

"You're shoveling her shit."

"...*Hers?*"

"That's right. Doniker's built right under."

"You're shitting me, right?"

"No, but she will. Dump a loaf on yer basket, she thinks yer takin' advantage."

Jack swallowed a surge of bile; Tommy smiled.

"There's a wheelbarrow behind the stall. Got a ditch out back for the leavings."

"I'm not gonna do it."

Jack dropped his shovel. Tommy glanced down at the abandoned tool.

"What was that?"

"I'm not gonna do it," Jack repeated. "I'm not gonna shovel some fat lady's shit."

"Then pack yours and leave," the dwarf replied calmly. "I'll tell Luna to draw yer pay. I could care less, one way or the other."

"I'm a performer."

"Not yet."

Jack knew there was no appeal. It was take it or leave it and he couldn't afford to leave.

Tommy kicked the blade end of the shovel and its handle popped into his hand.

"Here."

He handed Jack the implement.

"There's a shower set up behind the grabjoint when yer done."

By the time Jack finished clearing Peewee's latrine he was dryheaving and filthy and frustrated. By the time he had finished spreading the last of Peewee's offal, the midway was shut down. Nothing remained but a flotsam of paper wrappers and peanut bags, the detritus of natives returned to town that would, Jack was sure, be his first task to clear the next morning.

The sing-song of the calliope was long silent, the rides still. The calls of frogs had taken over, now, and the infernal buzz of insects. Jack scrubbed down in cold water fallen from a barrel rigged for an outdoor shower. He scrubbed a bar of lye soap down to a nub. His hair was stiff as a board and his skin raw, but he was clean. Which fact drew the unwanted attention of mosquitoes.

He cursed defecation, insects, and gangsters. He cursed Oliver Bladehorn. Most of all he cursed his own cursed luck. There could be a pile of gold buried under Peewee's bench and he'd spread shit for a century before he found it.

And there was no help in the offing, no ally, no confidant. The freaks down here were not about to trust him, no matter how much fire or crap he swallowed. He was a fool to think he could con a carney.

"God DAMMIT!"

He could not reach a skeeter sinking its probe between his shoulder blades.

"Let me." Cassandra appeared from nowhere.

And before he could decline she stepped quickly to his flank and slapped the offending insect dead.

"We should put some netting up," she traced the line of his spine with her finger. "Better than a smudge pot."

Jack scratched a bite furiously.

"I have some citronella oil in my trailer, you know. Will take out the itch."

"I just wanta sleep," Jack grabbed a towel.

"Sleep with me, then."

"Take a raincheck, Cassandra, all right?"

He was reaching overhead to kill the spigot when she asked him, "Why are you interested in Alex Goodman?"

Goosebumps on his back along with a sudden stir of tropical breeze.

"Got no interest," he mumbled. "Nothing special, anyway."

She circled her arms around his naked waist. She wore a translucent shift of some sort, a kind of peignoir pulled high around her multiple breasts. A narrow waist, he had not expected that and could not help but feel her legs, long and hairless and apparently impervious to the insults of mosquitoes. Her hair caught in the moon like a basket of pearls.

She smelled of jasmine.

"Alex Goodman," she pressed her hands flat on his butt. "What's Alex to you?"

"I met him. Had a couple of drinks. That's all."

"Sure, Jack? You sure that's all there is to it?"

"What do you know about Goodman?" Jack slipped his towel beneath her hands.

"Come to my parlor," she pulled away. "And maybe you'll see."

She lived as if on the road, in a caravan, a kind of customized wagon set on truck axles for tow. Her snake had the run of the place, apparently. Jack spotted the python right away, wound sinuously on a high-hung shelf crammed with plaster bric-à-brac of erotica.

Every possible variation of human copulation decorated the cheap and mobile interior. A mishmash of pagan relics completely unfamiliar to Romaine complemented the priapic display, a Zoroastrian barsom set between a bronzed Horus and a wooden post dedicated to the goddess Asherah.

"Leave your dirties outside," she said and pulled him a bathrobe off a hook.

Jack tried to ignore the snake and the statuary. He slipped on the welcome terrycloth and within moments was installed opposite Cassandra at a small hardwood table, perfectly round, inhaling some kind of incense lit with a taper by his hostess. She had already dropped her own robe to display twin cleavages on a single chest.

Jack found himself watching the rise and fall of her breasts. They were, all three of them, remarkably firm. Rising, falling again with the chant of some mumbled incantation. There was, naturally, a crystal ball between them. Jack wondered if he picked it up and shook it he might not see some domestic scene in miniature inside. Snow falling on a New England farm, say. Sheep grazing beside a crystal stream.

"In all fairness," he interrupted the prophetess's droning meditation, "I have to tell you I think this is a crock."

"That is Cassandra's Curse," the voice seemed not her own. "To prophesize and yet not to be believed."

There appeared to be no resentment in that statement. Perhaps a touch of melancholy. She reached out to take the translucent ball and Jack saw an elaborate analemma, its figure-8 tattooed down the length of an arm.

She cradled the ball with both hands. Eyes blinking wide open as a doe's.

Did it seem to glow brighter, the ball? What kind of trick was that?

"I see two men," the voice was disembodied. Remote. "You. And Good Man. But you do not touch. You do not meet."

Was that a smile tugging at that ripe, ripe mouth?

"The signs say that you have never seen Alex GoodMan. That he is, for you, a mystery. But not to meeee…"

Jack scowled contempt.

"Better oil your ball. I already said I met the guy. At a speakeasy. In Cincinnati."

Cassandra appeared not to have heard a word he said.

"You do not know him," she contradicted calmly. "And yet you seek him. Why is that?"

She wasn't looking into the ball, now.

"Aren't I supposed to be the one asking the questions?"

"Ask then," she opened her arms in invitation.

What was that stirring in his scrotum—?!! Jack jerked his hand to his crotch.

"It's not the snake," Cassandra smiled. "Not mine, anyway."

Jack felt himself go crimson.

"Goddamn it, cut the games! When did Alex get here? How well did *you* know him?"

"He came to Kaleidoscope a year ago," she replied directly. "Perhaps a little more."

A straight answer. Or…was it?

"You had to know him, then," Jack pressed. "He couldn't have been a stranger."

"No stranger to anyone, no. In fact, in many respects I would say he was exactly like you, Jack."

"Like me."

"Unsure of himself. Uncertain. Frail in a number of ways, addicted to compulsions over which he had little control. A man starting over."

"So what did he do before?"

"There is no 'before' for the man starting over."

"Not much of an 'after', either, apparently, 'cause by September he was dead."

"Dead, yes. You didn't need a crystal ball to see that."

"So what killed him?" Jack leaned forward to her. "What exactly? I need to know if what I've heard is true."

She gazed into her ball. He saw the three breasts rise and fall and his stomach lurched.

"Cassandra?"

He couldn't tell if she was listening. If she could hear him.

"What about Alex Goodman, Cassandra? Was Alex asking too many questions? Was he looking for something, maybe? Was he close?"

"Close—? To what?" She wove long, gypsy fingers about the ball, the glow from inside passing through the beds of her fingernails.

"You either know or you don't, dammit."

"I...see...a man," a sheen of sweat had broken as suddenly as if she had been doused. "I see a frightened man, but aroused. I see a woman as well, also frightened. An enormous woman. An Aphrodite."

"This is bullshit. You aren't telling me anything I haven't already heard."

Her eyes snapped up to meet his. Wild, feral eyes. "You have to pay."

Jack tried to rise from his chair and found he could not.

"The hell do you mean, 'pay'?"

"Prophecy is no good unless paid for. The old oracles understood that. They were wild, those ancient women. They took their geld in sex. Our word ecstasy comes from their rituals, did you know that, Jack? From their loins, their breasts, their lips...."

She was touching herself, her breasts, her pudenda.

"Men were known to die in coitus," she moaned. "Their hearts burst with pleasure! But some survived. The best. The strongest."

She leaned across the hard, round table. Jack tried again to stand, to withdraw, but again could not.

She smiled, her lips beckoning ripe as poisoned apples a mere breath away from his own.

"What about it, Jack?"

Her tongue teasing like a snake's.

"Feeling lucky?"

His erection jammed up beneath the table and the thought occurred that maybe this was the payment she really wanted, and he thought what the hell, he might as well—but then he saw her chest again.

"Jesus!"

He leapt from the chair.

"The fuck you trying to do to me?!"

"Do what people do, Jack."

"God-damned witch!"

There was a sadness in her face, but also a dreadful resignation. Cassandra The Prophetess threw a shawl over her crystal seer.

"The ball is dark."

"Cassandra. Please!"

"That is all I can do."

The next day's work detail did not, as Jack expected, take him back to clear the littered midway. In fact, Friday morning found the gambler unexpectedly and blissfully free of Tommy Speck's sarcastic supervision. Instead he was told at chow to repair to Peewee's tent in service of her elephant.

A truck trailer piled high with hay awaited. Jack unloaded bale after bale beneath Ambassador's reproachful inspection.

The animal snorting on its chain tether. Those African ears stirring the moist morning air. Jack stumbled over yet another bale. Ambassador once again snorted contempt.

"Look, yer honor, you don't like the way I'm doing this? Do it yourself."

As if in response to his imprecation, the elephant's massive head dipped, the chained tether straining taut as the bull lunged toward the trailer. Jack scrambled for safety, but there was no need. Ambassador leaned over the trailer, curled a bale of hay onto his trunk and plopped it onto the tentside stack neat as aces.

"The hell you need me for?" Jack muttered. But he chipped in anyway, man and beast now combining their efforts to finish the task in short order. Jack was headed back to his shack feeling pretty good when a commotion from among the caravans drew his attention. Loud voices. Strident. Angry.

Romaine jogged past the Sugar Shack and lion's pen to find Flambé pitching a fit outside his caravan.

"It was here in my truck! ALL of it! And it's GONE!"

A score or more of geeks and working men convening, now, from all about the camp. Jack saw Tommy Speck pushing through the milling crowd, Luna Chevreaux tall and calm in his wake.

"It's gone!" Flambé appealed wildly. "GONE!"

"Easy, Flambé," Luna commanded. "Now, what's missing?"

"FIFTEEN DOLLARS!"

Fifteen clams?! The old queer was in a hussy over fifteen singles?

But Jack cut his chuckle short when he saw the reaction of the freaks around him. A sinister silence was fallen over the misshapen community.

Flambé turned his attention straight to Jack.

"There's only one man here new to us."

All eyes swivelled onto Romaine.

"That's a pretty quick call," Luna Chevreaux cautioned calmly.

"But Flambé's right, he is the only one we don't know."

"We know he's not here for fifteen dollars," Luna replied and Jack tried to keep a poker face.

She knew what he was looking for? Is that what Luna meant?

But Chevreaux's attention was not at present directed to her new brodie. She was scanning the carneys, looking over the heads of everyone except The Giant.

"Where's Blade?"

Heads turned with a murmur of queries. Two heads in the case of Jacques & Marcel.

"Try his trailer?" Tommy suggested.

"His trailer," Luna struck off in that direction and every single geek followed.

Charlie Blade's trailer looked like a suitcase on wheels, posters from a hundred shows pasted on scarlet walls peppered with the

impact of his throwing knives and sword. Billboards from Maine to
California pasted like marquee on a rolling nightclub.

The up and comer was propped on a set of milk crates outside
his rolling home, eyes glazed over a cigarette burning to the nubs
of his fingers.

Luna marched straight up to Charlie's crated stoop. Tommy
Speck took one flank, The Giant her other. Other residents spreading in a large crescent behind.

Charlie smiled languidly.

"Morning, Boss Lady."

"I need to see your trailer, Charlie." Luna got straight to the
point.

"You ain't seein' nuthin'," Blade lipped over his cigarette, and
a chill seemed to settle.

"Giant," Luna's eyes never left Charlie as she addressed the
camp's strongman.

"Yes, ma'am?"

"Kick in the door."

The black man had barely started for the trailer when Charlie
pulled a sword from a crate.

Jack saw it coming. He leapt between the black man and Blade,
caught the edge of the sword on his brass knuckles and then stepped
inside to kick Charlie hard in the balls.

Blade went down swallowing his privates on the sandy street.

"...Fuggin'...bitch!"

"The door, Giant."

Took one size eighteen boot to kick the door off its flimsy
hinges. Luna ducked her head to enter.

For a few seconds there was nothing to be discerned other
than the sword-swallower's mumbled curses, the gentle rocking of
the trailer on balding tires, the chassis squeaking in accommodation
of Luna's shifting inspection. But then the *thud* of something substantial could be heard as it was dumped to the trailer's wooden floor
and moments later Luna emerged.

The lunar lady raised one hand to display a syringe to the

gathered carneys. In the other hand she displayed a sheaf of green-backs and a bindle.

"Ten bucks for the smack would leave…" she counted the one-dollar bills remaining. "…five bucks change. Give this to Flambé, would you, Tommy? Tell him I'll make good for the rest."

"How 'bout the snow?"

She did not reply. Instead she handed the stash to Giant.

"Put it back inside."

"No!" Blade pulled himself to his knees. "You can't! You got no goddamn right!"

"You know the rule, Charlie."

A low, feral growl rippled through the gathered congregation. It rose a pitch higher as Charlie crawled back to reach the cover of his trailer. Higher it rose!

Jack felt his skin crawl.

Charlie Blade blubbering now like a baby.

"Please don't! PLEASE!!"

It happened in seconds. The freaks rushed Charlie's trailer like piranha onto a mired cow. Charlotte and Jenny and Jacques & Marcel and Frankie and Cassandra and all the rest, all the other half-men and bearded women, the limbless and deformed who removed from the midway seemed immune to violent activity of any kind, snapped in a fraction of a second to become a pack of jackals.

They ripped the shutters off the trailer's windows as though they were eyelids. They tore into the flimsy walls as if they were flesh. They gutted the interior as Charlie wailed from the ground, hauling out the entrails of the young performer's life, ripping it to shreds as he watched.

A saturnalia of destruction.

Only Luna standing above the fray. And Jack outside of it.

"What's 'the rule'?" Jack shouted above the frenzy.

"You don't steal from another carney, Jack. Not even a penny."

"But he's on heroin, for Christ's sake!"

"He can ride any high he wants," Luna replied, pitiless. "But not on a carney's back."

Flambé arrived finally with a nozzled metal can. Charlotte, sweet Charlotte, struck a match with her webbed hands to the torch soaked in that fuel, handing it to The Giant.

"FIRE IN THE HOLE," the black man bellowed.

The freaks scattering from the trailer like evil children, their anatomic digressions making for a cruel discoordination of effort, an unnatural swarm. They came crawling or staggering or waddling away from Charlie Blade's trailer carrying everything he ever valued out with them. Props, clocks, silverware. Clothes and photos and memorabilia. Swords, of course.

Charlie's property redistributed in an instant among the performers of Kaleidoscope.

"DON' LET THEM, LUNA!!"

Charlie begging, now.

"LUNA, DON'T!!"

She nodded once to The Giant. He tossed the gasoline inside. Then the torch.

"NOOOOOOOOO....!"

An inhalation of flame, then, as if the trailer itself were swallowing a fiery sword. Then an orange ball billowed, rising like an orchid. Black, black smoke. Blade staggered briefly toward the ruins of his home, his life, but the heat beat him back. He fell to the sand, sobbing. The carneys jeering. Whistling derision.

"Jesus, Tommy—?" Jack turned to Speck. "Tommy?" Tommy Speck collected a vile wad from his cheek and spat it to the earth.

"Fuck him. Serves the chump right."

Chapter nine

A Brodie—*the carnies'
laborer, a mule, muscle.*

The moon seeped through a scud of clouds that night to provide a capricious illumination. A pall of tar and timber smothered the usual aroma of pine needles and damp earth. Jack was nursing his first beer since coming to this godless place, the first alcohol of any kind that he'd seen since the beginning of his indenturement.

He hunkered over a mason jar of homebrew, sitting at the base of an enormous tidewater cypress that sentineled the railway leading to Peewee's tent. The Princess's fabric palace glowed in the near distance like a child's magic lantern. Jack could see silhouettes cast onto the canvas by the lamps inside. He could see Ambassador's thrown shadow, the trunk dipping for water into the tank at the foot of Peewee's bed. He could see The Fat Lady, too, her ample figure distorted by the play of screen and shadow and sultry breeze. Propped in her bed reading—what? What tale of romance could compete with *this* life?

He would like to believe that Cassandra's sexually charged prophecy was simply a ploy, an attempt to pump him for information, find a hole in his story. The whole business with the lights and ball was just hooey, wasn't it? Not worth two minutes' thought. On the other hand...? Something about the encounter in the gypsy's caravan lingered. How could Cassandra know with such perfect conviction that Jack had never set eyes on Alex Goodman? He hadn't, of course—but how could Cassandra know that fact for sure? Prob'ly she didn't know, he told himself. It was just part of her act. On the other hand...?

Could there have been some genuine witchcraft at work in the sibyl's warren? Some revelation that he had missed, or cut short? Jack took a long swig of homebrew. Must be going native to be thinking like this! Crystal balls? Prophecies?

Still...Jack set his jar of beer aside. What if there was something he was missing?

He made sure he wasn't seen on his way to Peewee's pavilion. He entered the tent and ran the maze of clotheslines leading to her boudoir in total darkness, emerging to see Ambassador content on his chain at the tank beside Peewee's massively reinforced bed. An electric fan was propped on a stack of books at her side.

Jack tapped on a quarter pole.

"Princess? May I come in?"

She smiled over her book.

"Now, that was nice. The way you asked."

"Figured I had to improve over my last attempt," Jack said and stepped inside.

She put her text aside. *Candide.* Jack recognised the French etiology if not the work itself.

Did Peewee *parlez francais*?

"You been here, what—a week?"

"Eight days," he replied. "Or all my life, depending how you look at it."

She had enormous dimples when she smiled, Jack noticed. Dimples an inch deep.

"A week and a day for the man starting over," she sighed. "And have you found what you're looking for?"

"No," Jack looked her straight in the eyes. "No, I haven't. I guess that's why I came to see you."

"Me?" she brushed a corn-silk curl from her eyes. "I hate to tell ya, Jack, but I ain't exactly the fount of all wisdom. Fount of some things, maybe, but I ain't got the book of life in here anyplace."

"I don't need anything that complicated, Princess, but there's something I gotta locate, it's important, and I'm pretty sure Alex Goodman had what I needed. Or at least, I think he knew enough to steer me in the right direction. And I know there's at least one other person down here knows, too—"

"Know for sure?"

"I guess more like hope. Got no choice, really; I have no other place to go."

"Sometimes you can't find somethin', you gotta just let it go, Jack."

"Wish to hell I could. It's not for me. I don't find what I'm looking for, me and my family, well—let's just say we're gonna be looking over our shoulders for a long, long time. If you get what I mean."

The massive head dropped ever so slightly.

"I know that feeling. I do."

"No grins, is it?"

"Come up here," she commanded. "Stool over there, pull it up."

He gathered up a low-back beside the supporting pole and complied.

"Gonna tell you a story, Jack. About a little girl. She was a petite little thing, at first. Charming. Precocious, even. She wanted to play the violin—oh, yes! But Daddy said, no. And then her fingers got too fat and her joints riddled with gout. Her mother wanted her to play. Her mother said she had the soul of an artist. Her mother was never ashamed. Never distant. She could play like an angel. And this little girl was educated, too.

"But her daddy was a cold man. Distant. And when the little

girl got fat she became an embarrassment to her father, and on her nineteenth birthday he committed her to a sanatorium. You ever been to a mental ward, Mr. Romaine? It's hell. It is a living hell even if you are insane, but his girl was not insane, Jack. No, no. She wasn't loony. She was just fat."

Jack cleared his throat.

"How'd you get out?"

"Money. Orderlies at mental institutions are chronically underpaid, which makes them easy to bribe, and cheap. My mother managed it. One graveyard night a pair of orderlies wheeled me down to the infirmary. But instead of putting the juice to me, or dropping me in the cold tank, they had an ambulance waiting."

"And you came down here with your mother."

"I came down here, eventually," she corrected him. "But Mother—"

A single tear ran down the bowl of her face.

"I think Daddy must have killed her."

"Jesus. And your old man, does he have any idea where you are?"

"If he did he'd come for me, I'm certain," she sniffed. "And I would most certainly be trapped again in a living torment until I died...

"Have you ever met a man who would put his own child in hell, Mr. Romaine?"

"I know a candidate, believe me."

She drew in a long, soughing breath.

"Then you know the only thing you can do is to stay far away. Stay far away. Far. Far!"

Ambassador stirred at the tank.

"It's all right, Ambassador," she smiled. "We're all right, baby."

Jack lifted the corner of her sheet.

"Take it easy, Princess."

He wiped her face gently. Probably the first time he ever actually looked at her face properly.

"Thank you," she smiled and dimpled.

He started to retreat.

"No, wait. Wait."

She gathered his hand into her own. Was like putting a walnut inside a glove.

"I don't think anyone down here knew Alex, really, except me. I don't know what you're looking for, but I can tell you Alex didn't have anything of value. Anyway, if he did, he never mentioned it."

"I don't think it's the kind of thing he'd likely talk about," Jack squeezed her hand. "Did he mention any kind of, say, investments? Anything like that?"

She snorted.

"The only thing Alex took stock in was a bottle."

Jack took back his hand and Ambassador jerked his trunk to challenge.

"Shit, what'd I do?"

"Nothing, nothing," Peewee patted him on the arm. "He's just reminding me."

"Of what?"

"My bathtime."

She swept her bedsheet aside.

"I'm ready, Ambassador."

His trunk uncoiled to wrap beneath her lap as though she were a log.

"The hell's he doing?!" Jack scrambled off his stool.

"Taking me to my tub," she smiled coyly.

The massive bull draping his Princess gently over his twin tusks as gently as a towel. Hefting her like a forklift from her bed.

Jack retreated another yard.

"You sure this is smart, Princess? After what happened to Alex?"

"How else am I to get to my bath?" she seemed amused.

The ground trembling as the rogue bull swiveled to the water tank. Ambassador lowered Peewee still wrapped in her shift into the cool water. She slid off his tusks with a delighted squeal. Then a long, luxurious sigh.

"Only place where I can move, really," she said slipping out of her nightgown.

Jack found himself tempted to look. But Ambassador stood guard over his lady's balneation like a palace eunuch.

"The water! Marvelous!"

She leaned back and her breasts bobbed to the surface like kegs.

"I wouldn't mind your staying, Jack. But we don't know each other well enough. Yet."

Running her hands to her crotch.

"I'll just show myself out." Jack found the railway.

"Sweet of you to drop by," she called after him.

Jack turned back, briefly.

"One thing, Princess: You don't have to look over your shoulder here. Nobody's gonna let anybody take you from this place. Nobody."

She smiled sadly.

"*Merci, monsieur. Bon nuit.*"

Jack was long asleep when a Packard coupe pulled away from the apartment attached to the Kaleidoscope Café, heading west for a drive to Tampa. He was not there to see Tampa's midnight train hoot its imminent departure. A thick fog shrouded the man and woman who waited at a bench that was gathering dew beneath the station's shallow-peaked shelter. Could you have penetrated the fog you might notice that the woman was unusually tall, a head taller than her companion even while seated. The couple, though closely seated, did not appear intimate. Were Jack present he would have noticed the worn medical bag placed like a border between that pair of mismatched thighs.

"All aboard for ALBANY, ATLANTA…CINCINNATTI!…."

The porter's baritone summons nearly swallowed by the fog.

"Don't forget your hat." Luna Chevreaux handed Doc Snyder a boater.

It was not Doc's usual derby, this headpiece. It was a summer hat, gaily ribboned and flat-brimmed. Made of straw.

"Be careful, Doc."

"And yourself."

Iron valves hissing, a brakeman waving his flag, the plaintive complaint of a steam-driven whippoorwill, and Kaleidoscope's physician was swallowed into the morning mist. Luna remaining behind, tall and silent and alone.

Was a good hour after midnight when Jack Romaine was jerked from a fitful sleep.

"Get up, dammit! Get yer ass up!"

Tommy Speck jumping up and down on his goddamn bed.

"The fuck, izzit five awready?"

"It's the twins!"

A scramble of brogans and trousers and suspenders, then, Jack stumbling after Tommy to reach the Siamese brothers' neighboring cottage.

Cassandra was ahead of him, flat against the corrugated wall.

"They're sick," she offered that prediction. "I tried to ask them, I speak a little, but—"

"Let me take a look."

Jack raised Tommy's lantern to inspect the twin faces, rigid as logs on their rude bed. Both of the twins were pale, lips going blue. Marcel appeared to be the worst of the two; his face was clammy to the touch, his neck and shoulder swollen to the size of a gourd.

Jack took a hand. Cold. He leaned close to inspect the fingernails.

"What is it?" Tommy prodded.

"The fuck would I know?" Jack leaned down to Jacques.

"(Jacque. Jacques, my friend. Can you hear me?)"

"Jack? *Oui.*"

"(How long have you been like this?)"

"(Minutes. It started with Marcel. He said he could not breathe. We—! Cannot…breathe!)"

"(Is Marcel choked? Did he swallow something?)"

"(No. A bee.)"

"What was that?" Tommy asked.

"Bee stung him."

Jack verified the welt swelling over Marcel's shoulder.

"We need Doc," Jack declared.

"He's out of town." Cassandra reported that fact as if she were to blame.

Jacques gasped violently.

"(Oh, God!)"

Marcel's head rolling back.

"GIVE ME SOME ROOM," Jack fumbled for the knife in his trousers.

"What in God's name—?" Tommy trapped his fist.

"Lemme go, Tommy, he's gotta breathe."

"Have you done this before?" Speck did not let him go.

"Couple times. I was a corpsman."

"Let him go, Tommy!"

"…awright, awright."

"Cassandra, take the globe off the lantern. Use the oilcloth, you have to, but get it off."

Jack took the naked lantern and ran the blade of his knife back and forth through that white-hot flame.

"(Jacques, listen to me. I have to open your brother's throat. His *throat*, do you understand?)"

"*Oui.*"

"Tommy, Cassandra—hold their hands."

Cassandra and Speck rushed to either side of the bed. Jack allowed his crude instrument to cool a moment.

"(Mary, Mother of God,)" Jacques croaked. "(In our hour of need we beseech thee—)"

"Hail Mary, Mother of Grace," Cassandra joined in.

"Good luck," Tommy added his own benediction as Jack probed gently with his fingers to find the spot. There it was, the cricothyroid, just a notch in the voice box. Couldn't go too far, though. Or too deep.

Jack plunged his knife into the gap.

Jacques' protest was no more than the cry of a kitten. Marcel was past pain.

"Did it work?"

"Depends. They've got separate airways, but my guess is they're sharing a lung or lungs. Anyway, it's all I can think of.. Only thing I can do."

A small geyser of sputum and you could hear it, the whistle of air through the gash in Marcel's throat. Jacques swallowing air like a goldfish moments later with the shared ventilation.

"C'mon, Marcel. C'mon, buddy."

A whistle of air and then his eyelids flicker and then Marcel was back.

"(Don't try to talk,)" Jack directed. "(I cut a hole for you to breathe, I'm gonna put in a tube so it stays open, so just stay still, Marcel. Let your brother do the talking.)"

"I need some kinda tube," Jack turned to Cassandra. "Something that'll hold pressure, doesn't have to be big."

"I've got a fountain pen," she offered.

"That all you got?"

"Only thing close."

"Go get it. Tommy, use the cap. Cut off the tip. We got any alcohol?"

"We're a beddy, ain't we?"

"Douche the cap with whatever you got. Burn it. Pour on some more. We'll worry about the wound later."

He leaned over Jacques.

"(Has this happened before?)"

"(Yes, once. A wasp.)"

"(Did they pack him in ice?)"

"(Ice, yes! I had forgotten.)"

Jack looked up to see Luna Chevreaux flanking The Giant at the cottage door. The Giant bending low to peer inside.

"We heard they was sick."

The first words Jack had ever heard the man utter.

"We need ice," Jack appealed to Luna. "Lots of it."

"From the café, Giant. Hurry!"

The big man seemed to glide away.

"When did it start?" Luna entered the shack.

"Don't know," Tommy replied. "I just heard Jacques croakin' and came and got Jack."

"I've got the pen!" Cassandra announced breathless from the door.

"Got it."

Tommy Speck snatched the cap off Cassandra's pen.

Jacques reaching over to caress his brother's face.

"(I will never leave you, Marcel!)"

The siblings hanging each to the other like a life raft.

"(Always I am here! Always!)"

"This do?" Tommy handed Jack the cap.

"It'll have to."

Jack slipped the makeshift breather into Marcel's trachea. He'd have to rig a pledget of some kind.

"You got any gauze?"

"Not sure," Luna apologized.

"Find out. I need adhesive tape, too. And quinine. Surely with all the fever down here you've got quinine?"

"We'll look," Luna seemed glad to have a task. "Cassandra, can you check the infirmary?"

"Really important we get that medicine," Jack grated.

"We will," Luna assured him. "I'll go back to Tampa if I have to."

Back to Tampa?

But at that moment, Jacques reached out to take Jack's hand.

"(Will we live?)"

"(Of course,)" Jack replied and turned his attention to Jacques' conjoined twin.

"(Marcel, I need to know if you're getting enough air. Blink once for 'yes', twice for 'no'.)"

Marcel blinked once and quickly.

"(Good. Now we're going to ice both of you down and get you some quinine. You can beat this thing, my friends. Just try to relax, that's important. Let us do the work.)"

"Will they make it?" Luna whispered privately.

"You always tell 'em they'll make it," Jack kept a smile for the brothers' benefit. "The hell is that ice?"

"Coming fast as we can."

"Sorry, it's just—I never like to lose a man."

"You're doing fine."

"Hell of a time for Doc to run off."

"He had…business. In Florida."

"When's he due back?"

"Could be a couple of days," she replied as if it were an apology.

"Well, I ain't gonna brodie 'long as these two are in the woods."

"Of course not."

"Put me a cot in here, I'll be fine. Maybe some coffee."

"I'll send over breakfast. How about for the twins?"

"Water's the big thing. Lots of it. Maybe some broth or consume for nourishment. Nothing they have to chew."

"Doc should be back in a couple of days," Luna risked a return to that subject.

Jack pocketed his knife.

"Couple of days it'll be over."

Jack sealed the tracheotomy with ordinary adhesive tape and for five nights afterward never left the side of his unusual charges. Every morning one of the performers brought breakfast and coffee, usually with a fresh orange. Jack mixed the quinine got from the carney's infirmary with orange juice in an attempt to make that prescription more palatable for his patients. He applied warm, dry compresses to the site of the rough surgery. Jacques & Marcel never complained. Occasionally Jack would see the twin heads turn in unison, inches apart, each man inquiring as to his fellow's disposition, Jacques speaking easily, Marcel stopping the hole in his throat for some hoarse reply. Each brother offering encouragement to the other.

Three times a day, Jack took a temperature. Three times a day he took a pulse.

"(Am I checking one heart?)" he asked his patients, "(or two?)"

Marcel smiled with Jacques' reply.

"(We share.)"

The pulse was erratic at first and did not settle into any sort of predictable rhythm until the third day. The swelling and fever subsided more quickly; by the second day there was no more need for ice. As would any nurse, Jack urged water or juice at every opportunity. The twins had good appetites, though Marcel was reduced to soup while Jacques could eat anything he liked.

Nothing to do otherwise but watch and wait. Tommy brought the Tampa paper over from the cookhouse each morning. Jack had forgotten how much he looked forward to a paper, even a Tampa paper.

Some news from home made Tampa headlines: President Hoover was set to visit Cincinnati. Jack couldn't actually give less of a damn. He was more concerned that the Reds finished out their season with a meaningless loss to the National League champs. And who the hell ever played baseball in October—?! At that rate, half the country was going to be following football before the World Series even started.

There was another kidnapping, some millionaire in Detroit got his kid snatched. Just like the Lindberghs, everybody had an opinion about this one. The most recent scandal centered on the prison riot in Denver. Thirty screws taken hostage. Five thousand inmates holding shivs over their guards.

The latest *Tribune* reported that the Denver warden was refusing to negotiate with the prisoners. "They can go to hell," he said, which pretty much guaranteed that his flatfoots were going to get their throats slit.

Business was running pretty much as usual, Wall Street getting richer and richer though Jack briefly noted a back page editorial that whined about the dangers of trading on the margin. Jack skipped that story. The only stocks he was interested in were certificates that belonged to Oliver Bladehorn.

On the morning of the sixth day, Jack removed a jerry-rigged tube from Marcel's tracheotomy. There was no sign of infection.

"We're going to leave the wound open," Jack informed the twins. "It'll heal on its own. You can put on a bandage to keep it clear, if you want."

Jack plopped into his nurse's cot feeling better than he had in days. He slept through the day and on through the next rose-fingered dawn. When he woke he found Tommy Speck and Luna Chevreaux propped like pigeons on either side of the sleeping brothers.

"How are they?" she asked him.

Jacques' arm was still thrown protectively over his brother's chest. Marcel was better, much improved in fact, which Jack was relieved to see. The twin's face and upper torso were returned to something like recognizable proportions. Jack swung out of his cot and walked stiffly over to the twins. He checked their foreheads one at a time for fever. Nothing obvious. The pulse seemed normal, though there was something underneath, some occasional susurration not encountered in his other experience. But there was nothing he could do about that.

Jack reached for a Pall Mall and a match.

"I think we've over the hump."

Luna rose from her ottoman.

"Thank you, Jack."

Tommy Speck was grinning ear to ear.

"I never saw a brodie do anything like this!"

A brodie! Speck called him a brodie!

An unfamiliar emotion filled his chest.

"We still need Doc to check them out," he cautioned. "But everything I can see looks copasetic."

"Wouldn't have made it at all without you, Jack." Tommy squeezing his arm like a familiar.

Jacques stirred awake to see his visitors.

"(How is Marcel?)"

"(He's fine,)" Jack assured him. "(You're both fine.)"

"(You saved two lives this week, *mon ami*.)"

"(Can't afford to lose our musicians, can we? Especially two such distinguished performers.)"

"(We do not play that well.)"

"(Better than any Siamese I ever saw.)"

Luna's smile lit Jack up from the inside. Something warm, there, that he had not felt in a long, long time.

"Why don't you grab some chow?" she suggested to Jack. "See me when you're done."

Was still early in the morning when Jack approached Luna's café, and even in the short walk across the street he sensed a change in atmosphere that had nothing to do with climate. Veteran performers who normally disdained even to acknowledge his presence met Jack's eye squarely as he crossed the street. Some dipped a chin briefly. Jo Jo, "The Russian Dog-Faced Man", even spoke.

"Mornink to voo, Jock."

There were a score or more of geeks waiting inside Luna's café, obviously lingering late over coffees or orange juice. Gregory Lagopolus, the performer who kept the dead-born twin growing out of his chest always fully dressed, greeted Jack from a table he shared with two ordinary boys. Had never even occurred to Romaine that the geek might have sons of his own.

"Bonjour, Jack. Bravo."

Nods and smiles from every booth and table seconded Lagopolus's voiced sentiment.

Jack was not accustomed to ever feeling embarrassed, so why, now, in this company, was the color rising?

"We are proud to be associated with you, my boy," Flambé crossed over to slap him on the back and with that the other performers rose like deacons to lay hands or flippers or some other sort of truncated member on their now-accepted brodie.

"Set yerself down, Jack." The command came from Half Track.

Jack produced his required two bits.

She pushed the coins back.

"Not this morning."

For a brief tour of moments Jack gave himself over to the cookhouse bonhomie. The carneys wanted every detail of the twins' ordeal and Jack's role in it. Now and then Tommy Speck would take over and you'd think a change of bandage or bedpan was brain surgery. In those moments, Jack could almost forget about Oliver Bladehorn and Arno Becker. He could almost dispel the fear for his family, that cloud hanging over his son and Mamere. He even managed, for a short while, to suppress the plain truth that while he accepted these people's trust and basked in their praise, he was in truth no more than a confidence man, a thief.

Whatever joy he felt could not last.

And sure enough as Jack devoured his free bacon and eggs and grits and got through his second or third mug of coffee, the feeling grew that his sins were too deep to be sponged away in any baptism. Because no matter what the carneys had come to believe, Jack knew that he was a Judas. He knew that he had been sent with forty pieces of silver not to save these people but to exploit them, to use them.

For a second, he had the overwhelming impulse to come clean, to tell all the gathered citizens that he was here to rat, to steal. That he was here to con the carneys on behalf of a bloodless gangster in Cincinnati.

But suppose he did confess? Suppose Jack threw himself on the mercy of Luna and her fellows—what then? Surely betrayal outranked petty theft on the geek scale of offenses. Wouldn't the carneys visit an even worse vengeance on Jack than they had on Charlie Blade? And why should Jack expect any mercy?

Jack left the café trying to ignore the knot in his gut. He had already decided to avoid Luna Chevreaux. Better to be shoveling shit than risk unmasking himself in a vulnerable moment. But that decision was taken from his hands when Luna turned from a conversation she was having with The Giant, standing outside her apartment, to greet Jack on the street.

"Jack, you eaten?"

"Ah, yeah. Just."

"Hold up, I'll join you."

The Giant bundled off on some chore and Luna strolled over.

"Thought I might go to the river. Wanta come?"

"I prob'ly should check with Tommy."

"Tommy's off today. So are you."

They followed a sandy rut leading away from the café and apartment, past the sagging awning of the telegraph office.

She gave no hint of her intentions. No explanation. They left the familiar road in short order to reach a winding, single-file path crowded with brambles and blackberry vines beneath walls of cypress and pine. The morning was quiet, except for the fitful breeze. Jack watched the play of Luna's back as she led the way. The sway of her hips inside those cut-off trousers.

The stride of her legs seemed to pull wires from every other part of body. He watched the small muscles of her spine relax and contract with each step, the cerulean skin softer in the forest-filtered light. Her hair swaying coal black and uncombed.

She scooped a handful of berries off a low-hanging vine without pausing. He followed suit and picked up a swipe of thorns and she laughed. The path terminated at a rotting conglomerate of timber that used to be a pier. A boat badly needing paint was tied off. A motorboat, Jack realized.

"Check the fuel." She checked a gallon tank and primed the aging Gebhardt's carburettor, and within moments they were gliding down the Alafia River.

Luna settled at the tiller. Jack sprawled against a bait box amidships. The Moon Lady cut the inboard as soon as the current allowed, so that their boat drifted in silence. A slender mist clung like an orphan to water smooth as glass. Heron and egret plied the tributary for their morning feed. "Over there," Luna pointed, and Jack saw the v'd wake of an alligator trolling for bass or perch or unwary birds.

Even with the mist it was easy to see that the river was crystal clear, and pristine. There were no signs of human society on the water or riverbank, no homes, no houses, no buildings or camps of any sort. There were not even any fisherman out that morning. Plenty of fish, though, largemouth hiding beneath fallen cypress or in the roots of water oak. Waiting in that ample shade for a waterbug or moth to dimple the surface. Or some other insect. As they idled, Jack lit a cigarette, needing the glow of tobacco. He inhaled. And then a straw of water spat from the river to douse his fire and face.

"The hell was that?" Jack stared at the limp butt in his hand.

"An archer fish." Luna smiled as she tossed him a rag. "They can take down insects five, six feet above the water. Or cigarettes, apparently."

Apart from spitting fish and gators there were other hazards. Luna grabbed an oar to push off a cypress knee that ranged like the tusk of a rhinoceros just below the surface. Tear hell out of a boat, he was told. Keep an eye out.

It was good duty, Jack had to admit. After a short while Luna refired the inboard. Twin cylinders pumping *pocka-pocka* with a tang of gasoline. They were not pushing the pistons to any extent; the bow of their boat barely raised off the water. Even so Jack had to lean far over to dip his hand into the water running by. Not a sound rose above the skiff's baffled exhaust. A flight of mallards sweeping by like a squadron of aeroplanes, but silent, low to the water. They had just banked past a magnificent arbor of weeping willow when a raucous cry penetrated.

"Osprey," Luna nodded starboard and sure enough Jack saw a predator big as a buzzard preening on the peak of a bald cypress ashore.

"They feed on fish, mostly," Luna spoke above the engine. "But turtles, too. I've seen an osprey pick up a turtle and drop him from a hundred feet. Bust that shell like an egg!"

"My son would get a kick out of this," Jack sang back

"Your son?"

She cut the engine and again they drifted.

"You have a son?"

"In Chicago. Him and my Mamere. My wife was from France. Gilette. Met her during the war. She made it past the Germans and the gas and the artillery just to die over here of the damned influenza. So Martin grows up with me. Me and his grandmother."

"Good kid?"

"All American. Babe Ruth and baseball and every hero you can name. 'Cept for his father; I haven't exactly made that list."

"Fathers don't have to be heroes for their sons."

"Don't they?"

"No. They just have to be fathers."

"I strike out on both counts."

A rib of clouds suddenly sabotaged the sun's warming rays. The river turning dark and damp and green as jade.

"Place ahead involves a daddy, of sorts." Luna started the engine with a turn of the flywheel. "If you'd like to see."

"Sure."

She leaned on the tiller and slid their shallow-drafting craft toward the far shoreline, banking again downstream for another short run. She throttled back abruptly.

"There. Over there."

Jack capped his eyes with his hands. A strange skeleton of iron rose on a spit of land shoved like a dwarfed peninsula into the river.

"What is it, some kind of animal cage?"

"It's a cage," she uncoiled a line. "But not for animals."

They tied the boat off and jumped onto land that you couldn't call dry; Jack sank up to his ankles. The cage rose in a rough dome eight or perhaps ten feet high and approximately the same diameter, set on a perimeter of railroad ties. Vines laced with briars sharp as knives twined through the gridded bars. Palmetto had broken through the dirt floor inside. Luna dropped the lockless chain which secured the bowl's gate, the links jangling briefly, like chimes.

"C'mon."

Jack followed her inside.

"Fella name of MacCready had a daughter he couldn't marry off," she began without preamble. "She was a sweet girl. Born with lots of hair."

"My son has a head of hair," Jack offered, but Luna shook her head.

"No. I mean hair all over. Everywhere. Like the fur of a cat. She tortured herself at first, trying to get rid of it. Trying to look like everybody else—pitiful. And of course that didn't work and when she got of age and none of the boys would have her and when her daddy got tired of the extra mouth to feed, he got the idea of putting her on display. Here. Right here in this cage.

"'The Cat's Cradle', people called it, and MacCready put his girl on exhibit naked, like some kind of puma for people to pay and see."

Jack saw how the cage was exposed to the river. Easy to see. He tried not to imagine.

"People threw their nickels and dimes and pennies into the cage. Then Old Man MacCready, he got the idea of dressing himself up in boots and a tunic like a damn lion tamer or some such. Got himself a whip.

"He just used it for effect, first time or two, but he found out quickly that if he lashed his girl some, the natives would go crazy. Start throwin' quarters instead of nickels. Sometimes even silver dollars, if he lit into her good enough.

"Wasn't long before people started comin' from all over to see 'The Cat Woman'. MacCready took to leaving her in the cage. Built himself a lean-to right over yonder. So he'd be close to work, I guess. Probably figured with her hair she wouldn't mind the mosquitoes. Not any more than an animal would, anyway.

"Some of the rubes didn't think she was genuine, so he'd force her to defecate in the cage, and if she balked or froze up or was just plain constipated, he'd beat her. She'd shit, then. That was always worth an extra buck or two."

"What happened to her?" Jack asked.

"One day MacCready's out here, all set for business as usual, only by now some palmetto had grown into the cage. Just like you see here. And the daughter had gnawed herself off a length. He had her eating everything from squirrels to fish guts for the crowd's pleasure, so gnawing a palmetto frond would have fit right in.

"There was a good crowd, apparently. And like any good barker MacCready took his time buildin' 'em up. Teasing them to a frenzy. Finally it was time for the real thing. The old man turned to show the rubes the whip and she jumped him from behind and drove a palmetto frond right through his eye.

"Of course, that happens you naturally jerk up on instinct to pull it out. That's what old MacCready did, and when he did she reached around with those nails grown long as a panther's and gouged out the other eye.

"Now he's blinded. She took his whip and beat him 'till he begged. Beat his sorry ass to rags. Wasn't anything the natives could do—they were locked out. Time somebody finally got the sheriff out here she'd bullwhipped Old Man MacCready to his death."

The river burbled by, smooth and serene.

"Christ," Jack shivered.

"Think you're a shit father? Just remember MacCready. Now, come on," she ducked out of the cage. "I know a happier place."

The morning's mist survived only in isolated wraiths now, tendrils of vapor coiled beneath a limb of willow or cypress. Luna trolled her boat off the river into a narrow creek, the boat's bottom scraping past a sandbar, but then the channel deepened and widened to reach a crater that appeared to be boiling water.

"This some kinda hot spring?"

"Artesian, at least. Ever seen one?"

"Can't say I have."

She was unbuttoning her boy's shirt.

"Swim with me."

She dropped her top, her shorts. Jack had never seen a woman so large or muscular except, he realized, in a circus. Lately he had been noticing that, her thighs, her back. The skin was just skin, seemed like.

"Time's a wastin'," she dove naked into the spring's cobalt boil.

Jack followed gamely. He stripped and dove in and his heart threatened arrest before he could break the surface.

"JAZSUS—!"

She hooted laughter.

"JAZSUS CHRIST!"

The water was cold as ice! It was arctic cold. It closed on his chest like a glacier. So cold his hands ached, his feet. Jack was startled to see that his fingernails were already turning blue and as for his balls—? He couldn't goddamn find 'em.

"Mother *ffff ffff*ucker!" he stuttered.

"You'll get used to it."

She rolled onto her back. The water coursed between her breasts and lapped into the bowl of her belly.

"I love this place," she padded over to the boil and Jack was amazed to see her body lift with the force of the aquifer's flow.

"Move around, Jack, or you'll freeze."

He kicked into a crawl to reach her, the water coming from below, like some great giant hand lifting.

"You don't even have to work!" he marveled.

She stroked over to meet him, that cold hand below, supporting them both. It was impossible to sink, perhaps even to dive, in the face of that artesian pump.

They kissed over the heart of the spring, deep and long. Her skin was not rough at all, Jack was surprised to discover. It was smooth and warm and toned as a trapeze artist's.

"You still chilled?"

"Yes," he had to admit.

"Let's get warm."

She must have felt his erection, Jack figured, and so when she broke free he did not know at first whether to follow. But when she reached the shallows and turned to him waist-deep and looked at him, he knew.

They coupled in the water like a pair of otters, her hair black and sleek down that marvelous spine. Two lovers at the spring's edge, the water boiling cold around them. Slowly, at first. Then more urgently.

"Hold on!"

She kept the lobe of his ear between her teeth.

"Hold it!"

But finally he could not. An osprey cried out with their climax. Jack felt the welcome sun on his back.

They swam afterward, briefly, leisurely, and dressed. Then back to the boat and the river, her breasts pressing through the khaki of her damp shirt to fill the hollow beneath his chest.

It had been so long since he had felt anything like this. Anything at all like it. The water sailed by, the bow lifting now with the throaty labor of its inboard.

"Is there anyone else like you, Luna?"

"You mean with my skin?" Her response was matter of fact.

"Yes."

She smiled.

"There are whole families of us. Doesn't hit everyone, but often enough so that where I grew up we weren't thought of as being particularly different than anyone else."

"That's good," he said.

"Good, how?"

"It's just I'd hate to think you were like that woman in the cage."

"I am the woman in the cage, Jack. Every geek ever born is. Difference between me and that poor girl—? I choose my cage. And I keep the take."

Luna seemed perfectly at peace on the silent way back. Jack was torn with warring emotions. He had never made love to anyone that he intended to use. Or to betray. Could he have Luna, or anyone like her ever again? Had something twisted in the years of cards and cheating and sad, speakeasy cons?

Jack dropped his hand into the silver river. Maybe this place was different, he told himself. Maybe down here, with these people, a man could really and truly start over.

Jack held onto that thought or hope or fantasy, the very possibility of a new life rising like the water from the spring, bearing him up. You didn't need a lot to live down here. You could make do. Martin would love it, he was sure. Clean air and fishing. And baseball, too, you bet. You could always find a ball and bat, but first—

First he had to find something else.

Chapter ten

Heat—*trouble with people
who are not carnies.*

Fist Carlton's dark mood fit the sky which hung heavy and filled with soot over Cincinnati's malarial basin. A number of things had conspired to put Bladehorn's legbreaker out of sorts. The Duesenberg, for one, had a punctured tire, which meant that Fist was reduced to manual labor under the scathing indictment of his boss's inspection. When Mr. Bladehorn wasn't happy, no one was happy. Oliver Bladehorn had only just received the second telegraph from his butterfly-in-the-making, Jack Romaine, hinting at unspecified information related to Alex Goodman that, surely, was bound to be solid.

"'Solid'? Bullshit!" Bladehorn raged. "Who the hell does that son of a bitch think he's fooling?"

"Let me at him," Fist offered. "I'll show him what's solid."

"D'you need reminding that it was your responsibility to keep my wife on a leash to begin with?"

"No, sir."

"Cretin. You'd done your job, I wouldn't have had my property stolen to begin with!"

The more frustrated Bladehorn got, the more he harassed, belittled and pestered his thug *cum* chauffeur. So Fist had more than his usual store of reasons for wanting a reunion with Jack Romaine.

Finally, Bladehorn had dismissed him for the day. Fist was grateful to be on his way home. He'd taken a pullcar down from the Hills, switching to another streetcar crowded with merchants, tradesman and stevedores on passage through the Basin's filth before reaching the always-clean markets of Over the Rhine. His own people lived here, solid German stock who since the war had become suspicious of outsiders, insulating themselves in neat little apartments and tidy communal quadrangles.

No guinea would get to you, here.

Fist passed a streetside cheese vendor and walked another block to turn between two buildings whose facing walls rose nearly windowless for four red-bricked stories on either side of a narrow alley.

The alley ran to a dead end at a solitary fire escape which was where Fist was headed. His apartment was at the rear of the tenement, up four flights and down a shotgun hall, its solitary window offering the only view of the bounding alley, but Fist would probably have been unable to recall the last occasion on which he entered his apartment by its street-facing door. For years he instead unlocked the heavy gate barring entry to the alley, relocked the gate, and then climbed the fire escape four stories to reach a landing at the heavy and double-locked door allowing entry to his modest apartment.

There was a serious purpose behind the unorthodox entry. Fist Carlton had no friends; anyone approaching him from an interior door or hallway he regarded as a potential enemy. By using the fire-escape and by gating the alley, Fist was not required to meet anyone. Carlton did not want neighbors to know his comings or goings. He never spoke to anyone from the tenement. If he met someone loitering beside the alley he simply broke a face or an arm and they invariably failed to return.

In earlier years, kids would scale the locked fence to throw catcalls or sometimes bottles at Carlton's landing. Fist tolerated those indignities stoically. Kids at play were more valuable than canaries in a coal mine. You didn't get ambushed with kids around. Not even in Cincinnati.

Fist had barely entered the alley when he heard a cat yowl from the fire escape. It was not a housecat, or at least this tom had never entered Fist's home. In fact, it had taken him weeks just to coax the animal to his landing, each evening after work teasing the cat with some snack or another until it was hooked.

"Can't wait, can ya?" the big man smiled.

A four-storey climb with his heavy coat and implements reminded Fist daily of his limitations. It was getting hard to mount those improvised stairs, but he managed, finally reaching the fourth floor's landing and the door that opened directly into his kitchen. The cat was waiting.

"Git," Fist kicked but the cat was already scampering from range.

The landing's door was set in a metal frame, secured top and bottom with deadbolts and an interior drawbar. Took two more keys to throw the bolts before Fist stepped into his kitchen. He immediately reset the door's deadbolts and threw down the interior drawbar. The cat complaining steadily outside as Fist made sure his home was safe. This was his habit. His routine.

There wasn't much to check—the kitchen opened onto a single room which doubled as bedroom and parlor. Nothing disturbed there. He inspected the loo briefly. A real bathroom, with facilities. No invasion to be discerned in the shitter.

Carlton then lumbered on squeaking shoes to peer through the peephole augered into the apartment's also-reinforced front door. No threat apparent in the immediate hallway. Fist released another pair of deadbolts, keeping the safety chain engaged as he cracked the door open for a view down the corridor. Nothing to see but a shotgun of peeling wallpaper and unwashed floor.

A gentle release of tension on the chain as Fist released the safety. The door swinging open to reveal an empty milk bottle perched on the frontier between his apartment and the hallway. Fist did not touch the bottle; instead he stooped to ensure that the ring of dust gathered at its base was undisturbed. Satisfied, Bladehorn's feared henchman then closed the parlor door, secured the locks and safety chain and only then discarded his coat, hat, truncheons and revolver in favor of the more domestic routines at day's end.

The cat by now pawing at the kitchen door.

"I know, I know."

Fist rolled up shirtsleeves to expose forearms the size of logs. He lumbered back to the kitchen, bent over an icebox to retrieve a package butcher-wrapped inside. It was Fist's habit to feed the cat on the landing outside his kitchen door. Once inside Fist did not like to unlock the kitchen door. More secure to tempt the cat from the window.

Fist had armored the window even more exotically than the door. The window itself was ordinary; a pair of bright brass keeps released the glass. The real protection came from a grate of steel mounted outside the window, a moveable grid set in a heavy iron frame welded directly to the fire-escape. The grate itself was a quiver of steel-pointed bars made to raise or lower in sleeves set into the window's sill so that it functioned like a portcullis protecting a castle's gate. No intruder could force his way through Fist's armored window, but he could easily raise it to defend the landing against any intruder.

Or just to be entertained by the cat.

Fist raised the window first and a stir of air wafted through the grating. A padlock and bar secured the grate's vertical bars in their iron sleeves. Fist knelt at the window to release the lock, the ungrateful kitty jabbing a tentative paw through those iron spikes in an attempt to reach the food now maddeningly displayed on the sill.

Fist raked a ring of keys viciously across the grate; the cat spit and backed off. Carlton released the padlock's hasp with a chuckle and pulled the bar free.

"Not long, now," Fist promised and took a grip of the grate's iron frame.

Even for a big man it took a shove to raise the portcullis clear of the window. A sawed off broomstick propped beneath to keep the grid raised.

"Here y'are," Fist displayed the goodies inside the butcher's paper.

The cat snarling frustration with the scent of salmon.

"You want it, you gotta come to the sill."

A short leap took the cat from the landing to the window's wide sill. Fist swatted the cat with a huge scarred fist. Just slapped the tom off the sill and back onto the fire escape.

A howl, then, the cat impotent and spitting. Fist laughing from his redoubt. Pleased with his entertainment.

"Stupid kitty."

Carlton played the game a while longer, tease and swat, tease and swat, frustrating the tomcat with the salmon. Fist was enjoying himself, really he was. He would not have been pleased to know that his recreation was being observed.

A rope anchored on a vent atop the building's roof supported Arno Becker as he hung flat against the building's brick face directly above Fist's now-open window. Becker could see the cat and mouse game below, the cat leaping to reach the salmon, Fist's arm emerging to swat the animal off the sill. It was not the first time that Arno had seen this game.

Becker was close enough to taste the brass smell of fish on his tongue, but even though his feet were now on top of the metal tongue which framed Carlton's grating, Arno maintained a tight grip on the rope which, still, supported his weight.

You had to be patient.

Finally, Fist Carlton decided he'd played enough.

"Supper for kitty," he abdicated abruptly and extended a meaty arm to drop the salmon on the landing outside.

That's when Becker let go the rope, his body's weight snapping the slender stick below and driving the portcullis like a guillotine into the windowsill.

A violent concussion slammed Fist to his knees. He felt nothing, at first. Something had jerked him back from the window and his head, he realized, had slammed into the sill. There was the taste of pennies in his mouth, that was all. At first.

But then he tried to pull back into the protection of his fortress apartment—

"WHHHAAAAAA?!!"

That's when Fist realized that his arm was crucified onto his windowsill.

He screamed. The tomcat screamed.

A thump of feet and a body swung into view at the still-open window. Suspended in midair outside.

"'Lo, Fist."

Arno Becker smiling from the other side of the guillotine.

"BASTARD!!"

Fist lunging with his unbroken arm for Becker's throat. Arno trapped that arm easily. Snapped a handcuff over the thick wrist and then secured the other side of the bracelet to the landing's railing.

Both of Carlton's arms were now trapped, stretched, and exposed.

Fist screamed again. Pain, this time, as tendons and connective tissue to the brain and back overcame nature's first, insulating provision against trauma.

Then he was cursing. Cursing Becker, God, Bladehorn. Cursing his mother.

Arno smiling. Patiently. Waiting for a pause. Finally, when his victim was merely sobbing—

"Where is Alex Goodman, Fist?"

"Wha—? Who?!"

Becker snapped a sap down hard over the pinioned arm.

"AAAAAGHHHHHH!!!"

Another string of blasphemy. Then he was begging. Begging and threatening, alternately.

"Lemme go…I'LL KILL YOU, BECKER!! Lemme go! GOD!"

Arno inhaling the aroma of the salmon pinioned along with Carlton's shattered arm.

"Alex Goodman. Where is he?"

"I…I don' know. Nobody knows!"

"Not what I want to hear," Becker chided.

"I can't tell ya what I don' FUGGIN' KNOW!"

"Then were is Jack Romaine? Hmm? Master Jack, don't tell me he's off on his own. Bladehorn must have sent him someplace."

Fist shook his head.

"No...NO!"

Arno stuffed the blackjack back into his jacket and came out with his knife.

"What you want left hanging, Fist?"

"You *know* what Bladehorn'll do duh me! You KNOW!"

"I know what I will do, and I gotta tell you, Fist, nobody's gonna hire a mutt without mitts, you follow me? And I'd love to have these fists, really I would. Mount the pair of 'em over my fireplace. If I had a fireplace."

"Oh, God...."

Arno placing his blade on the handcuffed arm.

"Awright, awright!"

Fist's forehead collapsed briefly in the blood now pooling at his window.

"...Boss gave him a train ticket, that's all I know. Someplace near Tampa."

Becker took a slice out of flesh.

"OH GOD!!"

"WHERE?" Arno demanded.

"Jesus, 'Kaleidoscope'! Yeah, that's it—Kaleidoscope, that's the place. South of Tampa, that's all I know, swear to Christ!"

"You don't have to swear, Fist—"

Arno smiled.

"I always know when a man's telling me the truth."

The tomcat hissing now from the fire escape.

"How hungry you 'spose he really is?" Arno wondered aloud and leaned over to slice a piece off the salmon.

"Wh—what?" Fist tried to pull away as Arno smeared the salmon over his shattered arm.

"The fuck—? Fuck, you doin'?"

And then more choice cuts taken from the kitty's meal to smear on Fist's handcuffed arm.

"You don' hafta do this!"

Fist's breathing becoming labored, sporadic.

"You don't!"

Becker wiped his blade on his corduroys.

"Once an alley cat gets a taste, what I hear—? He just keeps on gnawing."

Arno Becker lowered himself to the fire escape below. Fist Carlton howling curses and imprecations from above, but there was no one to hear.

There were no children in the alley.

Chapter eleven

The Fix—*the grease,*
the patch, the bribe.

N

ight had fallen with a harvest moon by the time Tommy
Speck wiped his feet on the horsehair mat just inside Kaleidoscope's
Western Union.

"Hiya, HighWire."

Addressing himself to the withered old coot whose fingers
tapped code, apparently, even when he was asleep.

The old man rousing from a stolen slumber.

"Anything snappin'?" Speck climbed a stool.

"Deader than a drunk's dick," the operator replied sourly.

"Just got back from Tampa myself," Tommy confided, as though
it were the greatest trick since Lindy's crossing. "Some of the acts're
beddin' early. Guess who I saw?"

"Couldn't hazard."

"Mel Dodson—remember Mel?"

"Worked for the man," the Union man affirmed. "Took a mile of railroad cars to pack in all the acts. A walkin' mile."

"Some show," Tommy whistled admiration.

"'Dodson's World Fair Shows'." The old trouper suppressed a smile. "Class act, all the way around."

"Boy a'howdy."

"Never used a net, neither."

"Hell, no!" Tommy bristled. "Not you, Wire."

"Not anybody on that show," the old-timer amended gruffly. "So how are things with ol' Mel?"

"They finally made him full partner," Tommy reported.

"Sumbitch."

"Yep. Fair payback fer bein' a general agent all these years."

"Then again life's hard and you die."

"I heard that," Tommy dropped from the ledge of his stool. "Well, if you don't have anything fer me to deliver, I reckon I'll be—"

About that time the telegraph chattered its salutation.

CQCQCQCQ....

"Hold up," HighWire swiveled back to key a go-ahead and Morse chattered like firecrackers over the wire.

Harry scrawled the message, double-checked his tape.

"Anybody we know?"

"The new fella. Brodie." HighWire was reaching for an envelope.

"Ya mean Jack? Jack Romaine?"

"That's the one."

"I can get it to him," Tommy offered brightly.

"It's marked 'Personal'."

"He's laid up. Got the squirts."

Harry frowned over the telegram.

"Does say immediate delivery."

"Harry, I take people their wires alla time."

"I shouldn't."

"How much is the damage?"

"Pretty steep, three fifty."

Tommy produced a Jackson.

"He can pay me back."

"All right, then. If yer sure it's copasetic."

"I'll run 'er over right now."

Tommy sneaked the message from the old man's hand like a pickpocket and skipped for the door. He was barely outside the telegrapher's tin shed when a pair of headlights speared him from behind. The dwarf turned to face the glare. A touring car had him crosshaired and he could tell it wasn't Doc's.

Tommy shielded his eyes against the running lights.

"This Kaleidoscope?" a disembodied voice floated from somewhere behind the wheel.

"Who's askin'?" Tommy stepped out of the spotlight.

Stars swam before his eyes. He didn't see the driver leave the car, but he heard the door open, all right. Shoes digging into soft sand.

Tommy backed away instinctively. A man emerged finally from silhouette. As Tommy's eyes adjusted he could make out a few details. A cityslicker suit. Shirt open at the collar. A flat-brimmed fedora. He was taller than your average rube. Hair and face looked white as chalk, but that could be the light.

A cigarette glowed briefly in the visitor's hand. A casual inhalation before he flicked it hissing to the sand. Embers following that flight like a miniature comet.

"I'm looking for a man," Arno Becker looked down on Tommy.

"Don't think I'm yer type," Speck replied.

"Movie star looks but cheap threads," Becker went on as if Tommy had not said a word. "Low quarter shoes. Dark hair, early thirties. His real name's Jack Romaine; I don't know what he's using down here."

The Packard purring like a tiger.

"Sorry," Tommy shook his head. "Dudn't ring a bell."

"That a fact?" Arno reached into his pocket——

And pulled out a five dollar bill.

"Hey, buddy," Tommy waved him off. "I don't know any movie stars and I don't know this Romanian or whoever the fuck he is."

Becker leaned down to stuff the bill inside Tommy's shirt.

"More where this came from. You see Mr. Romaine, or your memory improves, let me know."

Jack had crashed early into his kip. The first real hint of autumn poured through the shack's single and open window, a welcome breeze entering with the flood of an ochre moon. Something came between Jack's bed and that fallen illumination. A shadow rippling over the cot.

A hand reaching out to close on Jack's curled arm.

"The hell?!"

Jack jerked away to find Charlie Blade shivering beside his bed.

"I need a fix!"

He was coming down, Jack knew the signs, the sword-swallower trembling like a colt in a thin, puke-stained shirt. Smelling otherwise of urine and beer.

"Get outta here," Jack ordered.

"I need some candy. *You* know!"

"I know what I'm gonna do if you don't get your ass out of my crib," Jack pulled the brass knuckles from beneath his pillow.

The young man retreated a notch. But then—

"You wanna know about Alex Goodman?"

Jack felt ice water run down his spine.

"What was that?"

"Goodman," Blade repeated. "You don't think you got the skinny from these freaks, do ya?"

Jack curled the brass bangers into his hand.

"Just get me a fix," Charlie scrambled back. "Get me straight I'll tell you about Alex."

Jack considered a moment.

"Not here," he put the knuckles into his trousers. "We're gonna talk, I want to make sure its private."

The midway's Ferris Wheel framed a waxing moon in a motionless spider of iron. You would have to look hard to see the two men installed in the lowest seat of that ride. Jack rolled a cigarette of Prince Albert for Charlie Blade. The small, white cylinder of tobacco weaving in the young addict's hand.

"Thanks," Blade inhaling greedily.

Jack followed the smoke with a ten-spot.

"Should get you fixed."

Charlie tried to snatch a grab, but Jack held back.

"Not 'till you spill."

"Awright, awright…Few years ago I got in some trouble. Was in Tampa, I needed a patch, a lawyer. Somebody gave me a number, some mouth name of Dobbs. Terrence Francis Dobbs."

"Never heard of him."

"Yeah, you have. He got stomped to death by Peewee's elephant."

Jack worked to keep a poker face.

"Alex Goodman? You saying this lawyer Dobbs is Alex Goodman?"

"Goodman was his carney name," Charlie sucked on his butt as though it were the last tit giving the last milk ever to be had in the world. "But he was a lawyer in Tampa 'way before he started callin' himself Alex Goodman."

"And how do you know that?"

"'Cause, I worked for him. Sort of a sideline; this was three years back, and he had it made. Had his practice in town, real estate, stocks. Got short of cash—that's when he started bringing in merchandise from Cuba. You could say I was one of his retailers."

"Not talkin' about you," Jack warned. "So why'd this Gatsby leave the good life?"

"He was playin' the market on the margins and got behind. Tried to make it up with bolita and rum and cigars, which left him owing some pretty nasty partners, so he changed his name and hit the road as a fixer."

"Fixing what, exactly?"

"If you'd ever worked an opera you'd know there's somebody in every berg, town and pigtrail that's gotta be paid off. Might be the local sheriff, an alderman, a mayor. Somebody always gets greased.

That's what Dobbs did, only, on the show he didn't call himself Dobbs, he called himself Goodman. Alex Goodman.

"Didn't work out that well, though. He only worked one, maybe two seasons. Made his bed in Kaleidoscope a year ago, maybe a little more. Pitiful fuckin' case by then. Drunk on gin half the fuckin' time…"

This judgment rendered without irony.

"'Magine a guy like that humping The Fat Lady!!"

Charlie wheezing laughter as his cigarette burned down to his fingers.

Jack pulled out a paper for himself.

"I got questions."

"My meter just ran out," Charlie smiled crookedly.

Jack displayed the tenner and this time Charlie snatched it clean.

"First question I got isn't about Alex," Jack leaned into Charlie's fetid face. "It's about Kaleidoscope. This beddy. This place."

"Your dime."

"The hell does Luna pay for this operation? One show, one night a week? Can't possibly pay the bills. And half the geeks eating at the café never pay anything. Who's picking up the tab?"

Charlie was ironing the ten-dollar smooth on his thigh.

"All I can tell ya is couple of winters back, the whole shooting match was goin' under. The café, the carnival—everything. Some bank in Tampa was set to foreclose, what I heard, then a year later the bank gets its money. How? I don't know; I don't have the books. But I can tell ya that until a few months ago I could walk up to Luna and ask her to spot me a hundred, two hundred clams and I'd get it no questions asked.

"Word got out that if you needed a hand this was the place to come. Carneys drifted in from all over. Freaks. Juiced-out acts going nowhere. Even a couple of circus performers. How you think High-Wire got his job?

"Way it's set up, when you got money you pay. When you get more money, you pay back, an' in a bind you eat free. Get a roof over yer head. See the doc, you need to.

"There was no loans signed, no IOUs. But then I never seen any cash, neither, and with my particular problem—"

"You need the green."

"Dollars for doughnuts."

Jack displayed another ten-dollar bill; Charlie reached out greedily—

"Ah ah," Jack chided. "This one you gotta earn. Find out anything you can on your man Dobbs. Tell me anytime *anybody* goes to Tampa. And if you see anyone new in town—"

Blade gathered his slim green salvation.

"Don't worry. I'll let ya know."

Jack tossed about in his cot worrying over Charlie Blade's credibility. He did not doubt that a lawyer out of work was the ideal hire for a carnival's fixer. Jack had always known that carnival operators employed go-betweens to grease the natives in whatever towns they staked a lot. There was always some minister or misanthrope clamoring for a spotlight to accuse the carneys of peddling pornography along with popcorn. More strident voices saw in the freaks, particularly, darker signs of Satan and his works, and these voices could run a show out of town. Of course, the more the righteous or self-righteous clamored to banish the forbidden fruit, the more their community was enticed to sample it. Tommy Speck often chuckled that a preacher was worth a hundred billboards.

But you paid for advertising, no matter how you got it, the printer getting his geld for posters and handbills, the councilman or clergy getting silver for silence. It was not hard to imagine Terrence Dobbs, AKA Alex Goodman, employed in that role. Was easy as well to understand how a disbarred lawyer hoping, perhaps, to re-establish his practice in some other state would change his name in association with the interim employment. It was not the accuracy of this information that kept Jack awake in his cot. What worried Jack was that the only thing he knew of Alex Goodman came from Charlie Blade.

Surely the disgraced sword-swallower was not the only carney in the beddy who was familiar with Alex Goodman's other life in

Tampa? Surely the freaks and performers with whom Jack worked every day knew Terrence Dobb's history; like Cassandra said, there were no secrets in Kaleidoscope.

"Except mine," Jack amended aloud and suppressed the guilt that stirred.

Clearly, Luna and the other carneys in the community had decided to keep Jack in the dark about Alex Goodman's real identity and purpose. But why? Was it simply the freaks' tendency to distrust outsiders that made Luna and her fellows loathe to speak of Goodman? Were they protecting Goodman's identity? That was easy enough to swallow, and Jack would be happy enough to buy it, except for a couple of salient points—

First of all, this community was clearly getting revenue from someplace other than candy and hootchy-kootch. Secondly, Alex Goodman was connected to Sally Price and Bladehorn's stolen money. It was possible, of course, that the carneys kept silent simply out of loyalty to Goodman, but was there a less noble reason for silence? Jack was convinced that the carneys knew something about Goodman's role in their community that they were not going to reveal to a mere brodie.

But was this distrust directed at all outsiders coming to Kaleidoscope, or was Jack its specific target? Jack swung from his cot and reached for a cigarette. "Don't get loony," he muttered to himself. After all, it was natural the geeks wouldn't open their souls to a newcomer. And Jack had to admit that since he had saved Marcel & Jacques, he seemed to be entirely assimilated into Kaleidoscope's odd assortment of parts. Everybody from The Bearded Lady to The Alligator Man greeted him warmly. He hadn't paid for his coffee in a week. And then there was Luna.

He could still feel her skin, smell her hair in that cold, spring-fed water. Her legs around his waist. Coupling like a pair of goddamn otters. Warming after. That alone was enough to assure Jack that he had turned the corner, wasn't it? That he had gained Luna's trust, and Tommy's, and the others?

He had swallowed fire, hadn't he? He was one of their own.

Jack had not anticipated being embraced so suddenly by the

mercurial family of freaks, or so warmly. And Jack was surprised at the changes in his own perception. Only the day before he was gabbing with Friederich over a wheelbarrow of the man's completely exposed testicles with no feeling of revulsion or fascination. He enjoyed playing cards with Charlotte and Jo Jo and Jacques & Marcel. And making love to Luna he never once thought of the color of her skin.

But for a man living a lie, the warm greetings and café banter now freely offered by these malformed and unusual people made Jack uneasy, as though he had incurred a debt, as though he were cheating cards at a table of children. Didn't take much reflection to realize that it was in precisely these moments that Jack was reminded he *was* cheating these people, all of them, and that if Luna and Tommy and the other freaks had grown to trust their new brodie, it was not the fruit of any fidelity on his part, but the product of his fabrication.

Jack pressed his hands to his temples. It was hard to know what was true when you spent so much time lying to yourself. But what the hell could he do about that, now? He *wanted* to deal straight, that was what Jack told himself, but he had no choice! He couldn't tell Luna why he was down here or who had sent him or what he was really trying to find. What would she do to him if she knew? What would happen to his own family if the carneys discovered a con-man in their midst?

All night went the merry-go-round. From there to the Funny House, Jack stumbling through a hall of mirrors searching for the authentic face in the endless souls receding into infinity on either side. Which was the knock-off, the facsimile, the fake?

Was there a real Jack Romaine at all?

But the old defenses would reassert themselves. The old voice that had taken him from New York to Chicago to Cincinnati pushing forward to say, Listen, chump, it don't matter what game you got goin', you think these geeks are playin' straight? You think these freaks don't got a card up the sleeve?

The old, familiar rationalization:

Just because you're playing them, Jack, doesn't mean they aren't playing you.

That was what Jack held onto as he sought slumber in a

sleepless night. For all he knew Luna could be lying to his face. So could Tommy. So could they all. These people weren't telling him everything they knew, that was for sure. Not about Alex Goodman, not about their money. There was definitely something fishy going on and if Jack had learned anything since coming to Kaleidoscope it was that a carney could hide a lie behind a smile easier than a rube could wipe his ass.

It was possible, his own sins aside, that the generosity Jack had experienced since saving Jacques & Marcel was no more than a come-on, a turn, a shill. It was possible, signs to the contrary, that Luna did not really trust him. That she was using him exactly as he was using her.

There was no way out of the maze. He had to protect Martin and Mamere and the only way to do that was to get Bladehorn his property. Time was running out; Jack knew he couldn't keep Bladehorn at bay with telegrammed encouragement. Jack had to get the gangster his property and if that meant he was a rat to Luna and Tommy and the other freaks, well—to hell with it.

There was nothing he could do.

Those were the thoughts that robbed Jack of sleep that night and embittered the early morning coffee he was sipping the following day in the café when Luna came in, her hair swaying down that long, hard back, to hand him his first pay check.

"Here," she ran her hand through his hair. He tried to respond in kind.

"Four and a half bucks. Thank you, Boss Lady."

"Don't spend it all in one place." She winked, and then turned to Half Track. "I'll be gone most of the day, Jenny. Giant needs some lumber to repair the camels' paddock and we're short on hay. You need anything?"

"Nope," HalfTrack scooped sugar into a jar. "We're stocked up."

Luna bent to brush her lips on the nape of Jack's neck.

Sent chills down his spine.

"You all right?"

"I'm fine." He smiled reassurance and she gave him a squeeze on the shoulder before she swayed away.

Jack watched Luna leave the café and cross the street. If she was shining him, she was doing a good job. Jack sipped his coffee. Luna said she'd be gone for the day, but it didn't take a day to get lumber and hay. Didn't take half a day. Jack had made runs for supplies with Tommy and even buying lumber and feed and all the rest he'd never missed the noon-meal's flag.

Was there something else taking Luna's time?

Something else in Tampa?

Jack made up his mind to follow her. Luna would obviously bring back a load of lumber and fodder—failing to complete that errand would look odd. And Jack knew that any run for timber and hay meant she'd be taking the Big Truck, the sideboarded Ford that had towed Peewee's wagon from the train station. The Ford was the only vehicle suited for heavy loads and would be a snap to tail. But Jack would need a vehicle of his own if he was to follow Luna's. The Model T—Shouldn't be hard to borrow the flivver for a daytrip to Tampa.

Jack left the café and found Tommy filling the stock's tank with fresh water.

"I wanta bank my pay," Jack explained. "I got nearly seventy bucks in cash, countin' what I brought down with me. It's too much to have layin' around."

Tommy agreed and without a qualm gave Jack the coupe.

Jack let Luna have a good five minutes' start before he cranked the T and rattled off in pursuit. He had changed clothes in the interim, into a suit appropriate for a visit to a bank, but not the duds he'd been wearing when he arrived at Kaleidoscope. He did what he could to create an unfamiliar appearance, tossing aside his fedora for a planter's hat, a local straw-woven headpiece with a loose, drooping brim. Discarding his pin-striped shirt for a solid, cotton weave. A bowtie and new second-hand shoes. In that camouflage Jack pulled onto the Tamiami Trail.

He could not see the Big Truck on the narrow two-lane ahead, but was not worried. Jack knew that Luna's first stop would be to get lumber and feed. Griffith's Lumber was not located in Tampa proper, but was situated north of the city, off a rail-line's spur. There were a series of sawmills and warehouses and other businesses located not far from the Tampa train station along a variety of feeding lines. Businesses dealing in large quantities of timber or produce or retail goods loaded and unloaded cars of goods along these lines.

The blacktop took you almost all the way to the lumberyard. As Jack drove in he saw long stretches of cypress and pine and palmetto give way to the burned ruins of orange groves. The Mediterranean fruit fly had destroyed tens of thousands of acres of these and other orchards. Virtually every manner of fruit could host the insect; every form of that produce had had to be destroyed, even down to individual trees at residences in town.

Stiff penalties were enforced against any attempt to transport fruit of any kind. The *Tribune* warned travelers that every outgoing trunk, portmanteau and handbag would be inspected for hoarded samples of guava or tangerine. Even that meager contraband could spread the plague of the fruit fly to the entire southeast, the paper warned its readers, a prospect terrifying governors from Florida to the Carolinas.

The smell of petroleum and smoke wafted into the Model T's cab. Jack could see fires stretching in straight lines alongside the road and across barren fields. Ditches normally used for irrigation or drainage had been filled with motor oil to burn tens of thousands of acres of fruit. What had been some of the most productive soil in agriculture was now no more than a grid of darkened stumps. Jack turned off the blacktop and away from a horizon of devastation to find the clay road leading to Mr. Griffith's yard.

He spotted Luna's truck pulling into the lumberyard. He found cover for the Model-T behind a drying yard and stacks of field fence, kicked the door open to let some air in and surveyed the grounds. A pair of yardboys were already at work with The Giant loading twobys and lathe onto the big Ford. Then came the hay. He saw Luna step inside the one-story clapboard that was Griffith's office and for the next half hour the only thing Jack saw entering the yard was a

Studebaker coupe and a pair of deuce-and-a-halfs. The coupe arrived first. A tepid hoot from the driver and the man at the gate waved him through to a meager shade beneath a cottonwood near the office. Somebody employed by the yard, Jack figured. Or maybe a salesman. Sure wasn't hauling lumber in a Studebaker.

The deuces came in later, offloading barrels it turned out. The workers moving slowly, sweat shining on mostly black skin.

The morning's heat and humidity made the cab stifling hot; Jack finally got out and made a shade for himself in the bed of the truck. He had begun to think he had blown a day off, that Luna was on a routine errand, and taking her own sweet time about it, too.

When she left the yard, he almost missed her.

Jack was expecting the Boss Lady to leave Griffith's in her truck, naturally, with The Giant riding shotgun. But there was Luna Chevreaux, now, driving the Studebaker coupe! Jack realized that she must have had somebody from town bring out the car which meant that Luna had more on her mind than wood and hay.

Jack got the T's magneto firing, engaged the hand-operated clutch and pulled out to follow Luna south toward Tampa. He was fortunate to have a truck laden with shade tobacco to put between himself and Luna as he tailed the Boss Lady down the narrow black-top. They picked up perhaps half a dozen trucks on the road and as many automobiles. Jack began to resent his present chore; in other circumstances, he'd have taken the day off from pounding stakes and shovelling shit to tour Tampa's Gulf-Coast diversions. He might have admired the homes of rumrunners and cigar magnates. He might have paused to appreciate the Moorish cast of the city's architecture, minarets rising across the river at the Tampa Bay Hotel. Maybe get out on the water. Eat a decent steak. Hell, if he played his cards right, Jack could imagine living down here. Provided they did something about the damn flies.

If he ever got out from under Bladehorn's thumb, Jack promised himself a vacation with his son in this sundrenched city. They'd get a room someplace, get out on the water. And for sure he would take Martin down to Plant Field to see where the Cincinnati Reds camped for spring training.

There were carnal pleasures, too, and carnal opportunities. Tampa's tropical climate combined with its distinctive minarets to conjure images of harems and women and Arabian nights. The Green Parrot was reputed to be one of the quickest clubs in town. It was no problem for a man with gladrags and cash to find himself a honey at the Parrot.

Those idle thoughts jarred to a stop when Jack realized with a sudden sense of disorientation that Luna was not taking her car into downtown Tampa. Instead, the Studebaker continued west across the Hillsborough River before turning south to the still-new Davis Islands Bridge.

Jack had heard only a smattering of gossip concerning the Islands, even though it was big news for Tampa realtors. The Davis Islands were one of the first pieces of real estate to be created artificially, the islands no more than a series of landfills developed specifically for speculative investment. Some big money had been spent on the project. Before it was even completed, fat cat investors, bankers and crooks were cutting each other's nuts to crowd in.

So what was Luna up to on the Islands?"

The newly finished bridge spanned not much more than a hundred yards from the mainland to the Islands and it was over that abbreviated causeway where Jack Romaine now followed Luna's car. *Rump, rump, rump...*Jack could hear his tires as they hit the seams separating the bridge's spans. The smell of salt air and sea breeze rushing through the cab of his flivver.

Seagulls and terns flew overhead, their lazy wheeling transformed in an instant with the plunge to beak some bounty from the salty water. There were people plunging into the water, too. Jack spotted a marina slipped with sailboats and other pleasure-craft, but he was sure Luna wasn't here for sailing, or any other recreation.

The bridge gave onto quiet, well-landscaped streets lined with palm trees and bougainvillea. Within minutes Jack had followed Luna up a paved driveway passing a well-tended display of palm trees and oleander to reach the grounds of the most spectacular hotel he had ever seen.

You approached the Mirasol Hotel on a drive punctuated with palm trees forty feet tall. Jack waited until Luna gave a valet her keys before sputtering past to find his own parking on the south side of the hotel. The automobiles in the garage made Jack's flivver look like a delivery van. He thought he had seen some pretty douche rides in Cincinnati, but this—!

The hotel and grounds embraced a sensibility even more exotic than what Jack had seen downtown. He found shade in a loggia supported by columns that looked to have been filched from a Greek temple. Finding his way back to the main entry he saw that every window and door in the place was arched like some kind of mosque. Jack recalled the article about the hotel he had read on the train down to Tampa. So was this Venetian Gothic? Looked like a cross between General Franco and Ali Goddamn Baba.

Still, you had to admire the work. Lots of detailing on the windows, the cornices, shields cast in plaster to decorate the stuccoed exterior. The hotel's main tower was six, seven stories tall with two wings offering spectacular views. The railings on the balconies were wrought in iron, all the castings turned.

Unless you arrived at the hotel by boat, you entered the Mirasol through a door flanked on either side by a trefoiled transom and French doors. A short hallway and a stroll past potted palms before you entered the Grand Lobby. Jack had no idea what you'd need a fireplace for given his experience of the climate, but there it was, an enormous hearth framed with fixtures of brass and iron. Fairly dark in the lobby, but a great view of the yacht basin below; Jack saw a sloop easing out from a slip, a soiree of gents and ladies playing croquet nearby on a lawn flat and green enough for billiards.

A tall ceiling overhead was carved like a mosque's interior into interlocking patterns of hexagons and squares. Like a kaleidoscope, Jack realized, and for a moment was tempted to spin on his heel for that effect. The wood itself was interesting, too, the entire ceiling finished in pecky cypress, that worm-eaten timber unique to southern forests. Everything in the lobby reeked of expense, the Chippendale recliners, the Corinthian leather binding the books in the adjoining library, the fireplace, the Persian rugs. The Mirasol was opulent, decadent, luxurious. A destination for foreigners and millionaires.

The fuck was Luna Chevreaux doing in a place like this?

The queue was five deep at the desk, rich folks not accustomed to waiting for anything waiting to be checked in. Clerks and bell-hops scrambling to accommodate. Jack scanned the faces and figures for Luna. No dice. Which meant she wasn't here for a room, at least not right away.

Jack strolled over to the concierge.

An artificial smile.

"May I help you, sir?"

"I'm looking for my party."

"Party, sir?"

"You couldn't miss her. Six feet tall, black hair, blue skin. All over."

"Ah! Miss Chevreaux."

"Yes," Jack did not miss a beat.

"The dining room, sir. And welcome to the Mirasol."

He picked up a paper from a divan in the lobby before entering the hotel's sun-filled dining room. The lobby was a little dark for Jack's taste, but the dining room was built to compensate, lots of tall windows and light. A mahogany bar was backed by a mirror must have been twenty feet long. There looked to be a hundred tables or more. Which one was Luna's? Jack considered a moment. Not the center of the room. She probably would not want a seat that would invite attention. But there were a score of screens and potted plants that allowed islands of privacy all over. She could be seated almost anywhere.

It took a while, but eventually he spotted her at a corner table behind a blind of ferns. A rattan chair, looked like. She was leaning over an untouched plate of shrimp and she wasn't alone. Jack could tell there was a conversation engaged in earnest. But he could not see Luna's companion. Maybe if he skirted the fern. Jack was about to improve his view when he got the sudden, sure feeling that he was being watched.

The maître d'.

Jack turned to find the headwaiter zeroed in on him as if he were a target. Jack was about to dash, but then reversed field to face the major-domo head on.

"I need a table."

"Are you a guest here, sir?"

"Meeting somebody," Jack improvised.

"Oh?" the maître d' took another step to close the distance between them.

"I'm treating my partner to dinner," Jack amplified.

"Partner?"

"From Sarasota. We're buying a carnival."

"I see." The man's curiosity immediately faded. He knew about carnival people. Let them stay in Sarasota.

"Is that table free?" Jack nodded toward a set of high-backed chairs.

"I believe so, yes sir."

"Thanks," Jack smiled.

He was seated without being discovered. A hedge of greenery was situated between his table and Luna's. The newspaper offered added cover. From behind that rag Romaine was able to see Luna through the ferns, but all he could see of her companion was a pair of well-brushed shoes and a pair of baggy slacks. A wreath of some pleasantly aromatic cigar haloed over the table.

Luna was animated in her discussion with her smoking companion. Jack saw her shaking her head vigorously.

"'No, now!'" he thought he heard her say.

And then she slipped an envelope across the table.

"Right away," she declared with heat.

Jack saw Luna's date place his cigar on a crystal tray, a clean hand extending from a shabby suit to take the manila folder.

Who the hell was this character?! Jack took a long moment before risking another glance at the smoke-wreathed table. The meeting was clearly concluded. The smoker had already retrieved his cigar. Jack would love to follow this gent. Run him to ground for a private conversation.

'Scuse me, bud, but what's your business with Luna Chevreaux, what's in the envelope and by the fucking way does it have anything to do with stolen cash and railroad notes?

But if Jack was going to follow the fixer, he couldn't let Luna spot him.

She was already rising from her table, turning—

Christ, she was headed directly for his table!

Jack slid from his chair, still hiding behind his paper, to beat a hasty retreat from the dining room. Wending his way carefully through the gathered waiters and tables and guests. Trying not to rush. This was no time to draw attention. No time to spill somebody's soup. And he had just about made it. Jack was two tables from freedom when he glanced, briefly, to the mirror above the bar.

And there was Luna, fixed on Jack's reflection in the frozen glass. Looking. Staring.

Shit!

He kept walking. He heard no challenge as he left the elegant room, but he kept walking anyway, never stopping until he was across the Persian-rugged lobby and through the arched doors.

Once outside Jack broke into a run and didn't quit until he was piled into Tommy Speck's Model T. By the time Luna emerged from the Mirasol's pleasant interior, Jack was merging with Duesenberg's and Packards on the far side of the drive. Luna waited for her valet alone, her bagman nowhere in sight. She must be able to see Speck's car rattling across the way!

But there was no challenge. No pursuit!

Jack felt his heart hammering in his ribs.

Slow down, he told himself. You made it. She didn't see anything, he told himself, as the Mirasol's *grande entrée* receded behind. It was a mirror, he told himself. She couldn't tell. Not for sure.

Jack clattered with the cover of other motorized tourists and pleasure seekers toward the Hillsborough Bridge, his hands shaking like a drunk's on the wheel. He'd give anything at that moment for a drink. Sell his soul for a pint of whiskey. He did not notice the cab trailing three cars behind.

He did not see Charlie Blade at all.

Jack returned to Kaleidoscope to find The Giant unloading lumber from the Big Truck, but Luna was not with him. By evening chow she still had not returned. Jack wolfed down a bowl of monkey stew, drank a pitcher's worth of iced tea and went to his shack. The afternoon's excursion had convinced Jack that, despite signs of fraternity, he was being conned, that in spite of his apparent assimilation into Luna's community, there was something going on, some unnamed thing that was being deliberately hidden.

The only source he could trust at all was Charlie Blade. Jack knew better than most that a junkie would tell you anything to get a fix, but it was Charlie who had confirmed Jack's suspicions that there was outside money coming into Kaleidoscope. And it was Charlie who had pegged Terrence Dobbs as the man taking the alias of Alex Goodman. There had always been the chance that Luna's one-time patch might have known something about the source of her money, but perhaps Mr. Dobbs AKA Goodman had been more deeply involved than that.

Maybe Alex had been a fixer with sticky fingers. Maybe he was the goose who stole the golden goddamn eggs.

Is that what got him killed?

And who was this character at Luna's hotel rendezvous? Was he just another alderman collecting a payoff, or was he Kaleidoscope's newest fixer?

The sun was well set when Jack finally rolled out of the sack. He struck a match to check his watch. Time pissing away. The performers would be gathered in the G-tent by now. If he was going to get the answers he needed, he was going to have to take a risk.

Jack arrived to find a tent filled with freaks mostly ignoring a bed sheet stretched tight between a pair of poles. A strobe of light and a clatter of celluloid threw a ripple of black and white images onto that makeshift screen, Marlene Dietrich stretching seductively beneath the big top. *The Blue Angel*—Jack recognized the film. But it was a crap game that had the freaks' interest. Penguin and Giant and Half Track crowded the pit. Friederich The Unparalled had chucked his wheelbarrow for the occasion, seated on his own scrotum opposite Pinhead and the Damier Brothers, who were fully in character as The Wild Men Of Borneo.

The only thing in the tent not in thrall to the fall of the ivory was the freak's mangy hound.

"Off, Boomer," Jack shoved the dog's snout out of his crotch on his way to the pit.

"Mind another player?" Jack displayed his roll.

"Why not?" Tommy Speck smiled. "Nothing better than takin' money from a brodie!"

Lots of laughter with that remark. Kidding all around. Somebody had brought some hooch. Jack took a long and conspicuous slug when the jug came his way.

"Go tiger!" Cassandra seemed to like her chances this evening.

Jack spread his cash carelessly on the straw.

"Let 'em roll."

He won a small pot right away. Then he pissed away those winnings, two bits at a time to different players. Spreading it around. Everybody was winning something off the brodie and within an hour everybody was loose. Lots of inside jokes, Jack still could not follow them all. Lots of winks and asides.

Was not hard to keep losing. People liked gamblers who lost and God knew he'd had practice. Jack had just about pissed his pay check away when it came his turn to toss the dice.

"Cat's eyes," he looked straight at Cassandra and threw.

And lost.

"Did I win?" Pinhead seemed startled at the possibility. "Tommy, din' I win?"

"Yes, ya dummy," Half Track groused. "Now, shut up."

"Does me in, boys."

Jack pushed his remainders into Pinhead's pot.

"Thag you," the man said sweetly.

Half Track shook her head. "Boy can't spell his name and he's gettin' rich."

"Lady Luck," Jack assured her. "Let's try sevens."

He threw again.

"Did I wiiinnnnn?!" Pinhead clapped his hands.

"I'm gunna flipper that boy to death," Penguin threatened.

"Gonna have to wait for me," Tommy chimed in and everybody roared.

Jack laughing along with the rest. Reaching clumsily for the jug.

"Half Track, tell me somethin', the other brodies, they like to gamble?"

"Sure. Hell, yeah."

"How about Dobbs?"

"Oh, sure, he—"

The dye clicked in instant silence. Pinhead looking around confused.

"Did eeeyeee win?"

Half Track did not reply.

"So," Jack stoppered the jug. "Apparently somebody here did know Mr. Dobbs. Or should I say, Alex Goodman."

"You never quit, do ya?" Tommy fumed.

"Not if I think somebody's pulling my chain," Jack shot back.

"What difference does it make?" Penguin shuffled uncomfortably. "'Dobbs', 'Goodman'—nobody here uses their real names. Nobody cares."

"You folks seem to care," Jack replied. "You seem to care quite a bit. Enough to hide it from me."

Half Track dragged herself up to take Jack by the shirt.

"Leave it alone, Jack!" she bit off the words. "Leave...! It...! Alone!"

She nearly tipped over as she dropped away. Jack reached out to steady her.

"Get yer hands off me!" she cried, and then, "Come on, Pinhead."

"Did eyeee loose?"

"C'mon, sweetheart," Half Track seemed suddenly to deflate. "Jenny's tired."

Pinhead rose dutifully, gathering the severed woman in his arms like a bag of groceries. The Giant collected the blanket, the dice. Jacques & Marcel would not meet his eye. A circle widened about Jack as the aristocrats of Kaleidoscope made their separate departures. Jack found himself finally alone with a siren flickering on a bed sheet and Tommy Speck.

"Here," Tommy jerked a telegraph from beneath his cap.

Jack fingered the envelope. "How long you had this?"

"So keep the tip."

Tommy left without apology. Jack tore off the end of the envelope and raised the telegram to catch the projector's lamp.

Slap, slap, slap—Emil Janning's masterpiece now completely unreeled.

Jack read his blunt summons. No way to stall this one; he had to find a phone. It wasn't hard to break into Luna's café. The street was deserted on all sides, the geeks retired to their trucks and trailers. HighWire was sound asleep at his wireless and Luna was nowhere in sight.

Even so, Jack entered the café looking over his shoulder. The back door would be easiest, he figured correctly. Just a tap of his knife dislodged the hooked latch which was the only barrier to entry. Jack closed the door carefully behind him, rehooked its flimsy latch before making his way carefully in the darkness to the counter and the café's hand-cranked phone. It took ten minutes just to get through, even calling collect.

"Mr. Bladehorn?" Jack felt like he was shouting. "It's Jack Romaine, sir, reporting as ordered."

Oliver Bladehorn accepted Jack's call beside the fireplace of his art deco mansion. Fist Carlton was sitting shrunken alongside, a mere manservant, now, holding the telephone for his boss in hands swathed with gauze. A cast on the one arm.

Bladehorn pulled a silk hankie from his smoker and pressed it to the drool seeping like sewage from his mouth.

"…So you tell me that our Mr. Goodman is deceased?"

Bladehorn's free hand sinking like a talon into the upholstery of his roost.

"Looks that way, Mr. Bladehorn."

"'Looks' does not sound definitive."

"Nothing's for sure in this place," Jack's reply came in scrawls of static.

"Did he HAVE ANY MONEY?" Bladehorn hated raising his voice.

"No, sir. Not a pot to piss in, from what I can tell."

"The situation here has not altered favorably, Mr. Romaine," Bladehorn scowling now at Fist. "I need my property. It has become a matter of some urgency, which means, and I hope I do not have to become specific, that it has become urgent for *you*, as well."

"I don't know what more I can do, Mr. Bladehorn."

"YOU CAN FIND IT!" Bladehorn bellowed. "FIND IT ALL!!"

"What if it was never down here, Mr. Bladehorn? Or what if there's nothing left?"

"Fifty thousand in cash and a quarter *million* in stocks cannot have simply vanished!"

"I'll keep pushing, sir. But you can't wring blood from a turnip."

"*You* can't, perhaps. But there's a man who won't mind trying."

Jack felt the hair on his neck rising.

"…What do you mean, Mr. Bladehorn? What man?"

"Why, your competition, Mr. Romaine," Bladehorn's voice was a menacing squeak in the receiver. "Your nemesis, perhaps."

"Becker? Here? How'd he find me?"

"Let's just say Arno has a way of ferreting out information. He knows about Kaleidoscope. He's almost certainly arrived by now, and I suspect will have fewer scruples in his efforts to recover my property than do you, Jack. In fact, if you can't find my property yourself, it might pay to simply follow our blonde friend."

"Following Becker's not a life-improving proposition, Mr. Bladehorn."

"Neither is disappointing me," Bladehorn replied shortly.

"Look, I'm busting my hump down here, awright? I'm not on vacation!"

"Mr. Romaine, if you want to see your family again—in Cleveland or whatever other hole you try to hide them in—you will do what it takes to satisfy my interests. Do you understand? You will follow, flog, mutilate—whatever it takes."

The line clicked dead and Jack had to remind himself not to slam the receiver onto its hook.

He took a moment to digest the new intelligence. Bladehorn had found his family. That was bad news. Nearly as bad as Arno

Becker finding Kaleidoscope. But surely if Becker were anywhere near the premises one of the freaks would have noticed.

Jack recalled his last soiree with Becker. Bastard must still have stitches. Surely he was not recovered enough for a trip to Florida?! But then came the voice that Jack could not ignore, the deeply frightened, pessimistic voice which went something like—

Who're you kidding, Jack?

The only way to keep Arno Becker away from a quarter of a million dollars was to drive a stake through the bastard's vampire heart.

No chance of a night's sleep, now. Jack paused before slipping out the café's back door. It was dark. There were no kerosene lanterns on the street, only a cloud-filtered moon to light the way. But Jack could see Peewee's tent through the pines, those twin poles raising her canvas like a pair of breasts in lunar composition. There was no light coming from inside, though. No magic lantern. No moving pictures on the sheets.

He pictured Peewee slumbering alongside Ambassador in her canvas mansion and smiled. Was reassuring, somehow, to envision the elephant standing sentry, cooling his mistress with the fan of those enormous ears. With that imagined comfort Jack left the shelter of the café's darkened door and stepped out onto the street.

"Hullo, Jack."

The voice came with the swift snap of a sap. A couple ounces of lead on a leather strap right behind the ear, a brief burst of stars, and Jack dropped like a sack.

Right into Arno Becker's waiting arms.

Tommy Speck was not able to sleep, which was unusual. Tommy had left the dice to nurse a beer on the wagon outside the tigers' cage. They weren't running a menagerie for the show; even Ambassador was off for the year. But Tommy liked the animals, the bigger the better, and Sinbad and Sheila were a never-ending source of mystery, cats caught wild who would, for the right trainer, jump through hoops of fire. Was easy to imagine the pair of carnivores as sentries, ever vigilant, ever ready to defend Tommy's sandy community, but what he needed now was a guard for his heart.

Tommy was not a man comfortable with divided loyalties. He did not enjoy spying on Jack, not even at Luna's direction. No matter what anybody thought of the brodie, he had to be better than the Aryan wolf who'd shown up at the beddy's Western Union door.

"I shoulda told Jack about the telegram," Tommy confided to the caged cats. "No matter what Luna says, I shoulda told him."

Tommy left the tigers unsoothed, taking a bead past the chow-house on the way back to his own downsized trailer. He was abreast of the Sugar Shack when for the second time he saw a Packard rumbling down the sandy center of Main Street. Tommy recognized the albino bastard at the wheel, his golfing cap jauntily cocked. But there was another man slumped on the bench seat alongside, a more familiar figure propped against the passenger-side door.

Was it—?

What seemed like a gallon of iced water flooded his guts.

"LUNAAAAAA!!" the sentry sounded his alarm. "LUUU-NAAA!!"

Chapter twelve

Stripping—*dismantling decorative members used on the various fronts, rides and equipment.*

A burst of stars. Then a jolt up his nostrils and into his brain. Like when you ate ice cream too fast on a summer day.

"Wake up, Pretty Boy."

Arno Becker's face floating in and out of focus. A sharp lance, then, like a cattle prod across his nose. Jack came awake, tears stinging his eyes.

"Ah. Better. Here."

Something cold and wet was forced to his lips. He sucked hard. It was good. Bracing. Arno took the jug away and turned to put it away. Turning his back—

Jack lunged, but something jerked him short in his traces.

He was bound to a tree. Jack felt the burn of the rope on his wrists, coils of hemp pulled so tightly around his chest he could hardly breathe. It was from a tent, Jack realized. Son of bitch, he'd pinched a rope from a tent.

"Too cheap to bring your own, Arno?"

Becker faced him again and shrugged.

"When in Rome—"

A pair of headlights kept Jack turned to face his kidnapper. He wanted to vomit, but that would be difficult strapped with his butt on the ground, a collar around his neck and a pine log draped like a two-ton breakfast tray over his outstretched and numbed legs.

His forearms and hands were tied to the tray. His shoes had been taken off, and his socks. He wriggled his toes.

"Still there," Arno assured him merrily.

"Wa…water."

No jug this time. Becker lifted a thermos of coffee from the Packard's radiator and splashed a sample onto Jack's face.

"FUCKER!" Jack writhed in his collar.

Arno pulled a deer-skinner's knife from its sheath.

"We ready to talk, now? Because we need to talk, Jack, and we may not have as much time as I'd like. Certainly not as much as you deserve, Jack-O."

"Look…" Jack gasped. "Cards up, right? If I knew where Bladehorn's money was, or his certificates, or anything else I'd tell ya, awright? I'm not stupid."

Arno sliced his knife a knuckle deep across Jack's abdomen. It felt like a hot wire passing just beneath the surface of his shirt, but Jack could feel a spreading seam of blood.

"That's in memory of our last conversation," Becker smiled. "Just a nick to get us started. Now. Where's the loot?"

"I dunno where it is, Arno. Jesus, if I did, you think I'd still be *here*?"

"I think as long as Bladehorn's got your whelp on hooks, not to mention Grandma, you'd do pretty much anything he tells you. Which is why we are having this reunion, Jack. So I can persuade you differently."

"You're gonna kill me anyway. Even if I knew. Which I don't."

"I am going to kill you, Jack, no doubt. But you can make it easy. Relatively easy. Or you can make it very, very hard."

Jack felt like he was strangling. He tried to move his arms, his legs.

"You don't really think those freaks give a shit about you, do you, Jack?"

"Bladehorn gives a shit," Jack hung in the ropes. "Not about me. About his goddamn property, though. And he won't let you keep it, Arno. You can find it, more power to you, but you'll never live to spend it. Bladehorn'll see to that."

"That weasel," Arno spit. "He's a dead man."

Arno leaning then to stuff a fist inside Jack's collar, twisting it. Jack feeling as though a stake was driving into his lungs, trying to breathe—trying!

"Y'see, Jack, you aren't the only man likes to gamble. It's just that Mr. Bladehorn's on a bigger table. The Market, Jack-O. Wall Street. Know what it means to speculate, Jack? Heh? It means you borrow against money you don't have at margins of twenty to one, thirty to one. Invest in some copper mine in Bolivia or Paraguay, right? And if it hits it's just like blackjack, and if it doesn't—?

"Why, you just borrow more. You borrow against the next big hit, but you can't lose them all, Jack, nobody can. And Bladehorn, just like you, never knows when to cut his losses."

Arno jerked his hand out of the collar and Jack heaved air like a newborn.

"The only thing between Bladehorn and the wolves right now is a man with a busted arm and no fists."

"Jesus!" Jack gasped and Becker squatted in the beam of the headlights.

"So tell me what you know, Jack. Any little scrap, ya never know."

"All right, then, all right," Jack felt he would rather be blind in the lights than acknowledge the pale amusement in Becker's eyes. "Alex Goodman—is an alias. The brains who set up the robbery, I think, was a fella named Terrence Dobbs. Used to be a lawyer, maybe some other things. Tampa."

"Very good," Arno seemed more angry than pleased. "And where is Mr. Dobbs?"

"Got himself stomped to death by an elephant."

The knife pulled slowly and deep over Jack's knee.

A scream gargled in Jack's throat.

"I don't have time for jokes, Jack."

"IT'S TRUE! ASK BLADE! CHARLIE BLADE!!"

"Another name? Very good, Jack. I must say for a man knows nothing you are positively brimming with information."

A wail broke, strangled and ashamed. It was like a bird that Jack could not keep caged. He felt himself pissing in his pants.

"Go on," Arno sneered. "It won't make you feel better, but it'll be a treat for me."

Jack bawled openly. Desperate sobs of terror and shame.

Arno enjoyed himself a moment.

"All right, then," he said finally. "For the doggy in the window: Where is the cash? Where are the stock notes? They must be in the camp somewhere."

"…I don't know!"

Arno inspected the toes of Jack's feet.

"This little piggie went to market—"

"Look, I followed Luna to the Mirasol, all right? She meets somebody, I don't know who, but you can bet it's got something to do with Bladehorn's loot. She gave him an envelope; he took it. That's all I saw. That's all I know!"

"—this little piggy went home."

"NO!" Jack jerked like a puppet against the log, legs twitching impotently, trying to pull away, trying to wrench that massive pine from its roots!

"One joint at a time." Arno seemed happier. "Just to make sure you're not holding out on me."

Jack's scream began even before Arno leaned on his knife. An awful lamentation rose higher and higher again before it fell to a chorus of pleas for mercy or for death.

Would be easy in that racket to miss the far-off call of a calliope.

*   *   *

Luna gathered her posse in minutes and in minutes more was hurtling over the Tamiami Road, stripping gears as her truck careened around sharp curves and narrow shoulders. There was not a lot of moon to help the truck's dimwatted lamps. Adding to that was a hazard of gnats and night-time feeders splatting their innards on the windshield.

Luna knew better than to use the wipers.

Tommy was riding shotgun.

"Look sharp," she commanded.

"I'm looking!"

"He won't be on the highway."

"Must be a dozen feeders off this blacktop!" Tommy yelled. "A hundred!"

"Not hard roads," Luna rejoined. "Was a Packard, right? How far can you go in this sand in a Packard coupe?"

The hound howled from the bed of the truck. The Giant perched at the sideboards with the others. Boomer bayed again and Luna fishtailed the truck to a stop.

"Tryin' to wreck us?" Tommy gasped.

"Listen!"

Luna killed the engine. The radiator creaked. Insects buzzing. A gator coughed from some slough of water. And then a scream rose distantly, like a panther mating in the pines.

Boomer lunging against his leash.

"THERE'S A ROAD!" The Giant pointed from his vantage.

It was a county road, a feeder. Crushed rock.

"LET'S GO."

Luna fired the truck to life, spinning tires from the asphalt in a bolt for the limestone spur.

Jack got water, finally, real water splashing over his bloody head. He came to whimpering like a puppy. Shivering.

"Look at your foot, Pretty Boy," Arno commanded.

Bloody nubs of bone tapping the pine like a blind man's stick.

"And we got another foot to go."

Jack slobbering shamelessly.

Arno grunted.

"You really don't know where it is, do you, Jack? All this time and you still don't know."

"Ah…ah tried!" Jack wailed like a boy trying to please an angry father.

"'Tried' is a word for losers, Jack."

Arno jammed his knife into the sand. Worked it a moment.

"Hate those excuses, 'Tried and failed', 'Try and try again'. Y'see, I don't *try* anything, Jack. I either do something or I don't. Right now, for instance, I'm going to kill you."

Jack's trembling head might have been taken for a gesture of assent.

"You're going into shock, Jack," Arno frowned. "'Man doesn't handle stress well when he's in shock. Pity. 'Cuts' my pleasure short, if y'know what I mean. And who better?"

Jack heard the gurgle of a jug into a cup.

"Here y'are. Last drink."

Becker shoved the cup past his lips before Jack realized it was gasoline.

Arno laughing, now, winding a handkerchief onto a palmetto frond as Jack spewed fuel from his mouth.

"Heard you were a performer. Swallowing fire, is it? Flambé took a real interest, what I hear. Who says you can't teach an old queer new tricks?

"So how about you perform for me, Jack? Hah? Final act of the show, I promise."

"Nnnno! PLEASE!"

Arno scratched a match under the fuming rags.

"You were in the war, weren't you, Jack? Saw lots of lungs burned out, I 'magine. Not exactly the same, in fairness."

"Arno! No!"

Becker kneaded his torchless hand deeply into Jack's well-tended hair.

"I'm gonna make you real pretty, Jack. Talk about a freak? You'll fit right in."

Becker shoving the torch into Jack's face.

"Open up."

"Mmmmp!" Jack turned away.

"Blow me, Jack."

Here came the torch. Jack could see it coming, could feel the fumes of gasoline raw in his mouth, his throat!

Constant pressure, that's what Flambé had told him. Always exhaling—always! But Jack was spent, lapsing into shock. How much reserve could there be in his overtaxed lungs?

There was no moisture to protect his nose, his lips. But he couldn't keep his mouth closed forever! Jack could feel the fumes working down the canal to his lungs. An irresistible urge, then, to cough, to sneeze!

Becker jammed the torch into his face—

"BLOW, JACK."

And Jack blew. He blew his lungs. He blew his guts. He blew out his socks and in the end he lunged a torch of fire a yard long into the evening air and just when he was about to fall into the dark forever....

Arno Becker jerked the torch away.

Jack heaving air into his lungs like gravel through a sieve. His face blistered, burned.

"Not bad, Pretty Boy," Becker sneered as he poured another tin of fuel into the cup.

"Now let's see you do her again."

Jack knew he couldn't do it again. There was nothing left to offer. Nothing to give.

"Sucking wind pretty bad, Jack."

Becker was pouring gasoline onto a fresh set of rags, but a rough-running engine interrupted.

"The fuck," Arno turned, irritated.

You could hear the lumber of the Big Truck barreling down the lane. Headlamps cutting like a scythe across the tops of the pines.

"I may just have to cut this short," Becker sighed and dropped the rags and gas for his knife.

Becker kneeled smiling beside Jack.

"Maybe I'll just take the whole head."

Jack thrashed wildly as Becker pried to open a seam in the rope that collared his neck. A sliver of moonlight running down the blade of Becker's knife like a falling tear.

"You...stupid...fucking...Kraut."

"What?" Becker hesitated, the foreign headlights sweeping closer. "What was that?"

"I...know...where it is."

Jack slurring his words through the seared flesh hanging from his face like jowls.

"The money...the stocks...I know."

"You're lying."

The blade cold now on the skin of Jack's neck.

"You're lying," Becker repeated coldly. "You're just trying to stay alive."

"Kill me, then," Jack wiggled what was left of his toes, "and you'll never know."

The truck burst around the corner leading to their clearing, the headlamps framing Jack and his butcher in a grisly tableau.

A shotgun boomed. A small delay and pellets sprinkled through the pines like the first timid messengers of rain.

Arno smiling with his knife.

"Know what this means, dontcha, Jack? Means we get another dance. Once more around the floor, except next time there won't be an orchestra to bother us, I guarantee. Next time it'll just be you and me."

He slashed the blade down savagely. Something like a brand seared Jack's face.

"See if she'll have you now, Jack," Arno hissed.

Another blast from the shotgun shattered the Packard's rear window, but Becker seemed in no hurry on his way to the car. No rush apparent as he nursed the choke and ignition. Took a couple of tries but then the coupe's heavy cylinders roared to life, the tires spinning cochina and sand into Jack's mutilated face. Becker roaring onto the narrow feeder and head-on at Luna's big Ford.

She saw him coming.

"HOLD ON!"

The steering wheel jumped in Luna's hand with every warp and rut in the rocky straightaway. Everybody in the truck bed hanging on for dear life. Was pitch black and now she had Becker's lights in her face, the beam from those carbon lamps shattered on the guts of insects. But she couldn't let him go. Could *not* let this son of a bitch get away!

The truck swerved sideways; Luna hauled it back.

"He ain't backin' off!"

Tommy Speck cursing as he tried to reload. The lamps from the Packard blinding the road.

"HE AIN'T PLAYIN' CHICKEN, LUNA."

"GODAMMIT!"

Luna yanked the wheel, the truck swerved.

Becker slid by grinning like a gargoyle.

Moments later Luna was sprinting through the palmetto heedless of the briars tearing her skirt and skin.

"JACK—JACK—?!! Oh, God."

The thing before her slumped in a roped collar, arms roped to a cruel tray, legs paddocked. Blood dripped fresh from a face blistered and burned and split cheek to cheek. Flesh hanging loose with snot from the shattered nose. A foot at first glance looked amputated.

"Oh, God, Jack!"

He had to work his mouth like a baby to make sounds that Luna at first could not clearly discern—

"Izzy…Izzy gone?"

Jack awoke in daylight beneath the uncanopied tester of a four-poster bed. It didn't seem like a carney's bed. Too comfortable. Jack looked down toward his feet and saw a foot propped on a crate and dressed professionally.

His face was stiff.

"Jack?"

Luna pressed his uninjured hand into her own.

"Where...? Ouch!"

The stitches on his face limiting his speech.

"Where am I?"

"My apartment. Above the café."

He tried to remember where that was.

"Water?" he articulated carefully and she poured him a glass from a pitcher at the window.

The water was ice cold.

"Use the straw," she advised and when he did skin peeled from inside his mouth in ribbons.

"It's all right, Jack." Doc Snyder floated into view like an extra entering a camera's frame. "You have some burns, but they will heal. They will."

There was something Jack meant to ask. But he could not remember what it was.

Doc inspected his face.

"Not too bad, considering," the doc offered that assessment cheerfully. "Be some scarring, of course. Complicated the stitching, but we managed."

The doc straightened up to finish his report.

"No fluid in the lungs, which is a miracle. As for the rest—I don't think you'll be stealing bases, but then, you never planned a career in baseball, did you, Jack?"

Jack swallowed his water carefully. "How did you find me?"

"Got Tommy to thank for that," Luna answered. "He saw the bastard hauling you off."

She took his glass and pulled a chair to the side of his bed.

"Who did this to you, Jack?"

"Name's Becker," Jack swallowed painfully. "Sapped me from behind."

"But why, Jack? Why would he want to do something like this to you?"

"Not now," Doc was fitting a syringe into a vial of what Jack knew was morphine.

"This should take the edge off," Snyder assured his patient.

"Who gess the bill?" Jack tried to form a smile.

"My treat," Luna said.

Her breasts settled on the bare skin of his chest, firm behind a flimsy corset of cotton. She kissed him. It was a real kiss, right on the mouth. Not off to the side. Not some peck around the barn. Right there on what was left of his smackers.

"Here we go," Doc palpitating a vein.

A swab of alcohol cool on the skin. A little sting.

Luna rising blue as a midnight moon.

"'Night, Jack."

He woke late that night, disoriented and confused in Luna's wide, soft bed. The foot reminded him.

"Damnation—!"

Jack took a minute to orient himself. Luna had left a light on at the stand beside his bed, which helped. A welcome Gulf breeze whistled through the window half-raised alongside. Must be some weather coming. Jack's lips were cracked like peapods. He saw the pitcher iced and sweating at the window. A glass ready to hand.

"Room service?" Jack joked weakly but there was no one to hear.

He saw a bell near to hand on the bed stand. Grunted to reach it.

"Doc?"

He felt ridiculous ringing the bell, but there was no answer to that summons. He tried again.

"All right, then."

He tried to follow his good foot off the bed with the wounded one and damn near fainted.

"JESUS!"

Blood rushing to his severed toes

"Could use another shot," Jack croaked to no reply.

Where was a fucking corpsman when you needed one?

A pair of crutches propped handily at a bed stand. Jack grabbed those props, hauling himself toward the window and the waiting pitcher of water and caught himself in the mirror of Luna's vanity.

Some man or piece of man stared back from that mercury pane. An unfamiliar face, split like a gourd. The nose was swollen and broken, and the face—! A gash running from cheek to cheek was sewn like the seams on a baseball. His gumline was exposed from the pull of the stitches, pink and naked to the roots of his teeth.

Jack raised his hand trembling to test lips unnaturally parted. He tried to smile. Doc had done his best, but this was no marquee effort. No face for the movies, for sure, unless it was next to Lon Chaney's.

A murmur of conversation drifted through the window from the sandy street below. Someone talking. Jack turned from the mirror to switch off the lamp by his bed. Every beat of his heart sending a fresh throb of pain into his foot as he hobbled to the window's sill.

You could see the roof of the Western Union office across the way, the creosote pole outside silhouetted like a crucifix. The wire swaying in a mounting breeze that corrupted the conversation coming in snatches from the street.

Voices outside. Directly below the window. Jack placed his head warily on the board of the sill. Risked a peek—

Luna Chevreaux stood just outside her door in hushed conversation with some other person out of Jack's sight. Luna had donned a jacket and trousers against the breeze now gusting strongly enough to lift her hair. Then Jack saw a leather bag extended in a gloved hand.

Luna took the bag and her contact stepped from the cover of shadows into the moon's unclouded light. A man by his movement. Average height and build. Baggy, lightweight slacks that looked familiar and a jacket that could have belonged to a gypsy. No vest. Shirt open at the collar. Jack could not see a face; his perch had him looking almost straight down at the fella's hat. It was a boater, flat-brimmed and made of straw, with what looked like an orchid stuck inside the band.

The meeting was clearly over. Luna took the bag and the boater's wearer melted into the dark like a fucking magician. Jack pulled back from the windowsill but waited until he heard Luna's feet treading up the stairs before hobbling back to his sickbed and a feigned slumber.

He heard Luna pad into the room. Heard her pause at the foot of his bed before moving to the window. She poured a glass of water from the pitcher. He could hear the ice swirling.

Was there just a hesitation as she sipped?

A little hitch?

She took the pitcher with her when she left. The door closed finally and Jack stared into his pillow. How many midnight meetings had taken place in Luna's apartment since he had come to Kaleidoscope? How many trysts in hotels? Jack would love to be a fly on the satchel delivered to Luna's hands, but for some reason it was the man's hat that nagged him.

Something about that headpiece—the hell was it?

It was an ordinary lid, a narrow-brimmed cylinder with a wide band. Perfect for the dog days of summer; the straw let the breeze through nicely. They were called boaters, as if you had to own a yacht to wear one. And then Jack remembered Cincinnati and the Milner Hotel—the man who delivered Sally Price's cash and train ticket had been wearing a boater. The bellhop hadn't called it a boater, of course, but the description fit, along with the loud jacket, the cheap shirt and rooster-sock slacks. But the clincher was the ostentatious boutonniere; not many jakes stuck orchids in their hats.

Especially not a man hiding from sight.

The more Jack thought about it, the more convinced he became that Luna's bagman was Alex Goodman's proxy, the emissary between Kaleidoscope and Sally Price. But whatever the proxy's role, Jack was willing to bet that Luna called the shots. Jack was now convinced that Luna Chevreaux was holding Bladehorn's stolen property, even if she had not been involved in its theft. Would take a lot of mattresses to hide that much moolah; Jack could see how Terrence Dobbs' legal expertise would be useful. Maybe the bagman had taken over his role. Maybe in more ways than one he was Luna's latest greaser.

A light rap of knuckles and Jack turned to see a white-coated gent at the door.

"You should be asleep."

Doc Snyder frowning disapproval.

"I couldn't sleep," Jack prevaricated.

"May as well see to your dressing, then."

The physician settled down to slowly and methodically remove the bloodstained rags binding Jack's foot.

"Got a touch there, Doc."

"That's the morphine talking."

"Where'd you get your training? The war?"

"No, no. Tulane."

"I was a corpsman, did I tell ya?"

"Yes, Jack," Doc taped off the dressing. The smell of fresh bandages and disinfectant. "Now cut the yakking and get some rest."

Doc switched off the bedstand's lamp as he left the room, but Jack did not sleep. He knew he was close to finding Bladehorn's property, very close.

But so was Arno Becker.

HighWire's deep slumber was broken when a small tremor interrupted a recurring dream. The telegrapher had been transported in sleep to Milwaukee. A beautiful spring day. His wife and daughter smiled below, artificial smiles, for the rubes, as the young and athletic performer stretched his toes to grip the wire spanning from his platform high above the deck of a barge to a tower raised on the shore.

There were thousands of people gathered at the lake to watch, a terrific crowd. But the wind was a problem. The wind was rocking the water, the water was rocking the boat, and HighWire could feel a harmonic developing, that dangerous rhythmic undulation so feared by men on the wire. He pumped the wire gently, just a small jump to damp the growing threat, compensating for balance with his longpole, but it was not enough.

The cable was oscillating, undulating in collusion with the wind and the water and HighWire was not yet cleared of the barge. The wire swayed, swayed—! The pole lurched and HighWire felt himself—

"…Wake up, HighWire. Wake up, old timer."

The disabled performer was roused from sleep to find a Frankenstein shaking his cot.

"What the hell?!"

HighWire scrambled for his glasses to find a face stitched northeast to southwest with catgut. Incisors bared like a mad dog. A foot swathed and seeping blood.

"Jesus Christ, Jack, is that you?"

"I got to send a wire," Jack leaned over on his crutches. "Tulane Medical School."

"The hell are you doing up at this hour?"

"Can you send the wire?"

"Could send it just as well in the morning."

"I need it now. I don't want anybody knowing I sent it. And I'll need the reply as soon as it comes through."

The old man nodded. "Should I have Tommy run it for you?"

"No," Jack declined. "Just you and me."

It took a week before Jack got his cabled reply. It was a week of dissembling, at least on Jack's part. Luna fussed over him daily, bringing a meal or changing a dressing. He had swapped the crutches for a cane, but she would not let him negotiate the stairs by himself.

He saw Luna every day. Her smell brought an erection. Her skin, that sheath that used to repel him, was now provocative, erotic. He wanted to slide his belly and legs against hers. He wanted to run his tongue into her, over her. He wanted to feel her legs crush him with her climax.

But what woman would sleep with a Frankenstein?

Luna answered that question. She was shaving him. His first shave, a night-time shear. The bedroom's mirror let Jack watch as Luna worked between the fences of his surgeon's handiwork.

"I look like a monster," he proclaimed bitterly.

Luna never interrupted the patient stroke of her razor.

"You've got a lot to learn, Jack."

"Whadda you mean?" Jack's reply sounded paranoid even to himself.

She paused. "How long ago did your wife die, Jack?"

The question took him by surprise.

"Four...five years, I guess."

"How were things between you two?"

"Don't see the point of that question."

"Well, did you screw around, Jack? A little liver with the steak?"

"Go to hell."

"Did you?"

"No, I didn't even think about it."

"That's good," Luna wiped the cream off her blade with a towel. "That kind of loyalty—you don't see it often."

"No. You don't."

"Except with carnies," Luna amended. "That's where you keep striking out, Jack. You keep figuring the odds. Working the angles. But you really don't know what sets a carney's life apart from any other. You don't yet know what makes carnies different from bankers or doctors. Or thieves."

"I suppose you do?"

"Sure," she folded the straightblade. "It came clear to me in one crystal moment. I was still in my teens, had literally run away from home for the circus. Got lucky when I ran into one of the finest gentlemen on any midway. That would be Mr. Clarence Wortham. This was, what—? Nineteen fourteen. He gave me the billing, 'Luna The Moon Maiden'. So here I am with my first gig on my first run, first time on a train for that matter, and we go and have a wreck.

"Every carney knows about the Wortham Wreck. Forty-one boxcars derailed. Everything was either ruined or destroyed. I mean clothes and costumes, props and trailers—the animals. Terrible scene, putting down the elephants and such. Not to mention the sight of mangled human bodies.

"Was enough to make anybody give up the show, but not The Little Giant, no, sir; Mr. Wortham, he wouldn't have any of us followin' the banner. Said if we wanted out, he'd let us go, but if we wanted to rebuild he'd back whatever loan was necessary to get us back on sawdust.

"Most of us stayed. Mr. Wortham set me up with a pair of clowns. Mike and Milly, they were. Had themselves a carney wedding, which is to say no wedding at all, but I never saw two more devoted people in my life.

"He juggled on stilts. She worked the benches. They'd do three shows a day and still take time to teach me to juggle."

Luna scooped three oranges from the bed stand and within seconds the sweet-nectared balls were chasing each other in complicated variations that seemed to defy gravity.

She let the fruit drop with a synchronized plop to the sheets.

"Mike was strong as an ox but Milly was frail. Something with her lungs, everybody knew, but she wouldn't quit. Wouldn't let Mike quit, either. So next thing you know we're on a gilly to Toledo, opening for the rubes on a Thursday night. Mike's in the pit keeping his firesticks and balls and fake anvils in the air. Milly's playin' the straight. Gettin' bellies from the marks. It was pretty hard work and I can remember at one point I told Mr. Wortham, I said, 'Looks like Milly's slowing down.'

"Well, she wasn't slowing down, she was dying. She took a couple of staggering steps just after Mike got his fourth live torch in rotation and then she collapses right there in the pit. Right in front of everybody.

"Mike drops off his stilts and before you can say Jack Johnson he's got her in his arms. She's not moving. He's talkin' to her but she's not saying anything. So there you are. Man and wife. Mike and Milly in greasepaint and clown face. You could just hear the crowd suck in their breath—'What's wrong?' the marks are thinking.

"'Or *is* anything wrong? Is it just part of the act?!' You can just about hear 'em. So how would you play the rubes, Jack? If it was your wife in the ring, what would you do?"

She did not wait for his reply.

"Mike just puts on his funniest frown, picks Millie up and carries her for the curtains, but before he gets there—and I could see tears streaking his paint—he turns back to the stands and gives 'em a big-ass glowing smile and with Milly's hand waves 'em a goodbye.

"Just as if there wasn't nothin' wrong in the world. Just so the rubes'll think it's part of the act."

Luna collected the oranges and returned them to the bowl.

"Only a carney can understand the kind of love it takes to do that, the loyalty. Y'see, Jack, a carney, a real carney, always knows the real thing when he sees it."

She placed his shaving razor beside the oranges. The moon pouring through the flimsy curtains that barred the window.

"Lie back."

She straddled him in bed, shedding her blouse in one smooth pull over her head. The hair tumbling down black as onyx over that marvelous lunar skin.

A valley running down the middle of her abdomen. Her breasts gleaming dark in the peach moon. She reached gently for the buttons on his shirt.

Jack stopped her.

"Not yet."

If she was offended or hurt or even puzzled she did not show it. She did not insist. She did not demand an explanation, for which Jack was grateful.

He was unsure what was real and what was not in this crazy, kaleidoscope world. And even if Jack could believe that Luna was able to see past the blisters and stitches scouring his face there was another fear, deeper, even more unsettling—

Jack knew that Luna could not trust him.

How could he trust her?

Their lovemaking, the tender care—was it the real thing? Or were Luna's attentions no more than an act, a con, a hustle? Jack could not erase the exchange he had witnessed on the street below the apartment—were those honest earnings in that leather bag or a dip from Bladehorn's bucket? There were too many secrets to trust, bags handed over in the dead of night, rendezvous in dark streets and bright luxury hotels. And she could be ruthless; Charlie Blade was proof of that.

Jack wanted Luna. He wanted to have the totally abandoned frenzy he had already experienced in those strong arms. once again or a hundred times or forever He wanted to feel her legs locked in a vice around his hips. But before Jack could have that, he had to trust her. He needed one additional piece of the puzzle filled in.

Within the week that piece fell into place.

It was the reply to Jack's late-night telegram. He paid for the wire, scanned its contents, and then crossed the street to Luna's place. A mid-morning sun filled the café with an autumnal light. The other carnies were through with breakfast and dispersed to the midway in prep for their Saturday show. Luna looked up from her coffee to see Jack negotiating the back door on a cane.

"Moving around pretty well, there."

"Gotta get back to work sometime." He offered a smile.

"Coffee?" She was already pouring a cup.

"Thanks," as he spooned in some sugar.

"I notice you got your things packed upstairs," she took a stool. "There's no hurry, you know. You can take your time."

"Thanks, but I need to get back in the swing."

She nodded. "Be good to see you back."

"'Course, there are a couple things I'd like to clear up first."

"Clear what? What do you mean?"

Jack turned to face her squarely.

"It means for one thing that I know who Alex Goodman really is. That's 'is', by the way, not 'was'."

"Do tell."

"Did you know Doctor Snyder came here from Louisiana?" Jack spread his telegram on the counter. "See I know 'cause he told me so himself."

"Louisiana, yes," she kept a blank face. "So?"

"So I ran a check on his schooling. Sure enough, there's Doc at Tulane Medical School, graduating with his M.D. in 1915."

"I'd have been happy to tell you that myself, Jack."

"But you haven't told me his name, have you, Luna? Not his full name."

"What's in a name?" she quipped.

"A riddle," he replied, and read from the telegram, "'Doctor Alexander Bonham Snyder'. Now, you speak a little French, don't you Miz Chevreaux? *N'est ce pas?* So you probably realize that 'Bonham', a fine, Southern name, can be traced to the French *bon homme*, isn't that right?

"*Bon homme* can mean lots of things but one way to translate it, for sure, is literally, which would make *bon homme* a ringer for 'good man'. Not far from there, is it, to get Alexander 'Good Man'? Or why not Alex Goodman?"

"Must be something in your java, Jack."

"I saw him give you his bag, Luna. The man in the straw hat, that was Doc, wasn't it? And that was his medical bag. So what's in the satchel, Madame Chevreaux? Was it cash? Was it certificates of stock? Little of both, maybe?"

"You're treeing the wrong coon, Jack."

"But not the wrong carney."

"You sure of that?"

"I've know for a while that somebody's picking up the tab for a lot of bad debt in this beddy. I know a lot more goes back and forth to Tampa than timber and The Fat Lady. I saw you at the Mirasol."

"And what about you, Jack?" she retorted coldly. "What brought you down from the Midwest to snoop? Who are you really working for up there?"

"The hell should I trust you with that information?" he growled.

"TRUST?! You have the nerve to talk to me about *trust*? You've lied to me ever since you got down here! Telling us you met Alex over drinks! Just a whim got you on the train? 'Starting over'? My ass."

"You take property belongs to somebody else, Luna, they ain't obliged to play straight getting it back."

"Ah. But whose property is it, Jack? Who owned it in the first place?"

"You tell me."

She shook her head. "I can't, Jack. I won't."

Jack caught his reflection in the polished brass of the coffee pot. A distorted image, misshapen.

A freak.

"Look," Jack took a deep breath. "The man sent me down here, he's got my family, awright? My mother-in-law. My boy."

She regarded him a long moment. "The man who cut you. Is he after the same thing you are?"

"Yes."

"You can't get in his way."

"You think I want to? If it wasn't for my family I wouldn't even be down here!"

"Then go get your family. Get them as far away from Bladehorn as you can."

"So…" he pulled up. "You do know about Bladehorn. That about tells the story, doesn't it?"

"Half the story, Jack, and believe me half of this story is more a lie than anything you can imagine."

"So tell me the other half."

"I can't."

"Won't."

"Can't. You're not the only one with family to protect."

Jack shifted his weight. "Then just give me some of the loot. Something I can take back to Cincinnati. Give me the cash, if there's any left. Or the railroad notes—surely you haven't run through a quarter million in stocks! Give me whatever's left, *half* of what's left, and I'll tell Bladehorn the rest is gone, spent. He'll never know!"

She pulled a handful of bills from her blouse.

"This should take you pretty far."

"Not far enough."

"I'm sorry," her eyes were wet. "It's all I can do."

Chapter thirteen

Chilling the Mark—*getting rid of a customer before he becomes a problem.*

Arno Becker hummed as he held the spoon over the candle, watching the concoction bubble as wax dripped carelessly onto the hood of the sturdy Packard.

"Soup's on."

Charlie Blade shivered on the fenderwell of Becker's coupe, his eyes gaunt tunnels in a face stretched tight as cowhide.

"Gimme!" The syringe in the knife-thrower's hand had been ready for minutes.

"You must learn to delay gratification, Charlie," Arno chided. "Pleasures taken too quickly leave one unfulfilled. Sex, for instance. You want to delay the climax as long as possible. Make them beg. Same thing for murder. Or sex and murder—there's a term for that combination escapes me at present."

"God damn it, I gotchu what you want!"

"The cash and bonds? Really? Then kindly place them in the car."

"You know I can't do that."

"And you know the deal." Arno moved the spoon off its tapered cooker.

"Don't do that!" Charlie begged.

Arno smiled. "There's plenty more, Charlie. Quality, too, excellent product which you may see for yourself *if* you give me something I can actually fucking use."

"I followed Luna to the Mirasol," Blade gave it up in a gush.

"I know about the Mirasol. And Luna. Jack Romaine was happy to provide that information."

"Yeah, I saw Jack. But did he tell you about Doc Snyder?"

"The doctor?"

"Doc got to the hotel ahead of Luna. I was surprised, see, 'cause I heard Doc sayin' at the café he was goin' into town to stock up the infirmary. I tailed him, hopin' I could get a line on whatever pharmacy he was usin', someplace I might could get something for my habit, see—"

"You mean steal it."

"But anyway Doc, he didn't go into Tampa; he went out to the Island, to the hotel. He gets out of his car dressed like a goddamn fag, some kinda boater and corsage. Wasn't the first time, neither, I could tell 'cause the valets all knew him. Greeted him by name."

"Did you follow him inside?"

"Take a look at me—I couldn't get past the concierge. Romaine, now, he looks like a fucking movie star; he can get in anyplace."

Arno smiled. "Perhaps no longer."

Becker leaning over then to inspect the heroin cooking on the hood of his automobile.

"I believe we're ready, Charles."

Charlie lifting his syringe to the offered spoon.

"Don't spill," Arno said amused.

Charlie pulled the cloudy opiate from the bowl of the spoon into his hypo. Rolled up his sleeve. But then—

"Shit, I forgot my tourniquet!"

"Use your shirt," Arno advised.

Charlie laid the syringe beside its candle cooker with trembling hands, ripped off his shirt, tied off his arm.

"C'mon, baby!"

He thumped a vein with a filthy thumbnail; it swelled a distended pipe in an emaciated arm. He snatched the syringe off the hood.

"You ain't gonna regret this," he babbled to Becker. "I can get you more!"

"We'll see."

The up-and-comer sucking in deeply with the first, full penetration.

"Yeah…Yeah, *man*—!"

Charlie Blade pushed the plunger to the stop. A laugh of euphoria, or relief.

"Pretty good?" Arno inquired.

"Good?! Oh, daddy, this is the *best*…the best—"

"'S'matter, Charlie?"

Blade's head jerked back as though he were swallowing a broadsword. A croak gargled from deep inside his chest.

"Tell me, Charlie. I'd like to know what it's like."

"IT…! IT…!"

His head snaps down. His legs collapse. His hands claw the steel fender as Charlie Blade slides down the Packard's chrome grille to the sand. Arno leaned over to observe the needle still pulsing in the dead man's arm. Something like foam bubbling from that impervious throat.

"Was good though, wasn't it, Charlie? Best you ever had."

Once in a blue moon would a blue moon rise over the blue landscape of Luna Chevreaux's sleeping body. The Moon Maiden never wore clothes to bed. A dulcet breeze through the window encouraged naked, sensual slumber. Pleasant dreams. But a terrified clamor stirred Luna on her bed. An elephant's trumpet, repeated and panicked, calling like Gabriel's horn.

"What?"

Luna raised herself up on an arm to see a red glow flickering on her window like the reflected flames of some distant fireplace.

Jack Romaine saw it, too. He was tossing between dreams by the open window of his shack when the smell of smoke jerked him from sleep. Rising to see red tongues flickering above the pines.

"FIRE!"

Jack stumbling into the street on his cane.

"TOMMY! LUNA! FIIIIIIIRE!!"

A growing firestorm fed by the breeze and fueled by hay and timber and tar had already swept from the midway into the surrounding pine trees and tents and trailers. You could see the Ferris Wheel lit up like a giant, burning pinwheel. Jack broke into a painful hobble behind Tommy Speck and a score of other performers scrambling for buckets.

"THE ANIMALS!" Tommy shouted. "GET 'EM OUT!!"

The roar of tigers and the whine of horses now adding to the general panic. Flames billowing like sails on an awful wind as carnies scrambled to bring thimbles of water to the conflagration. Jack saw Penguin and Flambé brave a burning haystack to free the big cats from their cages. Lions and tigers turned out to meet the bears native to Florida lowlands, the cats' primal screams rising with the snap of resin and wood.

And then came the familiar trumpet, high and long, rising above the rest. Even in that din Jack recognized Ambassador's call and knew as well its source—

Peewee's tent.

"Oh, Jesus!"

He saw it right away, the Big Top sheeted in fire. A giant light for some giant moth.

"PEEWEE!" Jack forced himself to a run. "TOMMY, IT'S PEEWEE!!"

By the time Jack covered the fifty yards remaining between him and the Princess's tent a score of carnies had converged. The pavilion was combed in fire, sparks spiraling to heaven from its canvas roof, and worse, a separate fire raging inside.

"PEEWEEE!" The Giant bellowed. "PEEWEEE!!"

Peewee could not hear the calls from outside her tent. Nothing to hear above the fire's angry roar but the trumpet of an elephant going berserk. The Princess was trapped on three sides by a sheet of fire, only the tent's high wall saving her from suffocation, the smoke coiling black and noxious.

Peewee was screaming, sparks dancing like evil clowns on the tinder of her books, her bedsheets. There was one route to escape, but Peewee could not see it. A single, narrow section of canvas that had been soaked with Ambassador's afternoon bath was steaming but not yet afire. The rails which brought her meal cart led to that narrow exit. But even if Peewee had seen that escape, she could not take advantage. Any other woman would simply drop to the sawdust floor and follow the iron to freedom. Even a panicked woman or man might scramble on hands and knees from the bed's location to that steaming door. Either that or dive into the tank. Better to suffocate than to burn.

But Peewee could not crawl. She could not leave her bed unaided, anchored by six hundred and fifty pounds of unwieldy flesh to a linen box surrounded by tinder and tar and fire.

"AMBASSADOR!!" she screamed.

But her guardian paid no attention. He was a bull elephant filled with fear and blinded by smoke and the smell of death. The only voice speaking to the beast now was telling him to run! To flee!

Ambassador lunged in a rage against the chains and stobs that tied him to the ground. But then he used his tusks, lowering the massive head to pry beneath a length of that hated perimeter. Another gut-wrenching trumpet of fear and rage and then—

Peewee heard the chain break even if she could not see it.

"AMBASSADOR—!"

But the only thing speaking to Ambassador was the call to survive. Jack saw the bull come charging from the tent in a boil of smoke, dragging half a ton of chain like straw. Carnies scattering like quail before that mad rogue.

Jack whirling to find someone, anyone!

"GIANT."

The black man lumbered up, an axe loose in his hand.

"PEEWEE. WE GOTTA TRY."

The Giant visored his eyes with a raised hand.

"How we gonna move her?"

"*You* move her!"

The huge black man shook his head.

"Cain't. Hell, I couldn' drag her out."

"Wait a minute," Jack stumbled to the railway. "Wait a minute, what about the feeding cart? The cart, Giant! THERE!"

Peewee's meal cart was chocked in plain sight on the narrow rails and within seconds Jack and The Giant had their shoulders to the wheel. They had to get the cart inside. There was carnage all around, performers and workers scrambling in desperate efforts to save loved ones or belongings. Animals screaming at odd intervals. Some would not make it out of their cages.

Jack thought of the trenches, during a shelling. Or the machine-guns, whistles and spades and bayonets. Men screaming. How the hoot of gas or the crash of artillery numbed you, kept you from doing what needed to be done. He had to remind himself that there were no shells here. No machine guns. No barbed wire. But the smell of death was the same, that acrid aroma of fire and smoke and men pissing in their pants.

The heat from Peewee's tent hit them like a blast furnace. The rails picking up heat as they disappeared into the interior.

"KEEP IT UP!" Jack and The Giant were running, now, accelerating the iron cart like a ram aimed at a medieval keep. Faster—Faster! Jack latched on with both arms, kicking back with the heel of his good foot. Kicking hard!

They rode the cart through the break in Peewee's tent and into a theater of flame. Nothing to see but black, black smoke and then—

BAM! The cart slammed squarely into the side of Peewee's bed.

"PEEWEE!!" Jack called out.

"He...help!" she answered listlessly.

Her ragdoll nearly invisible in that valley of breast.

"GET ON THE CART, PRINCESS!"

"I...I can't."

"Yes, you can! Giant, help me."

The black man was already reaching beneath Peewee's shoulders.

"Awright, Peewee, you need to help us. Just roll over to the cart. Got it? Just roll over, baby, and we'll do the rest."

Her whimpered reply lost in the firestorm.

"ONE, TWO, HEAVE!"

Jack straining with the giant carney to roll more than six hundred frightened pounds onto the cart.

She barely budged.

The tent's center pole cracking ominously. Like a mast in a storm.

"Oh, GOD!" Peewee pulled a pillow over her face and Jack snatched it away.

"NO!"

He was choking himself as he leapt onto her bed and took her terrified face into his hands.

"LISTEN TO ME PRINCESS! I am *not* going to die in this place because *you* give up, you hear me? You *can do* this, Princess. Just rock with me, honey."

"Rock a bye?" she asked in refrain.

"Rock when we push, Princess. Back and forth! Hard as you can, baby!"

"I'll try."

"NO," and Jack slapped her hard across the face. "Trying's for losers! There's no trying, here, Peewee. Now GET READY. GIANT—?"

"READY, BOSS."

"ONE—TWO—!"

Peewee moving, now, back and forth, once...twice...

"NOW."

They heeeeaved together. The Princess rolled to the edge of her bed, teetered. That's when Giant planted his paddle-sized boot on her butt and kicked Peewee onto the cart.

"WE'RE ON."

Jack threw a blanket over Peewee and was back to the cart, but now all four walls of the tent were wrapped in fire and, worse, a raging ring of flame inside closed to block any escape. There was no way out except through the blaze and the smoke was so thick Jack could barely see his hand. He dropped to his knees by the cart and found Giant.

"WE...WE TRAPPED?" the big man was near panic himself.

What could they do? Jack felt his back on the side of the water tank.

"THE TANK, GIANT!"

"TANK?"

"THE WATER TANK. USE YOUR AXE!"

The Giant snatched up his tool. Two strides took him to the recently repaired tank. His arms bulged like Hephaestus as he swung the head true along the seam. Sparks flying with that awful blow.

"Hurry!" Peewee wracked. "Hurry!"

The Giant ripped the head free and swung again. And again. A boy's pee of water sprang along the riveted zipper.

"KEEP IT UP!" Jack urged. "KEEP IT UP, YOU BIG SON OF A BITCH!"

Another stroke drew sparks, and another. A wrench of metal groaning, groaning, the black man swinging still in a spill of water.

"GET BACK, GIANT!"

The big man leaped aside and as he did a thousand gallons of water split the tank like a gourd.

"GRAB HOLD!" Jack threw himself onto the cart with Giant as a wall of water slapped into them.

A small tsunami carried them along the rails. Princess Peewee rode that wave, breaching hell on the top of her iron cart. Jack and The Giant hung on 'till the wave washed out, legs pumping, pumping like pistons until they were free and clear, free and clear.

Free and clear.

All night the carnies groped to contain the fire, those without arms or legs laboring beside their neighbors. By the time the sun rose over the sultry Alafia the only structure standing was Luna's café. The late October breeze shifted by midmorning to stir flames and raise ashes in dervishes from the scoria that remained. Stumps of lumber and tires smoked like smudgepots. Trailers and caravanserai slumped on their chassis in black heaps. Kaleidoscope's misshapen survivors scoured the terrain like alien beings on an alien planet.

A charnel house steamed all about, the smell of flesh—animals roasted in their cages. And not just animals, Jack learned.

"Not Flambé!"

The man who trained fire-swallowers and elephants for decades found dead in his bed.

Half Track rustled up a late breakfast for the survivors. The Giant squatted over a plate of biscuits and syrup implacable as any Oriental. Doc Snyder was there, tending the wounded. Tommy had been badly burned when he gripped the scalding bars on the tiger's cage; Doc was advising the dwarf's wife to keep Speck's wounds open to the air.

Every carney was looking after his neighbor in one way or another. Cassandra was cooing reassurance to Pinhead. A child found solace of sorts in Jo Jo's fur-lined arms. Everyone had lost something of value. Many performers were without clothes; Gregory Lagopolus huddled with his sons in blankets, his parasitic twin hanging from his chest in a towel.

Tommy Speck trundled up to toss what looked like a scorched-out kerosene can onto the heap already piled at the steps of the café.

"How many is that?" Half Track spit.

"Six, at least," Tommy answered. "Lit 'em all around the camp; it ain't no accident."

The porch coming alive with curses or prayers. Jack remained silent. What would the carnies do when they realized he was responsible for this awful visitation? Or did they know already?

He met Tommy's eye. The little man spit into the sand.

Well, then. That was that.

"Anybody tracking Ambassador?" Half Track spoke up. "Any idea where he would be?"

"Georgia, perhaps?" Jo Jo offered and the carnies smiled bitter smiles.

"Maybe Luna's looking for him," Half Track spoke up. "I ain't seen Luna, any of yous?"

"Luna—?"

Jack's legs pushed him up from the porch as if they had a mind of their own. He scanned the porch.

"Has anybody seen Luna? Anyone?"

"Fighting the fire, wasn't she?" Cassandra asked.

"Did you actually see her?" Jack pressed. "Did anybody see her?"

No reply.

Half Track shifted for the café door.

"Maybe we should check."

Jack burst with a half-dozen fellow misfits into the stairway leading to Luna's upstairs apartment to find a neighbor noosed at the neck. But it was not Luna. What they saw was a man stripped of his shirt, his tongue thrust obscenely forward and purple with recent coagulation. A rope twisted cruelly around the neck. Slung from a beam near the ceiling.

"SLATE!"

Jack stood in shock with everyone else below the corpse of The Human Blackboard. It was Slate's gift that had doomed him; the hanging torso displaying a text freshly scratched into the performer's famously erasable skin:

…Finder's Keepers…

That cruel taunt raised in large, ugly welts.

But where was Luna?

"LUNA!" Jack stumbled past Slate to Luna's door and his heart stopped.

The door that secured Luna's upstairs rooms hung cockeyed on a single hinge, its mortise lock splintered and useless. Jack already knew what to expect when he stumbled inside. The place was ransacked, shattered mirrors leaving shards on the floor, tables overturned. The upholstery had been ripped from the parlor's chairs.

"My God!" Cassandra whispered from the landing.

"LUNA!" Jack called again as he hobbled to her bedroom.

Everything was spilled to the floor, her chest of drawers, her clothes and underthings. The mattress ripped to shreds.

"LUNA!?"

"She's not here, Jack," Tommy said quietly.

"Oh, shit. Oh, shit, Jesus!"

Jack reaching for a wall to lean on.

"Look here." It was the twins, Marcel & Jacques, who spotted the unsealed envelope propped atop her vanity.

The twins' hands shook like maple leaves as they cooperated to open the note.

"Read it," Tommy directed. "Go on."

"I have your moonpie held by the river. You remember the place, Jack. Bring the money and notes and come alone. Otherwise your Amazon will be missing more than her toes."

"We have to get her back." This from Doc Snyder.

"We *got* to," Half Track echoed and that refrain rippled through the room and out to the stairs.

"We gotta get Luna back."

Jack pushed himself off the wall.

"All right, then. But if this is gonna work I gotta come clean with you people. And you gotta be straight with me."

No reply at first from the freaks. Until Tommy Speck spoke up bluntly.

"The fuck should we trust you, Jack?"

"Becker was on the trail for your stash way before I got cornered into the job. Not sayin' that makes me less responsible."

"Sure as hell doesn't."

Jack paused. "Tell you what, should we get Slate down from that noose, first? Then I'll tell you everything I know."

The Giant lowered Slate from his hanging tree and carried him downstairs. The message "Finders Keepers" was still clearly visible. They laid him out on a table. Cassandra covered the amazing human slate with a sheet and then they all convened in the chowhouse.

Where Jack for the first time in his life played his cards straight.

"I'm under a gangster's thumb, fella name of Oliver Bladehorn, up in Cincinnati. Bladehorn sent me down here looking for property he claims was stolen from him. We're talking about a sizable chunk of cash and a quarter million in railroad certificates. But I ain't the only one looking for the loot.

"The man who torched your town, hung Slate, and snatched Luna is a cold-blooded killer name of Arno Becker. Becker's been after the loot for a while; he followed me down here. He knows, and I know, and most of you people know that Luna's got control of Bladehorn's property. Now, if I don't fetch the goods and turn it over to Arno, he will kill Luna, no doubt. And he'll enjoy himself while he's about it."

The carnies taking that declaration still as so many stones.

"It's down to the wire," Jack went on quietly. "A straight swap is what he's offering—cash and stocks for Luna. But I can't make the swap until somebody turns over the stash. Now, I know somebody down here was in on this from the beginning. Somebody or bodies from Kaleidoscope had a connection with Jerry Driggers and Sally Price and copped themselves a fortune off Bladehorn's old lady."

Jack turned to Doc Snyder.

"Was it you, Doc? Aren't you Alex Goodman? Aren't you the man in the straw hat?"

Snyder affirmed with a nod.

"But I'm not the man controls the property," he said.

"No? Then who is?"

For a long moment no one offered anything at all. It was Tommy Speck, finally, who spoke up.

"Ask Peewee," he said.

A pair of hay bales and a blanket were all that was left of the Princess's palace. A bald cypress provided her only shade. Peewee hugging her ragged doll to a thin, cotton shift, her eyes wide and vacant. Humming some lullaby, Jack couldn't make it out.

"Princess," he knelt beside her. "Princess, we gotta talk."

No response.

"Luna's in trouble, Princess. It's about the money. Do you know where the money is?"

Peewee shifting her marbled eyes inside that wide skull to stare straight into Jack's.

"You know where it is, Peewee?"

"Sure I do," she said. "I'm the one who stole it."

The ground came up to meet Jack's ass.

"YOU?"

"Me," she sighed. "See I am, I was—Oliver Bladehorn's little boy."

"His—?!"

"His son," Peewee nodded. "*Was* his son, anyway, though there was always some difference of opinion on that point. On my birth certificate you'd see a name, all right: Oliver Peter Bladehorn, but if you checked my sex you'd see where the doctor scrawled 'Undetermined'.

"I was a hermaphrodite, Mr. Romaine. Male and female organs from birth, a *real* freak."

"And your father…he was embarrassed?"

"No."

She managed a chicory smile.

"He was disgusted."

"…I'll be damned," was all Jack could find to say.

Princess Peewee fluffed her cotton shift about her enormous thighs. "First thing Daddy did was to rewrite my birth certificate: Sex, Male. They started giving me shots, but it didn't produce, shall we say, the desired effect.

"I developed horrible problems. He used that as an excuse to put me away. A sanatorium. I was fifteen."

Jack tried to imagine that predicament, a double-sexed adolescent sentenced to a house for lunatics.

"The doctors performed some 'procedures' while I was there," Peewee pawed at her eye with a pie-sized hand. "Things they would *never* do in a normal hospital! It left me with one sex, not the one Daddy wanted, but it also started me gaining weight. By the time

Mother broke me out of that hellish place I weighed nearly five hundred pounds."

Jack tried to imagine that scene. An ambulance backing up to a loading dock. A crew of men with, what—? A cart? A gurney? What would they have used to offload their quarter-ton contraband?

"Mother had her chauffeur bribe a guard at the hospital to get me out. Then Jerry Driggers and Sally Price drove me to the train station and loaded me into a boxcar for New York. Mother was waiting. She had booked passage for two to France and included my name with hers on the manifest. The idea was to make Dad think that I was on the boat with Mother, but in fact I never boarded Mother's ship. Instead, Jerry was supposed to wait for a week and then put me on a freighter for London. The plan was for Mother to resettle with me in England, but only when she was sure we were out of Daddy's reach.

"The last time I saw my mother was in New York. She told me she loved me. And she wanted me to know she had a will. Mother had her own estate, you see."

Jack nodded. "Your dad said he married for her money."

Peewee sighed. "Was a sizeable estate before he squandered it. But there was some cash and railroad stocks that she managed to hide. Was to be our nest egg. To start over. But then Mother's ship went down in the North Atlantic and I knew if I tried to claim my inheritance, Father would declare me incompetent, put me back in the sanatorium and take everything for himself.

"So what'd you do?"

She shrugged. "Far as Daddy knew I was drowned at sea with my mother. So I let him believe I was dead and paid Jerry Driggers a pretty penny to bring me my cash and bonds."

"So that's how Jerry got involved."

"Wasn't hard. Mother told me the safe was under her bed. Beneath a really nice Persian. And she made sure I wouldn't forget the combination: One-Eight-Nine."

She smiled.

"January eighth, 1909. My birthday. I gave Jerry most of the cash, took the money that was left and all the stocks and came down here. To Kaleidoscope."

"How'd you hear about Kaleidoscope?"

"The sanatorium. The Elephant Man."

"Elephant Man?"

"Not the original, just an inmate with elephantiasis. Did a forty-miler in New Jersey before he got sick. He was talking about this place where no matter how different you were, you'd fit right in. It was in the middle of nowhere, he said. Good people in Kaleidoscope, he said."

"I'd say he was right," Jack agreed.

"When Luna took me in she didn't know I had a dime. First week I was here I told her everything. I was worried my father would find me. Still am. I have nightmares. Initially, I was worried Jerry Driggers would give me away. Dad would know from Mother's will about the cash and stocks and here was Jerry, her driver, splashing money all over town.

"Terrible to say, but it was luck for me when the cops killed Driggers. No way he could betray my secret from the grave. But I had another problem—Sally Price."

"Sally knew about the will?"

"No, but she helped Jerry bounce me from the loony bin and she knew my mother paid handsomely for that service. When the cops found all that cash on Jerry, Sally knew my father would be looking for her; that's why she got herself thrown in prison! I wrote regularly to reassure Sal I'd get her out of town."

"That would be the doctor's assignment."

"Doc Snyder, yes. He was my proxy in Cincinnati. But it wasn't Doc who was Alex Goodman. It was *moi.*"

Jack grimaced. "Something else I got half-right."

"I don't know what happened to Sally. Doc went to Cincinnati and left a train ticket and some cash. I was supposed to meet her."

"I saw you at the station," Jack nodded. "Looked like you had just come in from someplace."

"From St. Petersburg," Peewee nodded. "I had been down the

day before to set Sally up with a job. Got her one, too, with Barnum's show. Then I took the train back to Tampa to meet Sally, but she didn't show. And that was—what? Three weeks ago."

Jack hesitated. "...Sally won't make it, Princess."

"She's—?"

"Becker killed her." Jack felt himself blushing. "I found the letter you sent to Sally, and her ticket. How I got down here."

"Oh, Lord!"

"Princess, I hate pressing you, but what did Terrence Dobbs have to do with all this?"

"Well, Terry was a fixer, wasn't he? See, I had around twenty thousand in cash, but the stocks were in Mother's name and Mother was dead. So Luna goes to Terry and first thing he does is fake a birth certificate for my mother, can you imagine? With that proof of identity, Terry used his brokerage in Tampa to backdate a sale in Mom's name so it would look like she cashed in her certificates before she died."

"Slick. And what did Dobbs get for that piece of work?"

"Fifteen percent, which should have been enough, but then *he* gets in trouble, loses his business and next thing you know he's back to see me."

"To blackmail you."

"He said he'd tell my father everything, if I didn't get him more money. Said he'd put me back in the sanatorium!"

"But Ambassador put an end to that plan, didn't he?"

"Ambassador stomped on him, Mr. Romaine, that's for sure. But he didn't kill him."

A sullen breeze brought the smell of carrion.

"I killed Terrence Dobbs," Peewee's voice was flat. "He was a perv. Was easy getting him to the tub. And once I got him between my legs—? I drowned him."

She smiled sadly.

"That's what upset Ambassador. He thought that Terry was hurting *me*."

Peewee blinked back tears.

"So what's Daddy holding over you, Mr. Romaine?"

"Gambling debts. And my family."

Her hands fluttered.

"He knows I'm here?"

"No, no, Princess, he still thinks you're dead at the bottom of the ocean with your mother. And that's all he's ever gonna know."

"Oh, God!" she wailed. "If I could only believe that!"

"You *can*," he told her. "I can fix your pop, Peewee. I can fix Becker, too, but first I've got to help Luna and for that—I need the money."

A moment hung like rain on a tent.

"Get The Giant," she said finally. "I'll show you."

It took some time to repair the track that allowed Peewee to direct Jack and The Giant to the smoking remains of her bed. They brought shovels and axes and buckets to a tangle of twisted metal. The bed's brass tester sagging like spaghetti. Smoke rising to a sky now open above. There was still an ankle's worth of water in the tank, collected below the seam to support a scum of ash and pine needles.

"You'll have to dig it up," Peewee said and pointed to the charred remains of a poster.

"…Under the bed?" Jack guessed it first. "You hid the cash under your bed!"

"Just like mother," Peewee said.

Jack shoveled away ashes and dirt to find a metal trapdoor. Reaching down to grab the iron handle—"Dammit! It's still hot."

Giant dipped a bucket into the tank, and steam rose hissing from the door. Jack wrapped his shirt around an iron handle. The trap opened, pulling up a cloud of ash from the cavity beneath. Jack's eyes teared; he beat away airborne cinders to peer inside a tin-sided keep.

"There's a safe," he announced.

"'Member my birthday?" Peewee dimpled. "'Cause if you do you can open it."

Jack laid his axe aside and favoring his injured foot, lowered himself to the safe below.

"Let's see what we got," he grunted with a spin of the dial and immediately heard the clutch-type driver's *click, click, click.*

"One…Eight…Nine…"

The heavy tumbles fell with a discernible *snick*—

"Happy birthday."

Jack pulled a leather bag from the safe. It was a medical bag, he realized. Doc Snyder's bag.

He tested its weight.

"So how much is left, Peewee?"

"Something over two hundred thousand dollars," The Fat Lady replied.

"Two hundred—?! GRAND? LEFT?"

"We invested," Peewee shrugged. "Terry wanted us to trade on the margins but Luna said, no, be conservative. And then just recently we converted all the stocks to cash—that was why Luna was at the Mirasol, to sell everything."

"You telling me you took two hundred thousand Washingtons out of the stock market and put it in a medicine bag?! Why? Way the market's going, year or two, you'd be a goddamn millionaire."

Peewee rolled massive shoulders. "I read the papers, Jack. Lots of people trading paper. Way too much speculation. You see what's happened in Tampa? Ever occur to you it could happen on Wall Street?"

"No," Jack replied bluntly.

"I don't think anybody knows how much debt is stacked up in banks all over the country and when it all comes due—stocks aren't going to be worth a hill of beans."

Jack shook his head. "If I had two hundred thousand in that game? I'd let it ride."

"Ah, but then you never knew when to fold, did you, Jack?

He gathered a wad of hundred-dollar bills in his hand.

"Think it'll be enough?" Peewee asked.

"Becker's not gonna sell Luna cheap," Jack replied and placed the bills in his hand back into the bag. "But a hundred grand should do. I'll just tell him it's all that's left."

Chapter fourteen

Platform Show—*a small, single-O attraction presented on an elevated platform.*

The *Betty Sue* rode a gentle swell on the boundary of the Little Alafia. Shrimp nets stowed with buoys and ropes on a dilapidated hull. A prisoner was wracked on a pair of barrels astern, hemp ropes pinning Luna Chevreaux to those staves like a butterfly tacked to cardboard.

The sun breaking in beams through a flimsy screen of cypress and willow. Luna could not wipe the sting of perspiration from her eyes, nor those of insects. Arno Becker hummed some desultory tune beside a kerosene stove mounted on the shrimper's deck. A blue flame licking a metal pot.

Becker dipped a spoon into his pot, sampled it.

"Mmm, no. No, it needs a bite more."

He cut off the head of a .45 caliber cartridge, dropping that bullet into the boiling cauldron of lead.

Luna biting her tongue in her rude saddle.

Becker glanced in his prisoner's direction and smiled. She looked nice, there, pinned back in pants and nightshift. All that blue skin.

He turned back to his pot.

"Most interesting thing I ever saw was in a carnival," he remarked conversationally. "Some hick show. A man poured molten lead into his nose and leaks it out of his eyes! Of course, he used mercury, didn't he? Boiled the lead for the rubes to see, but poured mercury up his schnoz. Some dry ice and sleight of hand would do the trick, wouldn't it? But I always wanted to try the real thing."

Luna strangling a curse as the pot boiled silver.

"Jack'll bring the money," she tried to keep her voice from trembling.

"For your sake, he'd better," Becker smiled pale and blue. "Or by the time I'm through with you people will turn their heads and puke."

"HALOOOO ABOARD," a voice floated in from starboard along with the *pocketa-pocketa* of a two-cylinder engine.

Becker checked his watch.

"Right on time. Pity."

Becker trained a revolver on Jack as he scrambled awkwardly from Luna's runabout onto the deck of Becker's larger vessel. Jack had the medicine bag thrown over his shoulder. He gained the deck, taking in Luna and the red-glowing pot at a glance. Arno pulled the hammer of his weapon to single action.

"Easy, Jack. You ain't as quick on your feet as you used to be."

"Hurt a hair on her head, Becker, and you won't be able to run far enough."

"I'll keep that in mind. Where's the cash?"

Jack tossed the bag at Arno's feet. Becker waved him portside before kneeling to open the satchel.

He frowned.

"This can't be half what these freaks stole from Bladehorn."

"Not even close," Jack admitted. "It's fifty grand."

"I don't play games, Romaine," Becker's lips were thin and tight below his albino face.

"I told you I could get the money; here's proof. You want the rest? Give me Chevreaux."

"I don't bargain."

"What—? You really expect me to come here unarmed and turn over the entire stash without getting Luna first? Would *you* be that fucking stupid?"

Arno mulled it over a moment.

"Well, put it that way. So what do you propose?"

"A swap," Jack answered shortly. "You get the balance of the property—"

"Which is?"

"Another fifty thousand dollars."

"That's all?"

"All that's left. Which means you get a hundred grand and I get the lady."

"Don't play me for a sucker, you son of a bitch. A hundred grand is all that's left? Who are you kidding?"

"There's some stocks left, sure, if you wanta fuck around for a couple of weeks to get 'em sold, but if you want cash, yeah, this is it."

Becker released the hammer of his revolver.

"I doubt that's entirely true, Jack. Lucky for you I'm feeling magnanimous. But I name the place for the exchange. And I name the time."

"Name 'em," Jack agreed.

Arno turned to stir his awful pot.

"The Cat's Cradle, then. You know the place?"

Jack fought an urge to shit.

"Yeah, I know it."

"Of course you do. Meet me at the cage. Six o'clock this evening. Bring everything that's left and, Jack, if I see anybody's mug but yours, *anybody's,* I will turn this whore's muddy hide silver."

"You're gonna be a rich man, Arno," Jack tried to sound calm. "Don't screw it up."

"*Bring me!*" Becker snarled.

Jack turned to Luna.

"I'll be back at six. Hang tough."

"Oh, don't worry, Jack," Becker leered. "She will."

Luna's café offered only a single window to view the descending sun. The sun sure fell faster in autumn, Jack noted silently. Not so quickly as in Cincinnati, maybe, but too quickly, still. Doc Snyder huddled with the last of Kaleidoscope's ragtag population over the medicine bag as Jack snapped a rubber band around a bundle of hundred dollar bills.

"I don't know whether Becker's got a getaway planned by car or boat. Won't know 'till I get there." He snapped the bag shut.

"I still don't like the idea of you going in alone, Jack," Tommy Speck spoke up. "You walk in there alone, he'll take the money and then he'll kill you *and* Luna."

"Maybe not," Jack replied shortly. "Once he's got his loot, the last thing Becker's going to want is to have the cops on his ass."

"Becker's not concerned about the police," Doc objected. "Don't tell us that."

"What I can tell you is if the bastard sees anybody around that cage but me, he'll kill Luna on the spot. Money or no money."

"There must be somethink vee can do!" Jo Jo growled.

Jack shook his head. "Don't. It's too risky."

"We're carnies," Cassandra joined with heat. "We're used to risky."

Jack was about to object again when Tommy Speck's wife intervened smoothly.

"Let's just everyone settle down. Jack—it's your job to deliver the money and look after Luna. That's your job. Don't worry about the rest."

Jack scanned the misfit faces around him. Only a few weeks earlier he had been repulsed to see such creatures. Not enough hair or too much. Not enough parts or too many.

But they all had eyes. That's all Jack could see now, were their eyes. He'd stared down a thousand players over a thousand hands of poker in dozens of places but he could not read a single face staring into his own in this café. Not a one.

"Do your job, brodie," Half Track said quietly. "Let us worry about the rest."

He hesitated to gather the bag.

"I feel...I feel like I've let you down. All of you."

"Just get Luna," Tommy pressed the satchel into Jack's hands. "Bring her home safe and everything's jake."

Jack prepared himself to meet Arno Becker fighting a pall of apprehension. There were any number of factors feeding his fear. Arno could not be trusted, obviously, and Jack did not have his familiar tools. The knife and knuckles which made him cock of damn near any walk could not be hidden from Arno Becker. The Hun was not about to let Jack come ashore with anything resembling a weapon. Not even a doughboy's shovel.

Even the cane was risky.

Jack had accepted Cassandra's offer of a heavy, ironwood walking stick. He needed that prop for his crippled foot, of course. And in the hands of a man with two good pins a cane was as good as a club. But Jack knew he couldn't plant himself solidly enough for a game of stickball, let alone combat. He couldn't swing a club. He couldn't throw a punch, couldn't run. He didn't need a walking stick. What he needed was a gun.

It was Tommy got him one.

"God made some men bigger than others," the spunky little fart said, handing Jack a snub-nose. "That's why He made Smith & Wesson put out an equalizer."

"Can't have it on me, Tommy. He'll frisk me, first thing."

"So leave it in the truck. Stow it under the seat. Just in case."

Jack did not reply that he already knew he would need a gun. Whether he got to use it or not was the question.

"Got yer roads straight?"

"Yes."

Jack had decided to avoid an approach from the river, choosing instead to drive to the cage. Doc and Tommy had already shown him the cut off. Straight down a sandy rut off the blacktop.

Jack wasn't sure what to expect from Becker, but whatever it was he'd rather face it on solid ground.

"Money's square?"

"In the bag," Jack tried to joke.

"Break a leg, then," Tommy declared and the gathered carnies murmured in benediction.

Jack could feel the familiar churn in his gut. He dreaded facing the man who had butchered him, dreaded the encounter to come. But these people were counting on him. He thought of Luna, alone with Becker. He could not let her down.

Jack turned off the hardtop onto weed-covered ruts snaking through a prairie of pine and palmetto. The sun was just kissing the tops of the trees as Jack eased Tommy's truck to a clattering stop on the bank above the Cat's Cradle's rusted hemisphere. He couldn't see the cage, at first. Arno Becker's Packard blocked the view.

But when he left the truck, Jack saw the cage. He saw Luna, too.

She swung naked from the roof of the cage, her arms tied at the wrists and stretched overhead. Arno was dressed for the occasion like a carney's talker, spiffy in tails and top hat. He smiled at Jack's ragged approach and turned Luna around on her tether. Round and round. Like a piece of meat.

"One thiiiin diiiime, ladeees and gentulmen! To see the AMAZ-ING MOON MAIDEN! She WALKS, she TALKS, she CRAWW-WLS on her belly like a REPTILE!"

"You son of a bitch," Jack stumbled over the rough ground on his cane.

Luna heard him.

"Jack—? JACK?"

"I'M HERE, LUNA."

A groan turned into a cough that wracked her whole frame.

"BECKER, GET HER DOWN."

"Ah, I see you have little stomach for the exotic, sir. But I encourage you to indulge yourself. You do want her, don't you, Jack?

You *lust* for her, yes? And why not? What man doesn't want The Moon Maiden, eh? And all for himself.

"But first you must pay. Pay, sir, and you may have her. 'Have' her, get it, Jack? If you still think she's worth having."

Jack leaning on his hardwood stick to drop the bag and cash at the cage's rusty gate.

"Fifty to match the fify I already gave ya. Come and get it."

"You packing anything besides that cane, Jack? Any other toys I should see?"

Jack slipped off his jacket.

"Turn around."

Jack limped to oblige.

"Trousers and crotch," Becker ordered next and Jack obeyed without comment.

Becker smiled. "Nothing like getting caught with your pants down, is there, Jack?"

Jack offered not a word in reply. He had expected some kind of humiliation. That was what Arno liked. That's how he got his kicks. And it didn't matter—as long as Jack got Luna out of that goddamned cage.

"Well, well," Arno completed his inspection. "How about that, Miss Chevreaux? Our boy's decided to play fair."

"What about it, Becker? Are you done playing?"

"Just about," Becker gathered Luna's long legs in his arm and yanked.

Her shoulders popped in their sockets and she screamed. A hoarse, high scream swallowed in the pines.

"GET HER DOWN, GODDAMMIT"

"I'm still having fun."

Don't look at Luna, Jack told himself. Don't look!

He kept his eyes caged on Arno Becker.

"Hundred grand will buy you lots of fun, Arno. But you don't get it 'till she comes down."

"Oh, I believe I could take it, Jack. But since you've been so sporting here—"

A switchblade opened in Becker's hand.

"Cut her down yourself."

Becker waiting with the knife. Inviting Jack into the cage. Luna groaning agony.

Jack could feel his legs turning to water.

"All right, all right, I'm coming."

"And drop the stick, Jack."

"Fine," Jack tossed the cane aside. Arno emerged from the cage, tipping his top hat.

"I leave the field to you, sir!"

The two men's eyes locked like vipers' as Jack eased into the cage.

"I need something to cut her down," Jack pointed out.

"Certainly," Arno smiled and tossed the knife onto the sand beneath Luna's feet.

Jack had barely turned for the knife when Becker slammed the cage-door shut. A chain rattling on rusty bars.

"Tell you what, Jack," Becker snapped a padlock tight. "I'll just leave you two lovebirds in your cage."

"Jack?!" Luna breathing was labored.

"Easy, baby, I'll get you down."

All he could do was lift Luna with the strength of his one good leg and reach high overhead—high! to cut the hemp rope stretched tight to the top of the cage.

The blade glancing off the rope to nick her wrist.

"Oh, baby!"

"'S'awright," she gasped. "Just…gemme down!"

When the rope gave she fell like a sack and took Jack with her to the floor of the cage.

Jack hauled himself to a knee.

"Luna? Luna, baby!"

"My arms—!"

"We're nearly there."

Cursing silently over the knots trapping her hands. Working the knife carefully. But Luna's attention was directed outside the cage.

"The car. Jack—his car."

"Fuck his car. Let him have it."

"Jack, he's got a gun!"

Arno Becker placed his heavy revolver on the dash of his coupe as he counted his money aloud.

"…forty eight thousand…forty nine…fifty grand. Plus the fifty I already have makes one hundred thousand exactly. You stiffed me a little, Jack, but what the hell—"

He gathered his handgun.

"What's money between friends?"

Becker stepped from the Packard pulling his revolver level on the cage. Jack and Luna trapped inside. Clinging to each other in that cruel iron ring.

"This is too easy, Jack."

Arno strolling over.

"Like shooting ducks in a barrel."

Jack shoving himself in front of Luna as Becker spun the revolver's cylinder.

"Stay behind me," Jack told Luna, which seemed to amuse Arno greatly.

Becker adjusted his approach so that he could sight through the grid of the cage's heavy bars. The revolver's barrel elevated slightly, then lowering.

"S'long, suckers."

The trigger-finger pulling—

But then a deep, sustained growl stayed the killer's hand, Becker turning from the cage to find a hound baring teeth an arms' length away.

"Fucking mutt."

Becker turning to his new target. Boomer launching himself furiously, seventy pounds of meat and fangs. The revolver bucked with a heavy explosion. The hound jerked sideways with a slug in his flank. The carney's bloodhound falling to the sand. But before Becker could fire again—

BOOM!

Becker ducked as lead shot sprayed the clearing.

"FUCK!"

Tommy Speck and The Giant popping from the cover of Tommy's Ford motorcar to charge across the underbrush. Another blast from The Giant's shotgun had Becker sprinting for his Packard.

Tommy now firing his carbine on the run. The Giant tearing yet another wad from Becker's Packard with his double-barrel. Becker jumping into his coupe, jerking the choke but jamming the starter. The engine caught just about the moment Tommy ripped a slug through the windshield and Arno fishtailed from the clearing before the cage. Emptying his revolver at Speck and The Giant through his passenger-side window.

"The tires, Giant!"

The black man dropped to a knee.

BOOM! A wad of buckshot too high into Becker's door.

Giant fired again, the double-barrel bucked, and you could see a fender well above a black tire chewed with shot.

"What's happening?!" Luna's hands latched onto Jack's arm like a vice.

"They ran him off! Those crazy saps!"

The Giant now running toward the cage.

"The fuck were you crazy bastards thinking?" Jack greeted the pair.

"Didn't you know they were coming?" Luna leaning on Jack to stand upright.

"When have I ever known anything?"

"Hang on, we'll get you out," Tommy said.

"How'd you get a car in here?"

"Pushed it." The Giant taking the chain in his hands. Pulling it across his chest.

"Be faster to shoot the lock, wouldn't it?"

The chain shattered so suddenly that the giant man almost lost his balance.

Jack rushed over to kick the door open.

"Thanks, big man. Now, stay with Luna."

Jack grabbing the shotgun as he turned to Tommy.

"Any chance of catching Becker?"

"If we got a tire."

Arno Becker made it all the way to the blacktop before he felt the tire.

"Shit."

Was a rear tire, passenger's side pulling the wheel. But not bad enough to stop, not just yet. Especially not when you were dodging buckshot with a hundred grand on your bench seat. All he had to do was get down the road a mile or two. There was always some sap on the highway would stop to help with a flat and when he did Becker would have a fresh set of wheels.

Arno wasn't about to let a tire spoil his getaway. Worst case, even if the freaks caught up to him—? Becker reached for the Tommy gun on the seat. Should have used the squirt gun at the cage, he chided himself gently.

Oh, well.

The steering wheel was jumping in his hand, now, and Becker could hear the tire in the back, *thump, thump, thump.* He glanced over to the side-mirror and saw a black Model T small on the blacktop behind—

"—We'll never catch him," Tommy chambered a shell into his Winchester as Jack pulled the flivver's throttle wide open.

"He's weaving!" Jack shouted. "I think you got a tire, Tommy!"

But Becker wasn't finished. They saw the rear window of the Packard shatter with a long burst from Arno's gun. Becker firing blind at the pursuing Model T.

"Jesus!" Jack swerved with the *ping-ping-ping* of .45 slugs into the Ford's metal frame .

Just the one burst and then Becker dropped the weapon for the steering wheel. You could see the hairpin curve ahead. Could see the Packard leaning on its chassis.

"STOP THE CAR, JACK."

The dwarf clutching his leg as he jammed a foot into the dashboard.

"You nuts?!"

"STOP THE FUCKING CAR!" .

Jack nearly lost control as he slammed on the brakes, the fliv-ver sliding sideways on the blacktop.

Arno Becker was halfway through the hairpin when he saw Tommy's Model T skidding to a stop behind.

Why? Arno wondered briefly. Why would they give up the chase?

And then a bull elephant burst from the ditch to charge the crippled Packard. Five tons of elephant closing at thirty miles an hours.

"*Sheisse.*"

Ambassador rammed the Packard broadside. The rear tire exploded, the car rolled in a sloppy waltz, once…twice…the Packard skipped off the blacktop like a hockey puck and slammed into the trunk of a yellow-heart pine on the other side of the road. One dip of tusks tossed the car off the tree and into the ditch. Arno Becker hanging upside down. The Packard spinning on its top like a turtle. Becker cursing and furious, scrambling to retrieve his machine gun.

Jack heard the Tommy gun's chatter. He saw the flash-flash-flash from the muzzle.

"YOU SON OF A BITCH!" Speck slid from his seat to the flivver's running board.

Ambassador backed off, you could see it, stumbling briefly from the mangled Packard that was now quiet in the ditch. He backed off, the bull did.

But only for a moment.

Becker was scrambling to free himself from his getaway car when he saw Peewee's elephant return for a steady, deliberate circuit around his mangled Packard. Arno knew he'd hit the fucking thing; he could see a rip of .45 caliber slugs along the bull's trunk and flank. But it was apparent that the elephant was not mortally wounded and had not been driven away. If was as though the Tommy gun had stung the animal to a more studied attack.

"Want more, do you?"

Becker was fumbling for a fresh magazine when he saw an enormous pair of eyes sighting him over the chromed ornament of the coupe's hood. Two eyes, huge and intelligent, staring into his own.

"*KOMMEN SIE!!*"

A massive head rising, as if to acknowledge that invitation. A final, furious trumpet and then the head dipped. The ground shook. And five tons of raging beast drove ivory spears through the windshield, through the steering wheel, and through the bastard screaming curses behind. A single jerk of the elephant's head and Arno Becker was fetched through the windshield impaled on ivory tusks.

By the time Tommy and Jack made it to the ditch, Ambassador was gone, swallowed by a jungle of pine trees and wetland. Jack approached Becker's car with caution. He could see a flat tire spinning lazily. Could hear the creak of metal, the hiss of a broken radiator.

He found Becker hanging from the windshield, a spool of entrails sizzling with blood on the Packard's steaming hood.

"Looks like Ambassador did our work for us," Tommy sat down hard beside his carbine.

"Looks like," Jack agreed and, peering into the car, located Doc Snyder's leather bag.

"Go ahead," Tommy dipped his head as though to grant permission.

Jack crawled over the hood and past Becker's gored corpse to retrieve Peewee's money.

"Didn't get a chance to spend any, did he?" Tommy joked weakly and slumped onto the ground.

"Tommy—?"

A dark stain seeping through the dwarf's trousers.

"Tommy, goddammit!"

Chapter fifteen

> Tear-Down—*dismantling the midway*
> *at the end of the engagement.*

Three days after Arno Becker suffered an end which was too merciful, Tommy Speck died. Bled to death, Doc Snyder gave that postmosrtem. Knicked in the femoral artery by Becker's chance round. Eileen Speck went into labor the day after her husband's funeral. It did not go well. The baby became breached in the mother's diminutive canal. With the mother's life in danger along with her child's, the doc had no easy choices. If he spent too long manipulating the infant, both babe and mother would surely die, but the only certain way to remove the baby was to crush its skull and abort, a procedure Eileen refused to countenance.

The only other option was to go in aggressively and get her baby out.

"I'll have to break your pelvis," Doc told the woman in her awful labor.

"Long as my baby lives," she grated.

"I can't guarantee that."

"Give it as much chance as you can,."

Doc managed to ratchet Eileen's canal to the point that the infant was successfully delivered. Tommy Speck's wife was able to hold her baby and even to nurse the child a short while before she succumbed to shock and died.

Eileen called her daughter a perfect flower, and thus she was given a carney's name. Flower was small but was not a dwarf. She was, rubes would say, perfectly normal. The spittin' image of her daddy, Half Track declared, grief tainting the joy which any birth brought to the community of Kaleidoscope.

Flower Speck would not grow up with her mother and father, but it would be untrue, as Jack now knew, to say she would have no family.

Luna found a wet-nurse for Tommy's daughter and lodged the newborn in her own apartment. Eileen was buried beside Tommy on a knoll of ground overlooking the Alafia River. The Little Alafia, naturally.

With that sad ceremony finished, the community turned with no guilt or remonstrance to pragmatic concerns. Becker was dead, but the carnies could not be certain they were secure from some other psychopath. They were certainly not safe from Oliver Bladehorn. And there was the matter of how best to handle Peewee's money.

Only a handful of freaks in the community had any idea where the money came from that paid their bills, doctored their children and supported their winter hideaway. Of those residents, only Luna and Doc knew that the money Bladehorn would kill to recover was Peewee's inheritance. Luna convened a meeting in the café to explain the situation and air opinions on the matter. Brodies and performers packed every stool, booth and chair, everyone listening quietly, without interruption, as Luna reported details of the portfolio from the Tampa bank that had invested Peewee's cashed-in certificates, explaining that it was Peewee's choice to use the money to fund her adoptive community and that it was also Peewee's firm decision to liquidate all assets to cash.

"How much do we have, then?" Cassandra asked.

"Little over a quarter of a million dollars," Luna replied and the café was suddenly quiet as a church.

"It's a blessing, of course," Gregory spoke up. "But if we are not careful, it can also be a curse. Money divides as often as it heals."

"Agreed," Luna said. "I'd be happy to show you every dime that's been spent, but make no mistake, this is Peewee's money. Do I hear any disagreement on that point? Speak now or hold your wad."

"I would like to talk to the Princess," someone spoke up and there was a murmur of assent. "I would like her to hear our opinions."

"Fair enough," Luna agreed and told Half Track to serve chow on the house.

All sorts of ideas got tossed over flapjacks and sausage and coffee regarding the disposition of Peewee's estate, some folks urging immediate distribution of the money, others wanting to see the entire stash reinvested on the stock market.

"Folks are making fortunes on Wall Street," Penguin opined. "Why can't we?"

Jack agreed. The market was always a sure thing, wasn't it, especially with a quarter million to play? But he knew that Peewee had a different opinion.

The carnies were convened before the Princess's much diminished throne when they received her edict on the matter. Nearly everyone was startled to hear Peewee say that she had cashed in all of her certificates and was not going to put a red cent back in investment.

Peewee frankly admitted that part of her caution derived from instinct. "But I also read," she said, and went on to outline more reasons for abjuring the market. "Take a look at Tampa. Terry Dobbs was a bigshot, once, and we all know what happened to him."

Peewee going on to remind the carneys that Tampa's economy was once considered bulletproof.

"But now the banks are broke, real-estate's tanked, and, worse, the city does not have a way to recover. You can't earn enough to rebuild what's been pissed away and nobody knows how they're going to cover the debt left behind."

The Princess finished the justification for her decision by

pointing out that the same speculators who doomed Tampa's economy were prevalent all over the country.

"My father lost my mother's fortune on Wall Street and there are tens of thousands of men just like Oliver Bladehorn who are buying paper with money they do not have. There are smart men, ruthless men, who are one stroke of pen away from disaster.

"Sooner or later the chips are going to be called in from San Francisco to New York and what will happen to the markets then? I don't know; no one knows. But what I *do* know is that now is not the time to think about getting rich. We have what we need. We should be thinking of ways to protect it."

"But we haf provided protected it, have we not?" Marcel spoke up with his twin nodding assent. "We have protected you, as well. And with all apologies, Princess, for our protection we haf suffered terrible losses. The fire. Tommy and Eileen. Flambé and his family. Not to mention our possessions!"

"Every time you get on the train you risk something," Luna interrupted sharply. "Every carney knows there are no guarantees and no free rides. We took a risk when Peewee came to us, sure, but we got a fortune in return."

"But all of us did not know we were at risk," Cassandra spoke up. "In fact, most of us didn't."

"You didn't turn down the help," Luna countered. "I have yet to see a single person here coming to me for money who cared where it came from. You, Cassandra—you came from a gilly in Toledo without a pot to piss in nor a window to throw it out of. It was Peewee's money bankrolled your act, bought you a trailer.

"It was Peewee's money built the chowhouse that we all share. She bought Ambassador and paid for his feed, and when Pinhead was jailed for manslaughter last fall who do ya think kept his neck out of a noose?

"Everyone here has been helped one way or the other by the Princess, but even if we hadn't, even if no one here had received the kindness of a single dime of her money, it shouldn't matter. We're carnies. The boss makes a fix, we back him up and I'm the boss in this beddie. I gave my word to Peewee that she could use her money any way she wants. It was hers when she came here. It's hers now. That's the gig."

"But is it safe?" Penguin asked. "And are *we* safe?"

"There's only one way to be sure," Jack replied. "Only one sure way."

For a breath or two no one said anything.

"So," Half Track broke the ice. "Who's gonna do it?"

Jack sent a pair of telegrams before he left Kaleidoscope for the return trip to Cincinnati. The first wire went care of her tending family to Mamere and Martin. It was a note of contingency, also of confession. "WILL FOLLOW WITH LETTER," the wire promised. The other telegram went to Spuds Staponski; Jack could not be sure how happy the Cincinnati businessman would be to receive a message from a fellah who mostly drank his beer for nothing. But, hey, he'd paid Spuds every penny he owed, hadn't he? And this was new business.

Jack traveled by coach, this time around. No sleeper, no first-class amenities. He still had a wad of cash left over from Bladehorn's initial advance, but had developed a sense of frugality in recent weeks. A sleeper was an unnecessary extravagance.

He did not indulge in cards or conversation, but the reason for that circumstance was very difference on this trip than it had been on the way south from Cincinnati. On the train to Tampa, Jack had been invited almost continually to the diner or card table or some woman's private sleeper. The handsome man with the tony suit and marquee looks found it hard to remain solitary. Not this time. Jack still had plenty of money. He had his suit. But no one was inviting him to gamble or drink or dance. None of the swells or their full-calved honeys.

Jack would catch them looking, his fellow travelers staring at the scar splitting his face. His blistered lips just healing with bright, pink flesh. The gumline pulled up in a kind of rictus from the work of scars and stitches. They were fascinated, these well-heeled sophisticates, and they were horrified. They tried to be discreet; Jack was familiar with that effort. He had made the same pretense only too recently himself.

There were no floozies dragging Jack over to the gramophone, no innuendo, or flirtation. Certainly no offer of sex. There were opportunities to gamble, but not with the real money, not with the gentlemen in the smoker who hid their eyes along with their cards when Jack passed by. All Lon Chaneys report to the caboose, please. If you didn't mind playing with hoboes. The children, at least, were unabashed in their cruelty. Laughing when they passed Jack in the dining car as though he were a treat provided for their Halloween entertainment.

He rose stiffly from his second-class seat to find breakfast in the diner. Morning meals were most democratic, working stiffs and new-lyweds sipping orange juice in the atmosphere of cigars and sophistication. Jack found a seat near the back and was on his second cup of coffee when a porter passed by with a basket of newspapers. Jack recognized the black man from his first passage, but was completely unrecognized in return.

"Paper, suh?"

"Not now, thanks."

Jack's hands never left the well-oiled bag in his lap. It was not a Gladstone or portmanteau but a smaller satchel, freshly scrubbed with saddlesoap. Peewee had provided it for a purpose.

"Paper for you, suh?"

The porter now engaging some dapper seated with a gaggle of cronies just beyond Jack's table.

"Paper?" the porter solicited again.

"Yes, I will."

A banker, Jack had gleaned that much from overheard snippets of conversation. He was a corpulent, self-satisfied tub of guts, vested, coifed and clipped. A pleasant sheen of oil in the hair. A wax of mustache. A man prone to giving orders and used to having them obeyed. He was seated with a wife half his age in a matched set of similarly attired professionals and their wives, men and women making a studied effort to exude what they took to be an air of sophistication. A breakfast of millionaires.

Jack noticed that the banker did not thank the black man

who placed the newspaper at his disposal. You could hear the snap
of the rag as it opened.

"That's Malcolm," the wife twittered to a younger woman.
"Can't eat his breakfast without seeing to business."

Her confidant nodded, a plump young thing kneading a
wreath of pearls.

"Seem silly, doesn't it? I mean, what's the point of making gobs
if you don't take time to—"

"Malcolm?"

A deeper voice interrupting the women's chatter.

Jack looked up from his table to see the banker rigid in his seat.
His eyes bulging from their sockets, arms and legs rigid as posts.

"MALCOLM?!!"

The well-heeled gentleman fell face first into his grits and as
his guests scrambled in horror Jack noticed the paper on the dining
car floor. A bold headline bannered the latest:

October 29th, 1929
WALL STREET CRASHES—RUN ON THE BANKS

The elaborately grilled gate allowing entry onto Oliver Bladehorn's
grounds was unguarded. Jack tested the barrier; it opened complaining on rusty hinges and he limped onto the grounds. There was no
sign of security patrolling the arc deco mansion. No crinolines or
croquet on the lawn. The long hedges of juniper and holly and aza-
lea had not been trimmed, he could see. The flowerbeds were filled
with autumn leaves, buried in leaves actually. The pleasant aroma of
maple in decomposition.

Jack followed the track of asphalt around the house proper,
through the trees. The roofline of the lepidopterary was easy to see
now that the elms had lost their leaves. There was not a servant or
valet to be seen anywhere, but Jack could hear a gramophone inside
the hothouse. The piano tugged at Jack's memory. Where had he
heard that record before?

It was in France. Of, course, in the infirmary. He could see

Gilette, now, gently padding the dust off a shining disk, carefully bringing the needle to a groove. Was it Mozart—? Mozart, yes. Or someone similar. Jack shifted the bag in his grip, turned the brass handle on the flimsy door and went inside.

Turned out it was not a gramophone inside but a radio. Oliver Bladehorn swaying to Mozart in a million swirling motes of color. Butterflies lining his arms like scales. A beautiful insect parting wings on the crown of his bald head as the gangster pinned its cousin to a board.

Something rotting inside. A fetid decay filling Jack's nostrils.

"They're getting edgy," Bladehorn brushed a monarch off his arm as casually as if he'd been expecting Jack all morning. "Time to migrate, I expect."

"Time to open the windows," Jack agreed.

Bladehorn's head swiveling like a turret on his shoulders. Like a barnyard owl. Something like a smile threatening to break over the drool seeping from his mouth. The insect preening unnoticed on top.

"Good heavens, Jack. Whatever happened to you?"

"Played with fire."

"Knives, too, apparently. I hope you didn't go to all that trouble for nothing."

"I found the property," Jack assured him. "Most of it, anyway. It's all in cash."

"Cash? An unexpected blessing. I don't expect you to be astute in these matters, Mr. Romaine, but cash is something very hard to come by just now."

"I know what it means to break the bank," Jack leaned onto a potting table. "Looks like you do, too."

"Point taken," Bladehorn wiped his hands on his apron. "But with my property recovered *I* can start over."

Bladehorn extending his hands like a priest accepting a child for baptism.

"Money lets you migrate, you see. Just like the butterfly. South, for me, most likely. The islands, perhaps. Someplace where I can safely cocoon. You return to me, I tell you in candor, Mr. Romaine, not a moment too soon."

Jack tossed the bag at Bladehorn's feet. A moment's irritation before he bent to retrieve it, the bald, polished head dipping as if in deference. The butterfly flitting from that gleaming skull.

Bladehorn opened the bag with trembling hands.

But then—

"What? What is the meaning of this?"

It was a doll inside the bag. Peewee's doll. Nothing but a Raggedy Ann. A childhood gift from a mother to her child.

"What…have…you…brought…ME?!" The Fat Lady's father now wringing the doll's neck.

"It's a birthday present."

"A birth—? The hell are you talking about?"

"You really don't know, do you? You sorry son of a bitch. You don't even remember."

"Do not trifle with me, Mr. Romaine! I am not as completely without resources as you seem to suppose!"

"I don't suppose anything, Bladehorn. I goddamn *know*."

Jack leaned forward to bring his skewered face to Bladehorn's.

"And what I know, Oliver, is that you've got bigger things to worry about than me."

"Becker won't quit worrying," Bladehorn snarled. "I *know* Arno; he'll find you."

"He already has—take a look. But guess what? During our long, long conversation Arno told me all about your problems. Bad investments. Wolves at the door. And now, jeepers creepers, the banks are busted."

"WHERE IS MY MONEY?!"

The dome of his head turning scarlet.

Jack backed off a step.

"I took your money," he said. "I took it, I'm keeping it, and there's not a goddamned thing you can do about it."

Bladehorn lurched toward the potting table but Jack snapped

the brass knucks out of his pocket and across the bridge of Bladehorn's nose and as the gangster fell back cursing, he palmed the handgun always handy in the drawer of the table.

"You can't do this to me!"

Blood streaming down Bladehorn's face, into his teeth. The son of a bitch looked like some kind of gourd, or maybe a jack-o'-lantern.

"WHO DO YOU THINK YOU ARE?" the gangster raged.

"I'm not entirely sure," Jack pocketed the gun. "But it ain't an insect."

Jack Romaine emerged from the Butterfly House to find four men with Thompsons waiting. Three of the faces were unfamiliar, but Spud Staponski's was the fourth.

Spud had not seen Jack since his trip south.

"Pretty Boy. What dog got hold of you?"

Jack pulled a thin sheaf of bills from his waistcoat.

"Five hundred bucks I believe is what we agreed."

Staponski took the cash, counted it.

"We square?"

Spud stuffed the bills in his pocket.

"Get outta here."

Jack limped on past. He could hear the heavy bolts of the Tommy guns slide back, the shuffle of leather soles toward the hothouse door. He was barely onto the asphalt track when a quartet of weapons shattered the brisk autumn calm. Glass falling like chimes out of tune into the house of insects. Jack glanced back to see thousands of butterflies soaring into the sky. Like kites cut loose from their strings.

Epilogue

A Gulf breeze flutters damp and humid late one December afternoon through a ballpark cleared not too far from the Little Alafia inside a grove of cypress and pine. A radio announcer gives a play-by-play of the action, a voice hoarse with excitement and distorted with static:

> ...the Reds have their pitcher at bat, Joe Dawson at the plate! We're down one in the bottom of the ninth. We've got two outs with two men on base. Two strikes and two balls on the count. Wait a minute...Dawson's backed off the plate. He's off the plate, he's pointing to center field! To the upper deck! The hell's this kid think he is, Babe Ruth?...

The radio blares from the trunk of a cabbage palm that marks the left-field foul line of this homemade ballpark. Jack Romaine laughs in shorts on a jerry-rigged mound. His son Martin, suntanned and handsome as a movie star, wields a bat over a croker sack. Mamere plays spectator from the shade of the trees. Luna lounges alongside, long and lazy, raven hair and blue skin arranged on a maroon blanket spreading on white, white sand. An infant props on Luna's hip, Tommy Speck's little girl. Absorbed in the mystery of oranges.

Jack winks broadly to Luna from the mound.

"C'mon, Dad!"

The young man leveling his bat across the sack.

"Gimme something I can hit."

"Awright, slugger."

The windup. The pitch. The ball snaps off Martin's bat like a Roman candle; the radio announcer shouting on cue from the radio with the play—"*It's a home run! A home run DEEP into the center-field deck!*"

Jack's son streaks the circuit of bags and slides to home in his father's arms. Luna cheers from her blanket. And if you wandered just a little ways behind the ballfield you would once again see—

"The Kaleidoscope Café." A busy afternoon at the beddy. Gregory Lagopolus and his unfeeling twin follow Greg's sons to a churn of ice cream. Friederich The Unparalled straddles his balls to take a turn at the crank. Pinhead brings a plate of hotdogs to Penguin and Half Track. Jo Jo and The Giant and the rest of their special family chow down with a cohort of other performers and brodies as Jacques & Marcel accompany the Hilton Sisters for a quartet of harmonized entertainment.

Some folks throw horseshoes; some play dominoes, or checkers. Jack Earl slaps cards with a dwarf not much taller than his boots. Cassandra displays her double cleavage over Tarot cards. Offering her special dispensation. And as for Peewee—

The Princess sips a daiquiri from her special spot on the veranda, a novel and newspaper near to hand. She can hear the latest from the ballpark:

... *The runners come in one-two and now the team's piling out to mob Dawson at the plate. The pitcher—Joe Dawson! What are the odds? Joe Dawson hits a home run to win the game!*

The Princess turns a broad, dimpled face to find a prince perched on the lip of her nectared tumbler. *Danaus Plexippus* fans his wings slowly, cooling the royal blood in those marvelous veins. Those russet wings shot with black. However, a close look reveals that he is not perfectly preserved; some discoloration along a wing that bears the tears of a bad-tasting encounter with a sparrow, or owl, or some other predator. He is only weeks removed from the cocoon, this hardy

traveler. He has not sired progeny, has not even finished his migration, but seeing him here in royal company there is no doubt—
His metamorphosis is complete.

FINIS

Acknowledgments

I owe interest in carnival life entirely to a talented and enthusiastic filmmaker, Robert Nowotny, who prodded me years ago to produce a feature-film script that was unabashedly *in genre* and set in a midway populated by carneys, cons, and exhibitionists. Many Floridians will recognize in the make-believe and nascent community of Kaleidoscope a simulacrum of the actual community of Gibsonton, a town near Tampa which still exists today. The community imagined in the novel does not chronicle the actual history of Gibsonton, nor do its characters, except in cameo. But even casual research of carnival communities, carney advertisements and playbills reveals a plethora of fascinating anecdotes and history which inform the novel and its avatar of people and place.

I owe many thanks to Ace Atkins and Leland Hawes, author and journalist respectively, for helping me research the Tampa area of the twenties. Similarly, I am pleased to thank Dr. Nancy Humbach for helping me research the progressive city of Cincinnati during that same period.

About the Author

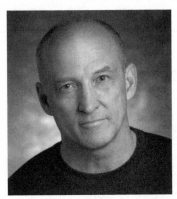

Darryl Wimberley

Darryl Wimberley has authored two critically acclaimed literary works, *A Tinker's Damn* and *The King of Colored Town*, along with the *Gulf Coast noir* series featuring Barrett Raines, Special Agent for the Florida Department of Law Enforcement: *A Rock and a Hard Place*, *Dead Man's Bay*, *Strawman's Hammock* and *Pepperfish Keys*. All are available from *The* Toby Press.

Wimberley has also garnered three feature-film credits. The screenplay for *Kaleidoscope* won Grand Prize Winner in a competition sponsored some years ago by *Fade In* magazine.

The author and screenwriter resides with his family in Austin.

The fonts used in this book are from the Garamond family

Other works by Darryl Wimberley
available from *The* Toby Press

A Rock and a Hard Place

A Tinker's Damn

Dead Man's Bay

The King of Colored Town

Pepperfish Keys

Strawman's Hammock

The Toby Press publishes fine writing,
available at leading bookstores everywhere. For more
information, please visit www.tobypress.com

1/7/09